Still Waters

Still Waters

PATRICIA HALEY

STILL WATERS

A New Spirit title published by Kimani Press in 2006

First published by BET Publications, LLC in 2005

ISBN-13: 978-1-58314-623-1
ISBN-10: 1-58314-623-7

www.kimanipress.com

Printed in U.S.A.

This book is dedicated to three very special men in my life—my brothers: Rev. Frederick Lane, Erick Lewis, and Fredrick Deon.

To my big brother, Fred, you've protected me as far back as I can remember. So many times you got in trouble taking up for me. I am so proud of the man you've become—a wonderful father, a dedicated minister of God's word, a great brother, a truly hardworking man, and a dependable son who has Daddy's high energy. You remind me of the Apostle Paul in the sense that when God called you to preach, you didn't seek approval from others or become overcome with doubt, you just went forward. I am so proud to have you as my brother. Not many sisters can say their brother stays in touch almost daily. I can, and I'm grateful. You're the best big brother I could ever have dreamed of having.

To my dear, dear, dear baby brother, Erick, words can't describe my love for you. Funny, fashionable, tall, handsome, loyal friend, generous, super supportive, well-liked, protective, and an incredible cook. You got both Daddy's dancing genes and his smile. You enjoyed life and didn't complain during challenges. You have the biggest heart of anyone I know. When you got paid, everyone around you did, too. Instead of focusing on receiving unconditional love, you so freely gave it to me even at the time of your greatest need. Your abundant love has made me a better person. I'm constantly encouraged by our friendship and the wealth of memories we share. You are one of the greatest blessings in my life. You proved that endearing love lives beyond the grave, and anyone who truly knows me will also know you. May your soul rest in God's perfect peace and everlasting love.

To my little brother, Freddy, who isn't so little anymore, I'm proud of the man you've become, with such a good heart. You're a loving father. You have so much of Daddy's mannerisms and laughter. Your encouragement means the world to me. You're a wonderful "little" brother. I missed out on the early years of your life but have been blessed to make up time in the last seventeen years, with many more to come.

We have more than just the same Haley blood; we each share a piece of our father's (Fred "Luck" Haley) heart. The three of you have blessed me, and for your presence in my life, I'm forever grateful to the Lord for giving me what no one else in this world has, Frederick (Rockford), Erick (Heaven), and Freddy (Arkansas) for brothers.

ACKNOWLEDGMENTS

Lord, you've guided me through the creation of another book. I acknowledge that *Still Waters* and every other story I've written wouldn't have happened without your presence and anointing. I thank you for your faithfulness, direction, and favor. May the literary gifts you've bestowed in me be used for our glory and may *Still Waters* be pleasing in your sight, blessing every person you intended to see or read this book.

Jeffrey Glass, you are the darling among husbands. Words are wonderful, but the level of appreciation you deserve can only be adequately conveyed through my actions and undying love for you, which will exist for as long as I live. I'm grateful for the memory of my beloved father-in-law, Walter Glass, an exceptionally loving and nonjudgmental man who was an amazing father to my husband.

I have a long list of loved ones connected by family or friendships, too numerous to name individually but no less significant. You know who you are. With the small amount of space available, I love and thank my dynamic mother, Fannie Haley Rome; her wonderful husband, Deacon Earl Rome; my loving stepfather, Deacon Bob Thomas; Lorena Skelton; my phenomenal little sister, Frances Walker; Jeraldine Glass; Brendon and Brice; Ophelia Haley; Rufus and Teresa Dismuke; Robert and Diedre Campbell; Donald and Mary Bartel; Leroy and Emira Bryant; Patricia Hill; New Covenant Church (Trooper, PA); Pastor Gus and Carolyn Howell; Ravi and Dorothea Kalra; Audrey Williams; Will and Kimberla Roby; Pam and Andre Seals; Vincent Alexandria; Stacy Hawkins-Adams; Nancy Arnold; Candace Hill; Nicole Bailey-Williams; Irene Brand; Maleta Wilson; Ernestine Jolivet; Thelma Gould; Shirley Johnson (Enoch-Pratt); Mount Olive (Lewiston, NC), Rev. Jones, Jr.; Teresa Smallwood; Andrea (AJ) Jones; Kelly (Dennis) Jones; Susan Irvin; Katy Boshart; Myla Meeks; Regine Hobson; the Washington women (Dear, Myrl, Rhonda, Andrea, Peg, and Wanda);

Penny Smith; Robin Green; Derrick Wooden; Shirley Burks; Hoyt Walker; and Ashley Burks. I appreciate the support from all my Haley, Tennin, Moorman, and Glass family members. I appreciate each and every person mentioned, as well as those inadvertently omitted.

What would I do without my advance readers:
Emma (John) Foots, Aunt Ada Tennin, Laurel (Lynn) Robinson, Dorothy Robinson, Dr. Leslie (Eldridge) Walker-Harding, Attorneys Tammy and Renee Lenzy, Kirkanne Moseley, Rena (Roscoe) Burks, and my incredible husband. Each of you has unquestionably made my stories better. T. Davis Bunn, you single-handedly challenged my writing and motivated me to continue enhancing my craft. I'm forever grateful for your mentoring.

Thank you sorors of Delta Sigma Theta Sorority, especially my own chapter—Valley Forge (PA): Pres. Theljewa Garrett and Ahoskie Alumnae (NC). Special thanks to a long list of independent African-American booksellers and book clubs, especially Extra Special Women (IL), Sistahs with a Vision (NJ), Sisters Empowered & Making A Difference (DE), Tabahani (CA), and Up All Night (CO).

Pamela Harty, you are a dream agent—encouraging, knowledgeable, and personable. You have made the business end of this job much easier. To the BET family, thank you Linda Gill and Glenda Howard for publishing *Still Waters* and for launching New Spirit.

As always, I acknowledge you, the readers. I write for two reasons. First, because it's a ministry God has called me to do. Second, I write to reach you. Thank you for touching my life, and may each of you be blessed in return.

Love…keeps no record of wrongs… It always protects, always trusts, always hopes, always perseveres. Love never fails.

—1 Corinthians 13:4-5, 7-8

Chapter 1

"I don't want a divorce." Mrs. Williams didn't flinch, not so much as a whimper. If the thought of divorce was offensive, she didn't let on. "I didn't get married to end up divorced. I don't want to be one of those women who ends up alone, and I definitely don't want my kids to grow up without their father, but I'm tired," she continued. "I'm just tired of trying to make him happy. If he would just act right, everything would be fine," she said as three of her sons came running up the aisle. "Junior, wait in the lobby for me and watch Baby Rick. I'll be right out," she told her preteen before turning back to the church mother. "That two year old can be a handful at times."

"I know six boys and a husband keeps you busy. I don't know how you find so much time to spend here at church with a husband at home."

"To be honest, I used to love working here at the

church. It was my only time away from the house, the kids, and Greg, especially when he gets into one of his moods like he's in right now. That's why I'm in no rush to get home today."

"Men need their space, that's all."

"Space? I'm the one who needs space. Don't get me wrong, I love my children, but six is a lot. I couldn't handle another one."

Baby Rick came charging in with Junior in pursuit.

"That's okay, I got him," Laurie said, corralling Baby Rick as he tried to breeze by. "Take your brothers and go to the car," she told Junior. "I'll be right out."

Mrs. Williams laughed openly. "You're still young, Laurie. How are you going to stop another child from entering this world if that's the plan God has for you?"

She'd stayed in the marriage believing it would settle down and get back to the way it used to be, back to when they were happy. If they were to have a chance, Greg had to get his anger under control. The more explosive he became, the more difficult it became and the less interested she was in concealing their issues from outsiders. In the meantime, she couldn't allow another child to sneak into the household, not through her womb. She had a plan, and it was to keep avoiding Greg's intimate advances until her body said the coast was clear. Menopause was far off, but avoidance was the best she could do for now, although there was a good chance that Greg's frustration wouldn't hold out much longer; with no backup plan in sight, fear whisked in.

"Got to take the good with the bad, honey. Marriage isn't easy but stick it out and let God get the glory." Easy to say for a deacon's wife married forty-five years. Mrs. Williams wasn't married to Greg Wright, a man whose moods riveted like a roller coaster—fast, slow, up, down, winding, scary, and at other times sprinkled with sheer exhilaration. Those were the times she was drawn to Greg, like when she first met him. Back then they couldn't stand being apart for more than a day. Now it was hard being around him for more than an hour. Something had to change. She knew it and hopefully God did, too.

Chapter 2

At least Sunday only came once a week. A reasonable person could endure three hours of just about anything, barring concentration camp torture, which was the closest analogy he could render for the weekly pilgrimage to his parents, the almighty Mr. and Mrs. Wright. Greg sat at the table nestled between two booster seats. His troubles swirled around, unbridled. Cheek resting on his tightly clasped fist, he plopped the pay stub and a few bills on top of the chipped veneer tabletop. Jolted back into reality, his body stiffened for a fleeting moment when the garage door opened. Greg knew he'd have to work hard in order to stay calm.

A millisecond was the only separation between keys jiggling in the back door and a stream of kids filing through the laundry room, making enough noise to put the Atlanta Falcons stadium of fans to shame. Greg eased to his feet but was overcome with a flood of Sunday school drawings thrust in his face.

"Daddy, see what I made?" six-year-old Keith said, pushing the paper into his father's view.

"Mine is better than yours," followed his seven-year-old brother.

"I got one, too," said a younger child.

Mitchell bypassed the bombardment of his father and went straight to the refrigerator. He was tall for a nine year old, particularly with a short mother and a father of average height. But tipping the scale at 175 pounds nullified any statuesque presence Mitchell might have commanded.

Junior stood at a distance.

"Boy, get out of that refrigerator. Get upstairs and get your clothes changed," Laurie yelled, lugging her purse, book bag, and the toddler.

"Okay, boys, I'll look at everybody's paintings one at a time," Greg said, sorting through the papers, trying to put them in some type of coherent order. "I can see that you've all done a really good job," he said to his pack of budding artists, sealing the accolades with a group hug, tight, not wanting to let go. This was his paradise, the family he'd created. They were the morphine that kept him going. "I'm proud of you."

"Are you going to take mine to your work again?" one of his sons asked.

"He's not taking yours," Mitchell said, gulping down a kiddy container of juice. "If he takes anybody's, it will be a real picture that I made, not some little finger paint thing you made at church."

"Mitchell, I said get upstairs," Laurie shouted. "That mouth of yours is going to get you into more trouble than you can handle."

"Stop yelling at the boy all the time. He didn't mean anything by it," Greg roared.

Silence rolled into the eat-in-kitchen like a Caribbean summer shower—brief, noticeable, and just enough drizzle to put a harmless damper on the festivities. Laurie bent over to set the baby down. Her eyes screamed back at her husband as their gazes met before she stomped out of the room.

Anger swelled in Junior. He caught up to his brother on the stairs, bumping him hard. "You're always starting stuff." He bumped him again. "I'm sick of you. Why don't you just leave?"

"You talking to me, Junior?" Mitchell said with voice cracking.

"Who else you think I'm talking to? You don't see anybody else on the stairs, do you?"

Mitchell shrugged his shoulders and kept quiet.

"Maybe I hate somebody else around here, too; maybe I don't."

"You hate me, Junior?" Mitchell whispered with tears forming.

"Nah, now get out of my way and leave me alone. Just

stop starting stuff, then I won't have to hate you and I won't have to hurt you, either." Mitchell ran to his room.

The fight on the stairs didn't stop the laughing and kiddy talk going on in the kitchen until Daddy made everybody go upstairs to their bedrooms. Daddy carried Baby Rick. When they got to the top of the stairs, he handed him over and said, "Take off Rick's suit and put that outfit on that your mother laid out for him this morning."

"What outfit?" Junior asked, mad inside that he got asked instead of somebody else.

"Boy, what's wrong with you? You saw that outfit laying on his dresser this morning."

Junior swallowed hard and sighed loud enough to feel retaliation but low enough not to let his father hear. "Come on, Rick. Let me help you get your clothes changed." *You're the only one who doesn't get on my nerves around here,* he reminded himself.

Before Greg walked away from Junior and Baby Rick, he added, "And get that room cleaned when we get back from your grandparents. That's too much mess for a two year old and a twelve year old to be making."

Two brothers per room swallowed the 2,200-square-foot house, which was a nice size 8 years ago for the young family, before the boys started coming and wouldn't stop. But there was always room for one more child. The boys wouldn't agree, especially Junior. Being the oldest, he had his own room before Rick was born.

Against his will, last year Junior was forced to share his bedroom with his baby brother. The age difference was a consideration at first, but it hadn't made sense to switch the other four boys around since they were already adjusted. The situation could be worse. He felt pleased that at least every one of his sons had his own bed. Not bad for six boys.

Greg opened the door to the master bedroom and found Laurie undressing. His eyes danced over her as he pushed the door shut, tight.

Laurie kept silent.

"What do you think about another child, a girl this time?" Greg caressed her bare shoulders. Preempting his hands from clawing at her any further, she jumped up.

"We need to get over to your parents. You know how mad they get when we're late."

"Forget my parents," he said, flicking his hand in the air, then breaking its force and letting it fall like a feather onto her shoulder, which was still in arm's reach. She dipped her shoulder and let his hand fall off. Crisscrossing her arms, she covered herself, hoping that would be enough to get him moving along another line of thinking. "Please let me get dressed so I can help the kids get ready."

Towering over her at five-foot-ten, his body easily nudged her until she fell back onto the bed. His slim physique with no hint of muscles sprouting from any region followed suit, completely covering her size sixteen body, compliments of her back-to-back pregnancies. "You never spend any quality time with me anymore," he said, stretching her hands out above her head and kissing her neck. "What happened to us? We used to be all over each other when we first got married. Now I can barely touch you without you pulling away."

Look around here, she wanted to tell him. "Greg, we're not twenty years old anymore. I have more to worry about, like the boys and taking care of the house. By the time I finish with my list of stuff to do every day, I'm tired."

"It's always the kids, the house, your church, your family, or something."

"Don't blame the church. You complained so much about me being involved over there that I stopped pretty much everything except Sunday service. So you can't blame God. I don't spend as much time with Him anymore, thanks to you."

"Okay, so you eased up on church, but you're always busy with the kids. You don't have any time left for me, and I'm your husband. I should come before the kids."

The kids, she thought, *I didn't make them by myself.* But she wouldn't dare broach that subject.

He continued lining the ridge of her body with tiny smooches, despite her frigid response.

"Greg, please, let's go. I really don't want to be late."

"Shoot, come on, Laurie, what's the problem now?" He snapped to his feet. She watched the blood vessels in his temples swell like a cresting river, then recess.

"What's wrong with you? You act like you don't want to touch me half the time. News flash, woman, you're my wife, which means I'm committed to you and you're committed to me. That includes everything," he preached. "What do I have to do to get some affection from my wife?" he howled with temples pulsating.

Laurie eased off the bed, careful to stay out of arm's reach of the brooding storm. Speaking up was good, but at what price? Fumbling to get her clothes on, she said, "Greg, why do we have to go through this? I'm not saying I don't want to be with you like that."

"Like what, Laurie? Like a husband and wife should be, as one, connected? You act like it's a bad thing," he screamed, taking a step toward her.

She compensated by taking a step back and rushed to pull the shirt over her head, leaving her view impaired for only a brief moment. "Greg, the kids can hear you."

"So what, those are my kids. They know Mommy and Daddy have disagreements. Don't worry about them; this is about you and me."

She knew he was approaching the red zone. The place on the thermometer where overheating was inevitable; the spot where the hose bursts, sending molten liquid spurting everywhere and painfully burning all in its path. "Greg, look," she said, slapping her hands against her thighs, "can we go to your parents, and then when we get home tonight, I'll do whatever it is you want me to do? Is that okay?"

He scratched his head with eyelids closed. "My

goodness, you make it sound like I'm some kind of an animal. I'm not trying to force you to do anything. This has to be something you want, too. Don't do me any favors," he said, slamming the door on his way out.

Laurie breathed a sigh of relief. It hadn't been pretty, but the little thunderstorm had blown in and out without any major damage, preserving enough energy to handle the upcoming phase two—dinner at the Wright's.

Chapter 3

The chatter coming from the boys in both of the back rows bridged the canyon looming in the front seat of the minivan, which Greg purchased right after their now seven-year-old Jason was born. It seemed like yesterday when they began struggling to make ends meet. Laurie had wanted the van desperately with two children already crowding their Nissan Sentra. Greg had finally gotten the job he wanted, but the pay was on the low side. After squeezing both car seats and a kindergartener into the car for a few weeks, Greg decided a new van wasn't a luxury, it was a necessity for his growing family. The fact that they'd purchased a fairly new home the year before with a steep mortgage hadn't deterred his decision. "We'll have to tighten up our budget and make it work," is what she remembered him telling her back then, back at a time when they dreamed together, when life was predictable, desirable.

Greg turned onto his parents' property and scooted through the gated fence, which was wide open as usual. The van crept up the long semicircular driveway, bypassing the first bay of garages and the twelve-foot, solid-oak, double front doors, easing to a stop about 100 yards before the pavement curved back around and headed back out toward the street.

The kids were eager to get out. Greg laid his head back on the headrest and gripped the steering wheel, staring at his younger brother's brand new convertible two-seater Mercedes-Benz parked a few car lengths ahead.

"Can we get out?" a voice asked from the back.

"Yes, you can get out, but"—Greg turned around to face all six boys in the back—"you all know how to act when you're in Grandma and Grandpa's house, right?"

No one responded.

"Right?" Greg reinforced in a stronger tone.

"Yes, we have to say thank you and please ma'am and no pushing each other," a little voice spoke up.

"Anybody push me, they're getting pushed back," Junior said.

"Try it and see if I'm playing," Greg responded. "Nobody better show off in there. I don't feel like dealing with any more mess today."

Laurie cut her glance his way, knowing he was subtly throwing her a message which she was in no mood to receive. She let his comment fly out the window with not even so much as a sigh of acknowledgment.

Rick tried to get out of his car seat. "Junior and

Mitchell, get out first, and then help the boys get out, too," Greg instructed.

"What a surprise," Junior uttered.

"Boy, I don't know why you're trying me with that mouth of yours. You have some kind of chip on your shoulder and I'm not going to let too many days go by without knocking it off. Now straighten up your attitude before you go inside that house. I'm not going to have you embarrassing me in here when you already know how to act."

Junior acquiesced and helped to get Baby Rick and his brother Larry out of the backseat as Mitchell watched the six year old jump out of the van like it was a jungle gym. The children hovered around the van, knowing not to take another step near the door until their parents were leading the way.

"You still mad?" Greg asked.

Laurie wanted to say, "What do you think?" but realized it would be a waste of four good words. Besides, why expend energy on a sore spot that couldn't heal? Might as well save all the positive vibes she could muster for the giant residing on the other side of those double doors. "I'm not mad, Greg." She ran her fingers through her hair with head slightly tilted toward him but not allowing her eyes to focus on him. "I'm just tired."

She cracked the van door open. "Keep Rick out of those rocks and, boy, put that twig down before you poke somebody in the eye by accident," she shouted to Larry, like a four year old could control the toddler. "Mitchell, take that stick from him."

It might as well be school recess for the boys because Greg paid no attention to the boys roughing it up outside the van. His discipline was directed at one person only—her.

"Well, if you go in there with a funky attitude, you know my parents will pick up on it, and I really don't feel like dealing with all of that right now. I have a lot on my mind, with the job, the bills, you know, a lot of stuff."

Laurie rolled her tongue around the border of her teeth and looked away from Greg in the direction of the children. She'd already heard this story before.

"You don't have to worry about me embarrassing you in front of your perfect parents."

"See what I mean? Can't you just leave our arguments at home? You have to let everybody and their brother know what's going on. I really don't want them knowing our business, so you need to get it together."

"Like I said, don't worry. I won't embarrass you, and I definitely won't let them know anything you don't want them to know." Filled with her lecture for the day on marital etiquette, she exited the van before he had time to toss in an addendum. She rushed to the back of the van, opened the storage area, and grabbed a carrying bag stuffed with pull-up diapers and toys.

When Greg came around the van, everyone moved in unison toward the door. "Can I ring the bell this time, Daddy?" Larry asked, jumping up and down. "Can I please, can I?" Before Greg could give the okay, Mitchell rang it.

"Now, why did you do that? You're just being funny at your little brother's expense. You're really asking for it," Laurie told her second oldest son.

Junior waited to see if that was the end of it, or if his mother would have to hear more yelling from his daddy because of something Mitchell did.

The massive wooden door opened and Mrs. Virginia Wright, a woman slightly taller than Mitchell, opened the door wearing a silk blouse accented with a pair of linen pants. Her nails were short and buffed to such a high natural gloss that it would take three coats of top shine for Laurie to get the same look. The woman's silky jet-black hair, which didn't show a hint of new growth, was pulled back into a tightly crafted bun. A Rolex watch, a pair of diamond stud earrings, and a tennis bracelet with enough glitter to blind a pack of deer were the only items of jewelry gracing her body outside of her wedding ring.

"Here are my grandbabies," she greeted with her palms up and elbows tucked tightly into her side. "And it's a bunch of you, too," she said, shifting her glance slightly upward from the children to Laurie's level. "Why, Laurie, it's always good to see you. Come on in."

Greg was the only one who greeted his mother and followed it up with a kiss on her cheek. "I don't know why, but I was halfway expecting the housekeeper to answer the door."

"Greg, you know the only work Lily does on the weekend is Sunday dinner. She's not here to answer the door for you anymore," Mrs. Wright said with a hint of pleasantry as she beckoned for the children to come in. "As a matter of fact, we haven't let anyone work weekends since you left for college sixteen years ago."

"I can't believe it's been that long ago since I left home for college."

"August fifteenth, a day your father will never forget."

"And won't let me forget it either," he said, with an edge.

Before tension claimed another soul in this mausoleum, Laurie found an out. Lifting Baby Rick, she said, "I'm going to take the boys into the kitchen and get them situated."

"That's fine," Mrs. Wright said without making a move in the direction of the kitchen. "Lily has made their favorite, chicken with macaroni and cheese." Approvals poured out from the boys. "She's waiting for them in the kitchen."

Laurie steered her men to the food, not looking back, glad to be moving along a path of fresh air.

Greg watched as his world walked away and braced himself for dinner.

"All we've ever wanted is the best for you," his mother said, letting her palm rest on his cheek.

"What I want and what you and Dad think is best for me hasn't matched in years."

"Well, there's always tomorrow, son. For today, let's keep the air clear and stay away from topics that might steer us all down a rocky path." She patted his cheek and released her tight jaws long enough to formulate the semblance of a smile. "Okay, will you do that for me?"

"Anything for you, Mom," he said, covering her hand with his.

Mom opened the French door leading into the dining room. "Look who's here?" she said, cutting through the merriment pouring out of the room.

"What's up, Greg," his brother Sterling Jr. greeted. Greg reciprocated, followed by an acknowledgment to his father, who was positioned at the head of a twelve-seat dining room table sitting on mahogany legs about the size of Baby Rick.

"I was wondering if you were coming?" his father said. "We were just about to get started when the doorbell rang." Dad continued placing the triangular-folded linen napkin in his lap. "Boy, you're going to miss your own funeral. I don't know how you hold down a job." No one dared interject as his father held court. "You're never on time."

"It's good to see you, too, Dad."

"Where's Laurie and the boys?" Dad asked.

"In the kitchen getting the boys situated."

"They need to get in here and say hello first. What kind of manners are you teaching those boys? I don't know why your mother lets Lily make two different meals. Those are a pack of thick, healthy boys. They can eat what we eat. I know that big one can eat at the table with us."

"You mean Mitchell, right, Dad? His name is Mitchell."

"I know what my grandson's name is."

"Why don't we all sit and eat," Mom jumped in. "The kids will be fine for now. Let them eat and you can see them later."

Laurie had the boys straightened out in the kitchen with Lily. She shuffled toward the entryway, letting time and distance rinse her thoughts clean—agitation didn't sit well on an empty stomach. She sliced through the dense tension without interrupting the conversation in progress.

"So how's the convertible running?" Greg asked Sterling Jr.

"Like a dream, big brother. You should treat yourself to one sometime soon. You're a hardworking man. Treat yourself to some real luxury. I know Laurie will let you buy a toy, right, Sis?"

She let her facial expression answer.

"Come on now. He's not a Yale man like us." Sterling Sr. pushed back in his chair and pierced his gaze on Greg. "You know he can't afford a convertible sports car drawing cartoons. Your Mercedes is a man's car and requires a man's job, not some part-time hobby that you're pretending is adequate to support a family you weren't ready for."

"Dad, geez, can't we at least get started off on a good note? Can I please, one day, just for once come into this house with my family, have a nice meal, decent conversation, and leave feeling like you haven't rolled over me with a semitruck. Just one time, is that too much to ask?" he said in a raised voice, which quickly trailed off to slightly above a whimper.

"Excuse me, I'm going to check on the kids," Laurie told them. For a house to be so big, it felt tight, choking, smothering, and to think, this was the place where Greg grew up.

"Ah, Pops, why are you so hard on my brother? He's a settled family man. Nothing wrong with that, right, Mom? You'd be happy if I got married as soon as possible and added a few more grandkids to the list, right?" Junior added.

"There's nothing wrong with raising a family. It can be a very rewarding experience if you manage to make the right choices," Mom said.

"Mom, don't you start in too or I'm out of here," Greg said, consciously not letting his voice dip down this time. Hold it. Hold it, he kept telling himself. Don't say anything you might regret later. Tough it out. He'd done it before, hundreds of times, and he could do it again.

"You know I didn't mean anything by it. You've done a phenomenal job providing for your little army at such a young age. I would have preferred for you to have gotten established before buckling down with so much pressure, that's all."

"This was my doing."

"And you say it so proudly, like going to law school for two years and then dropping out to take some penny-ante position with a no-name, second-tier company in order to take care of a family is a good deed, all because you couldn't control your hormones. It was bad enough that you settled for a part-time night school program, which I was willing to accept, realizing you weren't Ivy League caliber and a pseudo-law program was more suited for you. But after you had the second child, you quit," Dad had to point out.

"If I'm happy and not asking either of you for help, what does it matter?" He wanted to scream at his father but knew better. Disrespect and aggression weren't tolerated in Judge Wright's courtroom or in his house. In both places he was the law, and violators were punished mercilessly.

"It matters that I wasted a lot of my money on your childish pursuit of an education, one that could have gotten you off poverty row and into a more refined lifestyle."

"Dad, when are you going to get over the fact that I dropped out of law school because I didn't want to be a lawyer? I never did. That's what you wanted me to be. I tried to follow in your footsteps, but it's just not for me. Can't you be satisfied that at least one of your two sons did finish? Junior is the lawyer and I'm happy for him."

"Leave me out of this, man. This is between you and Pops. I don't want to be anywhere near the middle of this. As a matter of fact, I'm going out to the kitchen to hang out with my nephews. Excuse me."

"You don't have to leave, son," Dad pleaded with Sterling Jr.

Greg stood.

"Where are you going?" Mom asked.

"Going to get my wife," he responded, slinging his lap napkin onto his empty chair.

"Sit," Mom ordered. "Let's eat before the food gets cold. This discussion can be tabled for another time. Today is family day. Let's try to act normal, even if it kills us."

Chapter 4

Crushed black beans, processed and percolating, is what Greg had to thank for the aroma tingling his nose. Thirty minutes of fresh coffee brewing up close was the only benefit he could find in sitting so close to the vending machine area. His closet-sized cubicle, masquerading as a full-service office, would soon be retired when the big promotion finally came to fruition. A long time coming, but the moment had arrived, and just in time. With a $1,200 mortgage knocking at the door, feeding and clothing eight people on $2,800 a month after taxes and 401K deductions required a magician more than a college degree.

A coworker eased into Greg's cubicle. "Any word on when the promotion is going to be announced?"

Greg spun around in his seat. "I haven't heard a thing. I'm just waiting and hoping they do the right thing this time," he said.

"You really think you're getting it this time?" his coworker asked.

"Why not? All I know is that I should be the one to get the lead spot or something is wrong around here. I've been with this company for eight years and in this same position for three. It's time for me to get mine. I have a family to take care of and I need a real raise. So, yeah, I'm looking for this promotion to be mine. I deserve it."

"You do deserve it. Everybody in this department knows you're the best graphic designer here. When I got my promotion last year, I just knew you were on the list, too. The execs are crazy if they don't realize what an asset you are to this company."

"Why, thanks, man. I appreciate that. At least someone around here thinks so. You'll have to put a word in for me," Greg said, mostly joking.

"Huh, I don't think so. My input might backfire on you because I don't have any pull in this place. I'm just a peon line manager, like a guppy in a pond full of piranhas. I'm just trying to stay out of everybody's way," he said, letting his hands crisscross in midair without touching. I'd like to help out, but you're on your own. Good luck."

"Yeah, thanks," Greg said. Luck might be exactly what he needed. Probably wouldn't hurt to say a prayer, too; something, anything was worth trying. Besides, uttering a few words during his greatest hour of need was normal and couldn't constitute him as a religious fanatic. No, no, that was Laurie's bag. One carrier of religious craziness in the house at any given time was more than enough.

The morning crawled by and all Greg had to show for his time was a half-sketched soft drink advertisement. The stack of ten layout requests was vying for his attention. He jumped onto the company's intranet site and surfed to the home page. He clicked on Human Resources and navigated to Announcements. "No updates for today, man oh man." His head dropped as he blew out a breath of air that sounded like steam releasing from an engine. He sat uninterrupted. Finally he pulled his lunch from his desk hutch and unwrapped his turkey sandwiches, which looked like the amount of meat needed for a man's sandwich had been divided into three. He took a bite and plopped the snack-of-a-sandwich back onto its crumbled strip of cellophane. Stomach churning, he wrenched his hands, letting his glance roam around his desk. He pushed the lunch bag back on the desk and gripped the edge with both hands. He checked the intranet again. No news. He jerked back in his chair and wanted to let out a taste of his frustration but caught himself. What was taking so long? Everybody in the office knew today was the day. It wasn't definite that the team's lead spot was his, but who was more qualified than him? Eight years with the company, notable mention on three national advertisement campaigns, a bachelor's degree, and a couple years of law school to boot. He whipped out a pen and jotted down a column of figures.

2,800	
-1,200	*mortgage*
-125	*association fee*
-250	*utilities*
-70	*phone*
-600	*food*
-25	*diapers*
-100	*insurance*
-40	*cable*
-100	*credit card*
-75	*gas*
-25	*church for Laurie*
-75	*kids expenses*
$ 115	*(left)*

He circled the balance over and over until the imprint dug into the four pages underneath. Broke. The few months when he was fortunate, there was around $100 left to split between him and Laurie for pocket money. He rarely saw any of the so-called extra money by the time the boys got the extras they needed and Laurie took care of a few other odds and ends around the house.

School supplies, dentist appointments, and new clothes—all those expenses were coming down the pike in another month. This promotion was just the ticket. Since the new job paid about $25,000 more, he drew a line through the 2,800 and made it 4,300. He squeezed in lines for "emergency 200," "savings 200," and "van 300." Another 300 for college funds. He also scratched in "Laurie 300." It would be so nice to finally be able to let her have money for herself, not to be spent on the house or the boys, just on her. She could get her hair done and get a manicure or whatever it was she wanted from one of those girlie shops. Thinking about his boys and Laurie sent a warm charge circulating through his body, thawing out lingering parts of his frigid soul. She could buy a new outfit from time to time, too, like other women. She deserved it. She was worth it, and he knew it.

After making additions to the budget, there was more than $400 a month left for everything else. He could take $150 for himself. That's all he needed; so long as his family was taken care of, he was happy. Life was finally coming together. He reared back in the chair with fingers interlocked behind his head. He wouldn't be able to get a new sports car like Sterling Jr., not yet, but Dad would see that his profession of choice was finally paying off and ends were more than meeting, they were overlapping.

He took a bite of the turkey sandwich, savoring the taste, relishing the thought that they would soon be a thing of the past. He would soon be able to go out to lunch like most others in the office. The day of skimping and hoping was over. He surfed the net one more time and scooted closer to the computer. Flashing across the screen read:

New Organizational Announcement
Staff meeting at 1:00 pm in the large training room

Greg glanced at his watch. 12:47. Up and out, no haste. His heart was pounding; blood careened through his veins. His legs were moving up the stairs, two at a time, but it was slow motion. He busted into the room with head held high, letting his sweaty palms glide down the sides of his pants. The room was densely populated with the roughly 100 employees expected. Greg found a seat up front. It would be easier for the Director of Marketing to recognize him when the time came. That's how it always worked when someone was promoted. They got the token praises and handshake from the boss, several levels up.

Within a five-minute period the remaining crowd flooded the room and by 1:05, the program was in place. A couple of assistant directors talked about second quarter earnings. Greg could care less about changes in the free parking guidelines. Expansion coming to the cafeteria was worthwhile seeing that he would soon be able to eat at work. No more carting a sack lunch like his sons. He could toss the Monday through Friday meatloaf and turkey sandwiches out the window. Real food for a real man was just one of the little perks he'd earned with this promotion. A few more administrative announcements, and then it was time for the director to take the stage. Greg looked around and made eye contact with two of his coworkers, giving a slight nod and grin of assurance. *Straighten up,* he thought. *Be calm, but poised.* What would he say when they acknowledged him in front of the department? In all of his preparation for this time, he hadn't given his speech any thought. Okay, it was too late to dwell on it. A simple thank you would work well.

The director took the stage and silence swept the room. "This company would not have established such a tremendous record of consistent success without a dynamic group of committed individuals such as yourselves. I think you all deserve a round of applause."

The room roared. *Yeah, yeah, yeah,* Greg echoed to himself. *Get to the announcements.* He rubbed his palms against his pants again, hoping they would stay dry this time.

"You all deserve praise and recognition. However, with any team, there are those who tend to stand out, even among a room of qualified, capable individuals such as yourselves. When individuals go the extra distance to make this company better, they need to be recognized and rewarded. Therefore, it is my distinct honor to announce that we have selected a candidate for the Graphic Design Team Lead position within the Advertising Division."

Greg shifted his weight forward in order to spring up effortlessly when his name was called.

"Megan Hurley, please come forward."

Greg was already in lift mode before the words Megan

Hurley were able to get an emergency override signal to his brain, telling him to plop his behind back down into his seat. Greg's emotions ran around out of control. He squirmed in the seat and refused to look back into the crowd and give anyone an opportunity to read his reaction.

Applause and whistles saturated the space minus Greg's contribution. It took all he could muster not to bolt out.

"Megan, congratulations on your promotion. You are truly a valued asset in this company, and I want to welcome you to the management team." The director and Megan shook hands as she rattled off a few words of acceptance, each word feeling like a needle sticking in the bottom of Greg's feet.

"Well, I want to say thank you for the opportunity and I look forward to working with my new team."

"Again, congratulations and welcome aboard." The director clapped his hands once. "Okay, that concludes our team meeting. Let's have another record-setting three months, and I'll see all of you in October for our third quarter update. Thanks, everyone."

Greg hustled to exit the scene before people started asking him questions like a reporter pushing the microphone into a grieving person's face, asking how did they feel after encountering a personal tragedy. How was he supposed to feel when he was just robbed of a position that was rightfully his? One he had worked his buns off to obtain, making sacrifice after sacrifice, pouring his heart into each project. And what kind of gratitude did he get from this shiftless, no-account, backwoods, two-bit company—none. He wanted to linger in the stairwell but heard the door open a flight or two below. He sprinted back to his cubicle and immediately got on the phone to avoid being free when those who were sure to come by reached his cubicle.

But his coworkers didn't get the hint. "Man, I just knew you had the job. Your name was written all over it. I can't believe you didn't get the job. What are you going to do?"

"What can I do?" Greg said, slamming his hutch door closed.

"I don't know, but if I were in your shoes and did the kind of work you did, shoot, I'd have to talk to somebody in here, and if they couldn't give me a lead position, I'd probably be out of here. Simple as that."

"Yeah, right, you're trying to tell me you would quit this job if you didn't get a promotion?"

"I'm not saying I would quit. Oh, no, don't get me wrong, but I'm saying you're not me. You have serious skills. You know you can outdesign everyone in this department. We all know that."

"Obviously not everybody agrees with you."

The coworker tilted his head and pressed his lips together.

Greg logged off his computer. "Look, man, I'm out of here."

"It's only two o'clock."

"That's right and I'm out of here," Greg said, dropping his briefcase on top of the stack of unfinished drawings. "Let Megan meet my deadlines." Greg left in a huff. Tomorrow he might see things differently, but for right now, he had as much commitment to the company as they had for him—superficial and not worth acknowledging.

Chapter 5

Greg had his hand on the door leading to the stairway when his manager called out to him. "I would like to talk with you about your current position. Do you have a minute?"

He wanted to say, "Doesn't it look like I'm leaving?" without caring about the consequences but opted with, "I guess."

His manager didn't appear phased, but it didn't really matter to Greg. Letting someone else in the department feel a taste of his frustration might be just the medicine he needed.

The two gentlemen followed the wall around a sea of cubicles until they reached a conference room. Greg took a seat and kept quiet as his manager closed the door and took a seat on the other side of the table.

"Greg, I wanted to speak with you before today's announcement but we had a client emergency and I didn't get a chance to chat with you earlier."

Greg sat stiff, with eyes piercing. He could see but not hear the manager taking a soft gulp.

"You are a valued employee and I recognize the contributions you've made to the company."

This should be the place where the humble employee jumps in and thanks his or her superior. Greg didn't set a single word free. Valued employee had been used one too many times today. That title belonged to Megan, the real winner. What was the name of the team Michael Jordan and the Bulls beat when they won their second championship? Who cares. No one remembers the loser who came in second place.

"Greg, let's be frank here. I'm not going to blow smoke up your behind. I know you're disappointed about not getting the lead position. I really fought hard for you."

"Really."

"Yes, really," the manager said, laying his hand on the table. "And believe it or not, I have every confidence you can do the job."

"So what happened?" Greg sat stiff in the chair with his arms folded, determined not to blink.

"The rest of the management team wanted someone with more leadership experience."

"Leadership experience." Greg leaned onto the table separating him and the manager. "Megan doesn't have any more experience than I do."

"Well, that's not quite true. She's completed an M.B.A. program since she started here six years ago."

"I know exactly when she started," Greg said with a tone of indignation, "because I was the one who trained her." He reared back in his chair, letting his arm stay on the table. "And now you want me to report to her? Humph. That's funny."

"Actually you won't have to report to her. That's what I'd like to talk to you about."

Greg didn't go out of his way to make the scene comfortable.

"The entire management staff values your contributions and—"

"Right," Greg interrupted, "and that's why I didn't get promoted?"

"Greg, look, we need to get past this situation. We've worked hard to come up with an alternative track for you. We're offering you a lateral move to the Features Department."

Features was a demotion. Only untalented artists with limited potential found excitement working in the dungeon, a place void of any career light. It wasn't the position for a designer who was serious about developing his or her craft and making a career out of it, but if it came with a raise, it had to be considered. "Will I be eligible for the bonus pool like the team lead position?"

"No, unfortunately, you still wouldn't be."

"What about a raise? Will I at least get some more money?"

"No, not really. However, if money is a key concern for you, I can see if we can come up with a few more thousand a year."

Greg chuckled.

"Work with me, Greg. I'm doing the best I can with an awkward situation. I feel really horrible about this. I want you to know the executive staff has taken notice of your work and we're working on getting you into a management position as quickly as possible, most likely in a year, two tops."

"Two years?" All Greg could think about was the money. "I'm supposed to wait two years. I've busted my chops here. You know I have, and all you can tell me is that I should look for my promotion in two years, and that's probably no guarantee."

The manager didn't respond.

"See, that's what I thought. So let me get this straight. You're saying hang in there, Greg, keep working your behind off, and who knows, maybe a few years down the road we can do something for you. In the meantime, rot in your funky little cube but keep churning out those award-winning ads because we really value your work." Greg snarled and let his head bob up and down on his rotating neck. "Get the heck out of here. If you think I'm going to sit back and be used by this company or any other company, you have another thing coming." Greg used all his force to push away from the table, sending the chair wheeling back toward the blind-covered, floor-to-ceiling windows.

"I would like to discuss this further."

"I'll see you," Greg told his manager who was still sitting.

"Let's plan to circle back on this matter tomorrow."

"I'll let you know if I'm coming in tomorrow."

"What do you mean if you're coming in tomorrow? We have the entire soft-drink packet to finish and get out by close of business tomorrow and you're the point person on the project. You have to be here."

"Get your new team lead to handle it. She has all the experience."

"Greg, this isn't going to fly well with the executive team."

Greg darted from the room in the midst of his manager's plea.

Chapter 6

"Drinking doesn't bring clarity." That's what Dad had echoed after hearing case after case of DUIs that led to vehicular manslaughter. He dodged the looming cigarette smoke while making his way to the bar.

"Hey, partner, what can I get you?" the bartender asked, sailing a bowl of pretzels across the countertop.

Greg reached into his pockets, pushed the lint out of the way, and pulled out two five-dollar bills and two ones. "I'll take a beer." He tossed a five on the bar and shoved the remaining money back into his pocket.

"Tap or draught."

"Tap, light is fine." Greg spun around on his chair to hear the game playing on the TV located overhead in the back corner of the room. The cool drip of beer on his finger indicated that his suds of despair had arrived. "Thanks," he said and took a swig, wincing as the flavor infiltrated his mouth. The bitterness didn't compare with the bad taste left from work.

"Can I get you anything else?"

"Nope, unless you have a job."

"Ah, employment problems, huh?" The bartender drew a glass of beer for another customer sitting two stools down. "It's rough nowadays when your job situation isn't right."

"Tell me about it," Greg said, wetting his lip with the beer. "No matter how hard you work, you can't get ahead." Greg let his head hang down. "Sometimes you just get tired, man, you just get tired."

"I hear you, but you have to do what you have to do." The bartender wiped the counter around Greg's area. "Where do you work, my man?"

"At the advertisement company."

"Ah, you're over there," he said, shaking his head. "You have it made, don't you? I hear that's a good company to work for, good benefits and all."

"It's not all that. I've been working there for eight years and they've promised me so many lies it's not funny." Greg slicked the sides of the mug, erasing the beads of water covering the mug. "I tell you, I'm ready to get out of there."

"Is it that bad?"

"Yeah, they're racist for one. A man like me won't be able to get ahead. That's not going to happen. So it's time for me to make some other moves. I'm not going to sit around there working myself to death for thirty years. They're crazy if they think I am."

"You're not thinking about leaving them, are you? I'm not trying to get into your business, but we don't have a whole lot of companies like that around here. Paine and Augusta State are about the only other major employers in the area."

"Never know, I just might have to check them out. All I know right now is that I have to do something about this job. They don't respect me there, that's for sure. Today they offered me some petty job after they gave my promotion away to a lady I trained five years ago, and they expect me to be cool about it. Shoot, man, they're crazy." Greg gently spun his mug of beer between his palms. "They have another thing coming," he said, spinning around on the barstool to face the TV again.

"I hear you."

After watching the mixed doubles, women's quarterfinal, and men's singles matches, his second beer was half gone.

"Another one?" the bartender asked.

Greg indiscreetly eased his hand into his pocket and felt his few bucks. "No, I'm fine," he said, swishing the last bit of beer in the mug. "Two is my limit."

"Two? You barely touched the first one and you're not doing too well with this one." The bartender dipped a few glasses in the soapy water behind the counter and set them on a rack.

"I'm not a beer person."

"Having problems on your job and watching the Williams sisters lose all in the same afternoon requires a drink. Why don't you take a shot of gin, on the house?" The bartender grabbed a shot glass.

"Oh, nah, nah, that's okay. I'm good with the beer."

"Sure?" he asked, holding the bottle of gin in his hand, ready to pour. "It's on me."

"Nah, really. Thanks though, man." Greg pulled his last two dollars out and laid the tip on the counter. Payday was around the corner. It wasn't the first time a pocketful of lint would be his only currency between checks.

Chapter 7

Consistency kept chaos manageable. Six o'clock dinner. Seven o'clock clean the kitchen. The summer schedule was slightly different than the fall. School was out and there was no homework, which meant the boys got an hour reprieve on bedtime; instead of eight-thirty, it was nine-thirty, forty, fifty, fifty-five. How many times had she caught a glance of the kitchen clock during dinner? Greg wasn't one to miss dinner but work seemed demanding lately. Hopefully he'd be home soon and eat the meatloaf before it shriveled. She knew how much he hated dry meat.

She crept up the stairs and checked on each child. Baby Rick was sleeping on Junior's bed. "Everybody, take your baths and get ready for bed." She picked up Rick. "And keep the noise down so you don't wake him."

"You want me to put him in his crib?" Junior asked.

"No, that's all right. I'll let him sleep in our room."

Junior beamed with a look of approval. It wasn't so bad sharing a room with his little brother when Rick slept with his parents most of the time, leaving the room to Junior.

Walking past her sons' room, Laurie saw six-year-old Keith asleep and Larry was at his desk coloring with his tabletop light still on. "Turn your light off and go to bed," she said entering the room while shifting Rick's weight to her other shoulder.

"I'm waiting up for Daddy," he said, turning out the light and dragging to his bed.

"No, you're not. You're taking your little self to bed right now." She took her free arm and pulled the cover over his little body but wasn't able to bend down and seal it with a kiss as was normally done.

Water formed in his eyes. "But he promised to read Spiderman again."

His disappointment tugged at her heart. She knew no consoling words would suffice for a little boy who loved having his dad put him to bed night after night. Where was Greg? Whimpers pricked her back into the little boys' room. "Go take your book into Junior's room. He can read to you," she said softly, trying not to wake his brother.

"Do I have to?"

"Yes, now go," she said, flinging the covers back. "You boys act like you can't do anything by yourselves when your father's not around."

The preschooler slammed his book under his arm

and walked hard, not quite stomping into the hallway, muttering, "He doesn't read it as good as Daddy."

"That's okay, go on anyway. Otherwise you'll have to go to bed without a story."

Junior must have been better than the last option because no further rebellion was waged.

Laurie stood still, taking in the moment. Greg was a good father, no question. She loved him for that. Half the time she wanted to choke him for being so bull-headed; other times she wanted to love and protect his feelings. Through ups and downs, he was still the only man she'd ever truly loved, and a first love was hard to shake.

Chapter 8

Greg glided the Sentra into the driveway, coming to a slow halt inches from the garage door. He would leave the car outside tonight instead of making a bunch of noise by opening the garage door. The dome over the sink lit the kitchen well enough for him to find the refrigerator. He peeled a slice of meatloaf from the platter and planted himself in a chair at the table. He took a tiny bite and chewed it with the energy of a snail. He could have flicked on a light switch and been instantly transformed out of the darkness but opted not to. Instead, he stayed at the table, holding the slice of meat for a bit before laying it down.

He tiptoed up the stairs, careful that his eleven-thirty arrival wouldn't disrupt a house of sleepyheads. He gripped the master bedroom's doorknob and slowly turned it, pushing the door barely wide enough to sliver into the room. Without turning on the light he let his hand trace the wall around to the closet. He entered the walk-in closet, closing the door behind him, and flipped on the light. He was eager to find Laurie. Beer hadn't done much to drown his sorrows. Maybe she could.

Muffled noises and light peeking underneath the door woke Laurie, who had only been asleep since eleven o'clock. She stayed in the bed. Rick didn't budge, lying between her and the edge of the bed. Greg changed his clothes in a whirlwind and hopped into bed, snuggling next to her.

"Un-huh," she grunted, wiggling her shoulders.

Greg continued in his relentless pursuit of affection.

"Where have you been? I've been worried sick about you."

"What do you mean where have I been? I've been out, that's where I've been."

"You could have called," she said in a sharp, cutting tone.

"I had a lot on my mind and I needed some space. What's with all of the attitude?" he said, moving in closer.

"Will you please stop? Rick is in our bed."

"I'm tired of you putting him in our bed," Greg said, jumping up. He reached over Laurie and swooped up Rick.

"Why don't you let him sleep? It's already late."

"Because he has his own bed. I don't want him in our bed every night."

Greg deposited Rick into his own toddler bed with not much of a stir of protest from the baby.

Laurie had moved to the other end of the king-sized bed, out of arm's reach, or so she thought.

Greg picked up where he left off.

Laurie shook off his advances without comment.

"Don't start. I had a tough day at work. I don't need you to trip on me, too. I need you." He caressed her shoulders.

"I'm tired. I had a lot of running around to do today, and the kids wore me out this evening. I don't feel like staying up."

"You never feel like it," he burst out, pushing back from her.

Laurie's body froze. The deep voice of authority rushed through her limbs. If she could keep quiet, be still as a mouse being stalked by a vicious cat, maybe he would let her crawl away unharmed. Where was God? She had been practically living in the church, praying, seeking, begging for Greg to change, and nothing so far. Still more of the same.

"I'm tired of your funky attitude. You act like you don't want to be a wife. I have enough to worry about trying to provide for this family. The last thing I'm going to put up with is you treating me like I have the plague."

"Greg, it's not a big deal. I'm just tired tonight, that's all."

"You're tired every night. What are you doing all day to be so tired at night? Are you seeing somebody?"

What? The nerve of him. How dare he make that kind of accusation after all the kids she'd had for him. If he only knew just how much this wasn't about him. Even if she couldn't keep her vows to him, she desperately wanted to keep her vows to God about being faithful and seeing this marriage all the way through to the end, so long as it didn't kill her.

"Well," he demanded.

"No." Saying "what do you think" wouldn't be smart right now.

His tirade continued. "I'm the one working. If anybody should be tired, it should be me, but you don't hear me complaining. That's because I know how to handle my responsibilities."

Not his responsibility speech again. She didn't write the actual checks but was well aware of their financial distress. In the event that she might slip and forget, there was Greg, in full bloom, like a perennial flower with deep roots returning time after time without fail. Her eyelids wanted to snap shut, but his wailing wouldn't permit it.

Laurie reached over to turn on the light situated on the nightstand.

"Greg, you're going to wake the kids."

"So what if I do. This is my house. I'm the one paying the mortgage around here. If I want to yell at the top of my lungs all night long, that's what I'll do," he professed, sending shock waves rippling into the hallway.

Temples throbbing, rage rising. Extinguish his fire

while it was still containable. Take a deep breath and maintain control. The techniques she learned in the counseling last year were kicking in.

Greg paced the room with his arms floundering in midair.

"I might not get any respect at work, but you can best believe I'm going to get it here."

Let him rant out of energy, then he can take his black behind back to bed and let everybody else in the house go back to sleep, too. Laurie waited with bated breath for Rick to let out a cry. She prayed the boys would sleep past this latest sermon. She'd noticed the boys were developing a higher tolerance each year for their father's midnight madness episodes. Years ago, they would awaken, bawling their eyes out. Now they mostly rolled over, covered their ears with a pillow, and kept sleeping.

"I walk around here, broke, no money in my pocket, but do you hear me whining to you and the kids? I can't even go to the bar and afford a decent drink like other guys do. I can't afford to buy my lunch at the office. Isn't that a joke? That's the kind of sacrifice I'm making for this family. And your rejection is the thanks I get. Is it too much to ask for your support, a little love and affection?"

She could dash fuel on the argument by jumping in. Instead, she pulled the cover up to her neck and held on tightly.

"What do you have to say for yourself? Am I talking to myself?" he said, ripping the sheets back, exposing her T-shirt-and-shorts-covered body.

Shhh. Don't add to his agitation. Whatever Greg was going through came from somewhere other than their household. She hadn't known him long enough to be the source of so many of his woes in life. "Put the cover back and lay your sick behind down" is what she wanted to scream into his face. A glance at the clock displayed 12:15. She rubbed her arm across her eyes, which were closed. Could she please get back to sleep? It was after midnight. How much more would he require her to endure?

"I'm talking to you, Laurie. Geez, say something."

Within a hint of a second he was in her face. She jumped back instinctively. "Say something, I said." She prayed intensely, silently, with enough gumption to command a legion of angels to her defense, which is what she suspected would be required to protect her from this out-of-control man hovering over her, the one she refused to label as a husband in this instance.

"Greg," she said, shaking her head and clutching the covers like they were her lifeline, "you promised to never hit me, no matter how mad you get."

"Who said anything about hitting you? Don't go acting like a victim. I haven't touched you. Geez, give me some credit. You know I'd never put a hand on you, right?"

She didn't answer.

"Right," he spurted with teeth clenched together and sound and spit mixing.

"Right." Her voice wavered, with her heart skipping beats. She struggled to maintain balance. Her body was as close to the edge of the bed as she could get without falling off.

He pounded his fist into the pillow four inches from her head. “What else do you want from me?”

Laurie held her breath and continued to cry out in her soul for God. What would it take to get His help? Greg needed work, and she knew only God was capable of fixing him. She sure couldn’t.

“Turn out the light, I’m going to bed,” he snapped, like a balloon collapsing as the air seeped out.

She fumbled for the light without taking her gaze off the smoldering blaze called her husband. Sleep would be the final extinguishing factor for Greg, but she didn’t expect to get any rest next to this maniac. Bags under her eyelids were already in order, but they were better than a black eye any day. Thank goodness for small blessings.

Chapter 9

Play dead—possum—motionless, invisible. A temperature gauge could shed light on his mood. Had he calmed down, or was he still in an uproar? It was hard enough keeping the six boys settled without having added anxiety. She heard Greg moving around but didn't turn over to face him. *Go away, go to work, go wherever, just so long as it is out of the house, and in the process, send my old husband back.* She meant the man who whisked her off her feet when they first met; the one who showered her with affection and love before the children came; the man who made her feel secure, valued, and a woman. Apparently, when she wasn't looking, that man left and the new Greg eased in. Every now and then glimpses of the old Greg showed up, without notice or longevity.

"Laurie, you awake?" Greg whispered.

She held her response.

"You awake?" he said a little louder.

Realizing he wasn't going to stop until he woke her up, she grumbled an incoherent sound followed by, "Yeah, I'm awake."

He tried and tried to keep it together, but the anger felt overwhelming, boiling over on its own. Greg looked at his wife, the mother of his children, the woman he'd loved for fifteen years if he counted all the time he'd known her. He was sick of saying sorry. It seemed inadequate even to him. "About last night," he said, pulling his T-shirt over his head, "I didn't, I mean I'm sorry for what happened."

Her back remained to him.

"I know you're probably mad, but I'm sorry."

"Why would I be mad, Greg? What would that help?" Curt and disgusted is how it came across. A pinch of support would be a godsend, but she didn't give it. Hearing her tone felt like electricity trying to ignite a spark that was dying out. If she could let it go and attempt, for once, to see his struggle, to feel the weight that was close to bringing him down. Forget about what he'd learned in counseling last year on handling anger, life was real, fast motion. He couldn't help acting the way he did when he did. Relief needed to come from somewhere and soon, or he was going to explode.

"I can tell you still have an attitude. I guess I won't bother to tell you about work."

"You can tell me anything you want to. You will anyway. It doesn't matter what I say or think. We both know that."

"Wow, you really don't give a care about me, do you? Can't you see I'm going through something?"

"It's always about you, Greg. This whole family has to march to your beat. If you're mad, you want us mad! If you're sad, you're not satisfied until the whole house is down, too." She grunted. "We live by your rules. That's the way it is."

"What's with all of this mouth? Gosh, you sure have changed." Silence ducked in. "You act like I'm doing all of what I'm doing for me, and you know that's crazy. I'm busting my butt for you and the kids. And this is the thanks I get," he said, snatching his keys from the corner of the dresser, "attitude and innuendos." He opened the bedroom door. "Thanks, Laurie, for nothing."

He entered the hallway and Rick wrapped his little arms around his father's leg. Three sons followed suit.

"Daddy, when are you taking us fishing again?" Jason asked, the oldest of the bunch.

"Yeah, I want to touch the worms," Keith, the typical first grader, said.

"Me, too," Larry, the youngest of the three, said.

"You know you're scared of worms," Mitchell said, joining his younger brothers in the hallway.

"I'm not either," Larry responded.

"Yes, you are."

"Stop, I'm not scared, huh, Daddy."

"Mitchell, boy, stop picking on him. What I tell you about picking on your little brothers? You're supposed to protect them, not agitate them."

Mitchell sighed. It was difficult maneuvering down the stairs flanked by a pack of sons. Greg whisked Rick into his arms and gingerly descended the stairs.

The oldest boy emerged and dashed to the master bedroom where he found his mother.

Greg helped the boys with their cereal and juice. He slapped some sliced meatloaf onto two pieces of wheat bread, squirted a blob of ketchup in the center, tossed the bread on top, pulled the cellophane wrap from the drawer, and ripped off a portion. The ends clung together before he could get the sandwiches wrapped. He stuffed them into a brown paper bag. He kissed the boys on each of their foreheads and hustled to the car. The Velcro-attached digital clock stuck to the dashboard displayed 8:10, forty minutes later than usual. He dropped the car in gear and whizzed down the road, making tracks to work. In eight years he could count the number of times he'd gotten to work later than the rest of the staff. This was the day he had wanted to arrive early, before his boss.

The crisp mocha aroma skipped around the office making its presence known. Greg tossed his lunch bag onto the desk and logged onto his computer, crouching over. The main screen appeared and he navigated through the prompts, finally sitting.

Greg figured his manager must have been lurking in the aisle, because he pounced into the cubicle before the computer was fully fired up.

"We sure could have used you on the team yesterday.

It goes without saying that your input would have been invaluable," his manager said.

Greg didn't say anything as he worked through his e-mail in-box. From what he could remember, there wasn't a promotion with his name on it yesterday. His manager had another thing coming if he expected him to continue playing the fool.

Tom leaned onto the corner of the desk, closer to Greg. "We had to scramble in order to get the footwear campaign ready by end of day yesterday. Three of us ended up working until nearly eleven o'clock."

"Why were you working on the footwear campaign? That's my project, and it's not due until next week."

"You're right. Initially it was due next week, but we got a call from the client yesterday around two-thirty offering a fifteen percent bonus if the job was completed by this morning."

"Where did you get the layouts?"

"We pulled what you had on the shared drive."

Greg didn't have any words; of all times to be absent. He'd never missed a deadline. Could this job get any worse? It just wasn't his day or week or year.

"And since you weren't here and we weren't sure if you'd be in today, we had to pull together other resources," his manager continued.

"Really."

"Yes, really." Tom stood to his feet. "Do you mind if we jump into one of the conference rooms? We need to chat."

"Sure, let's go."

A short jog and they were nestled in the conference room.

"I understand that you were possibly disappointed about not getting the team lead position, but rest assured, we value your input."

Enough with the valued employee bit. Save that for somebody who believed it. "If that's true, why didn't I get a promotion instead of a lateral move and no raise?"

"Is it the raise? Like I said yesterday, I can talk to the executive team and see what they can do. I'm sure they can come up with a few more thousand a year."

Greg chuckled again, just like yesterday. The insulting raise amount was laughable then and even more so today hearing it repeated.

"Come on, Greg. I'm trying to create a win-win scenario all around, but I'm going to need your input?"

Greg leaned back in the seat with his gaze locked on his manager, who was shifting his weight in the chair and wrenching his hands on top of the oversized conference room table.

"I can't give you that."

"What do you mean?" Tom asked.

"I'm not accepting the lateral move. Why should I?"

Tom's glance circled around his feet. "I'm sorry to hear that. I was hoping we could work something out."

"Well, Tom, it looks like we can't, so now what?"

Tom sighed. "I'll have to revisit the proposal with my manager."

"Great, let me know what he says." Greg stood. "In the meantime, I have to get back to my office and finish the soft-drink ads."

"That won't be necessary."

Greg halted. "Why not?"

"Greg, this is awkward, but we were sure you'd accept the lateral move. So we went ahead and reassigned your pending projects."

"You did what?" Greg said in an elevated voice. He'd poured his heart into perfecting the soft drink layouts. It was some of his best work.

Tom sat up straight. "I'm sorry, but you weren't here yesterday afternoon and you had a deadline. What else could I do?"

Greg hurled word after word at Tom. The obscenity mixed with wild ranting drilled through the closed door and spilled into the office, attracting the attention of those located in close proximity. Employees began to hover.

Tom's body tensed, and his eyes widened. He clutched the table, pulling in tight as Greg got louder and closer.

A knock was heard at the door. Tom didn't move. Greg made his way from the other side of the table to an up-close position, looking eyeball to eyeball with Tom. "If you think I'm taking this crap, you have another thing coming."

The knock intensified. Greg snatched the door open and stormed out, brushing against the guy standing in the pathway.

Head aching, blood boiling. He had to get out and get away from these people before he totally lost it. Quit, that's what every molecule in his body was shouting. He wanted to. He should, but he couldn't. Where else could he go? What would he do? Laurie and the boys were depending on him. They were his life. This torture was for them. He sequestered himself in his cubicle. The advertisement jackets were shoved to the back of his desk. He resumed reading his e-mail, opening one after the other, clicking it closed almost immediately, replying to none. The words weren't processing. Forget it. He navigated to his bootleg game menu that a colleague from the systems team had secretly loaded onto his computer and kicked off a round of solitaire. It took thirty minutes to win a game that normally took five.

A call came in. The caller ID read Human Resources. Greg took a breath. He answered the phone on the fourth ring, catching it before the call went into the voice mail box. The soft voice on the other end requested that Greg come to the Human Resource office for a meeting with the director.

"I'll be right there." Greg wasn't sure how to react. Was it sinking in with management? Were they finally taking him seriously about being promoted? It was long overdue. He did the right thing, turning down the lateral move. He wondered what kind of a counter offer they'd concocted. No seconds to waste. He hustled down the two flights of stairs to the main floor, through the double doors, depositing himself in front of the HR director's receptionist.

"I'm Greg Wright," he whizzed off, feeling calm on the outside, but doing cartwheels on the inside.

"Please go right in, Mr. Wright. The director is waiting for you."

Greg bounced to the doorway of the office. The director beckoned for him to enter.

"Take a seat, Mr. Wright."

Greg did as asked. It had been more than a year ago since the last encounter he'd had with the director.

"Mr. Wright, it's come to my attention that you had an altercation with your manager today."

Greg tried to sit still in his seat but found it challenging.

"Several employees have raised a complaint that they were threatened by your presence."

"What?" he replied, fidgeting in his seat, propping his elbow on the arm of the chair and resting his chin on his bent middle finger with thumb and index finger pointed up, his eyelids refusing to blink.

"You understand why we can't tolerate such behavior?"

Greg's heart pumped fast, uncontrollably. Loser, loser flowed through his veins. Eyelids wide open, he was still holding ground.

The director opened a file on his desk. "I've taken the liberty of reviewing your record." He paused. "I'm impressed with your performance. You have consistently done well for us." He closed the file and set his reading glasses on top.

Thoughts raced through Greg's mind.

"But this kind of behavior can't be tolerated. Last year you were ordered to attend anger management."

"And I went."

"I know you did, but here we sit again with a similar problem."

"I wasn't trying to scare anybody. I just think that I'm due a promotion. I've done everything the company has expected and more, and I still can't get my promotion."

"The fact remains, we can't allow belligerent behavior. Every employee has the right to feel safe."

"So, what is this? Are you firing me?"

The director toyed with his glasses. "No, I'm not firing you."

Greg gasped.

"Not yet." The director flicked his thumb against the corner of the folder, also refusing to take his gaze off Greg. "But I am suspending you without pay for thirty days."

"Thirty days. Why so long?"

"Company policy. With one notation already on your record, we aren't left with many options."

"Will I have to take the anger management class again?"

"I can't order you to take the class again. However, you should seriously consider taking the class if you think it will provide the help you need."

Forget that class. If they treated him like a valued employee, there wouldn't be an issue. Greg was silent, but his mind wasn't still. No pay was all he could process.

It was almost time for school to start. The kids needed clothes, fees. What about the mortgage? He would hold it together in front of the director no matter how deep he had to dig. The satisfaction of knowing he was broken wouldn't saturate the office.

"What about my insurance?"

"We'll waive your copay during your absence."

Greg got up to leave.

"Mr. Wright, I suggest you take this time off to compose yourself and work on gaining control. We see you as a vital component to the company and would love to see you extend your career here with us."

"Am I allowed to go back to my desk?" Greg asked.

"Uhm, I'd prefer for you to take the rest of the day off, sort of a way to get this separation in progress right away. The sooner we start, the faster you'll be back here contributing to the team. Is there anything you absolutely need to have from your desk?"

Greg remembered his meatloaf sandwiches. They were the only other casualties of the day. He shook his head no.

"Good, then I look forward to seeing you in about a month. My assistant will overnight the necessary paperwork to you. Mr. Wright, I wish you well. I really do."

As Greg twisted the doorknob, he felt like the world was crumbling down around him. The pennies he made at least paid the bills. No money was a whole different arena. Dad would be glad to know he'd been right. His son's hobby wasn't paying off after all.

Chapter 10

Pouring ammonia on a flesh wound that was cut to the bone was an act of suicide but he had to do it. No one else was wiser than his father when it came to legal rights. No one else could really tell him what needed to be done with the kind of candor that Judge Wright could give. It would be like pulling a tooth without Novocain, but if he could hold up under the pain, relief would soon follow. Greg pulled into the circular driveway like he'd done countless times before. Mom was home. Her silver Mercedes-Benz S-Class was parked in front of one of the six garage doors. He couldn't jump out, run in, and spill his guts to them. He locked his arms over the steering wheel, letting his forehead rest on top. Courage was building, but anxiety wasn't giving up without a fight. In a whirlwind, before he could change his mind, he was inside the house, standing in front of his mother.

"Where is Dad?" he asked her. "I need to talk with him."

"He's playing golf with some friends," she said, easing the door closed. "What do you need?"

"Some advice on what I should do with my job," he said, planting his hands on his waist and dropping his head.

"You're still having problems with that job? I thought you were settled in by now."

Shaking his head, he said, "No matter how much work I do, they won't promote me and I'm getting tired of busting my chops for nothing. They've passed me over twice. I don't know what to do. I was really counting on a promotion. I need the money," he said, letting despair have front stage.

"Is that what this is all about—money? Because I can write you—"

"Mom, it's not just the money," he said, slapping his thigh. "I've worked hard. I've earned a management position."

"Your dad doesn't think that your career is going anywhere," she said, turning and strutting down the hall toward the family room. "Maybe you should consider giving up on this job and going back to law school, and not that night-school route this time. It was hard enough for you with one child, let alone six. I prefer you take the accredited full-time approach. It would take some doing, but I'm sure we could talk your dad into footing the bill. He's so disappointed with the choices you've made that

I'm sure he'd do just about anything to get you on solid footing." She stopped and faced him.

"I'm not asking Dad or you to rescue me. I don't need to be rescued. All I wanted was a few words of encouragement and maybe a little bit of advice. That's it. Is that too much to ask from my parents?" he bellowed, gaining momentum and volume with each word. "Good grief, all I ever get is a bunch of negativity."

Mom raised one eyebrow. Remembering whose house he was in, he snapped his senses back into check and wrestled his tone into submission. "Haven't I done anything right in life? Aren't you proud of anything I've done? I know Dad isn't, but what about you?"

"Baby, I love you. I'm very proud of who you are and what you're doing," she said, firmly gripping his shoulders. It's not your fault that your wife wants to keep having babies and dragging you through the financial abyss."

"Mom, don't blame Laurie."

"I'm not blaming anyone," she said, loosening her grip on him. "It's just difficult to sit back and watch you struggle so much at such a young age when you should be enjoying the fruits of life like Junior. Instead, you have six young children and a host of responsibilities with a wife who sits at home all day waiting on you to earn the money," she told him, taking a few more baby steps down the hall, with little progress being made in reaching the family room.

He wanted to defend Laurie, but right now having his

mom's acceptance was the only shred of hope he'd felt in months. It was flickering and he didn't have the capacity to extinguish it.

She locked her arm in his and detoured their route from the great room, famous for its wall of windows, and instead went to the first floor office. She stopped Greg at a leather side chair, beckoning him to sit. She went around the other side of the desk and pulled a checkbook and pen from the top drawer and began writing.

"Tell me what happened at work and maybe the two of us can figure out your options. Nothing is hopeless, Greg. You'll be just fine. You'll see," she said, handing him a check. "Is this enough?"

His eyes watered reading one thousand dollars. "Mom, you know I can't take this." He could use it, but taking care of his family by his own means was the only bit of pride he could still taste.

"Take it, son, please," his mom said, clutching his hand. "Your wife and your father don't need to know. This is our little secret."

"No, Mom, I don't keep secrets from Laurie, but thanks anyway."

"Take this check. If you don't need it, don't use it."

He embraced her and held on, savoring his time of comfort. For a moment, life was right, but this much peace couldn't last. He couldn't remember the last time something wonderful lasted long enough for him to enjoy it. Marrying Laurie was like a dream come true twelve years ago. She admired him like no one else had. She made him feel good about himself during the rough times. He couldn't imagine being without her. She made the difference in his life back then, but as solid as their relationship had been, it wasn't lasting. Nothing was. "It's just good having somebody to talk to, Mom."

"I'm always here. Don't you forget that," she said, patting him on the back. "You hungry? I have a nice Caesar salad waiting for us in the kitchen. Why don't you stay and have some lunch with me," she said, standing in the office doorway.

"Nah, Mom, I have to head out. Tell Dad… No, on second thought, don't tell him."

Walking out of the house, Greg felt his mother's listening ear had enabled him to dump a few rocks out of the heavy load he was lugging, but the remaining boulders were still weighing down his esteem. Sometimes it was easier just not thinking about any of it. "Is the garage locked?"

"I don't think so, why?" she asked.

"I want to borrow a few tools for a project I'm working on."

"It should be open. If not, the keys are on the rack in the mudroom. Be sure to close it when you're finished."

"Mom, no matter what happens, I love you."

"Go on, Greg, and stop being so dramatic."

He entered the set of garages located closest to the driveway through the side door and flipped on the overhead light. He slid sideways past the boat in stall one and the Range Rover parked next to it, stopping at slot number three, which was empty. Along the back of the wall hung three sets of golf clubs, hunting guns, a few tennis rackets, and a buffet of tools. Greg perused the wall and snatched the item he was looking for. He slid back out the garage the same way he came in and jumped into his car, hoping that his mother was out of eyesight. He reclined the passenger seat and set his tool on the floor, letting it rest on the seat.

Laurie expected him to be at work. No reason for her to believe otherwise. Taking the rest of the afternoon to suck in some air and solidify his plan without any distractions would be the next step. She would probably be glad to have him out of the house anyway. Her disdain for touching him said it all. She'd lost respect for him, too, just like everyone else. As long as she believed in him, he had been able to keep going. With her support lost, what was left?

The afternoon was sprinting by and Laurie wanted to get the floors vacuumed and dinner cooked before the boys got home. Beulah Grove Baptist Church was a blessing in many ways with the most recent being vacation Bible school. Having the boys home all day would be too much for her to handle.

The ringing phone caused her to sigh first and then gasp when she heard who was on the other end. There went a perfectly good day; it was now headed for the skids.

"Laurie, this is Virginia. I'm calling because I'm worried about Greg."

"What's wrong with Greg?"

"He's having more problems on that job of his and it's putting a tremendous burden on him He's concerned about being able to take care of you and the children."

"And how do you factor into all of this?"

She refused to call her by the name of Mom. Mrs. Wright hadn't earned such an honor. Laurie didn't feel comfortable calling her Virginia either. Basic respect didn't have to be earned. It was automatic for someone Mrs. Wright's age. That's the way she was raised, and this far into her thirties made it too late to change now.

"I'm his mother and apparently one of the few people in his life who's trying to look out for his welfare."

"Look, I don't know why you're calling, but Greg isn't here," Laurie said, clenching her teeth, tight, shut, hard. Fifteen years and she still gagged on Mrs. Wright's words. Whoever said marrying the man meant marrying the family couldn't have known the concept would carry so much cruelty.

"I know he's not there because he just left here."

Why was he spending lunch at his mother's? Laurie wanted to know but would rather let sewage back up in her house before asking Virginia Wright for anything, including basic information.

"Greg is going through a very challenging time in his life. As his wife, you're going to have to step in and help him through this."

"Greg and I don't have any problems we can't work out between ourselves. I thank you for your concern, but your worrying about me and my husband is unnecessary. We will take care of whatever needs to be taken care of over here."

"That all sounds well and good but this is a serious matter. Greg looked out of sorts here today. This is too much pressure for him. Have you considered getting a job now that your children are in school? Any help you provide is going to be a tremendous relief for Greg."

Laurie had no desire to respond. Not that it was any of Mrs. Wright's business, but they had decided when their first child was born that Laurie would be a stay-at-home mom. Greg grew up with a mom at home and wanted his children to have the same privilege.

"Hello, are you there?" Mrs. Wright asked.

"Yes, I'm still here," Laurie said.

"Well, what are your thoughts about getting a job and helping out?"

"Greg wants me to stay home with our kids and that's what I'm going to do until my husband and I decide we have to do something else."

"The children are in school."

"Not Rick. If I go back to work, who's going to take care of him—you?"

"You know that's not feasible. However, I will contribute to his daycare, gladly."

"Oh, you'll contribute to his daycare. How kind of you to help me take care of my baby. You're just the perfect grandmother."

"Laurie, your remark is uncalled for. I'm just trying to help you and my son live a decent life in spite of the obvious poor family planning you've done."

"Why, you are just full of advice today, Mrs. Wright. You really are something special."

"Like me or not, I'm going to look out for my family. Your tone is inappropriate, but that's not going to change my opinion. You have a lot to learn, young lady, about marriage and what it takes to hold one together. I've been where you're trying to go. You could learn from me."

"You and Mr. Wright don't have any idea about what goes on in this house," Laurie told her.

"You'd be surprised."

"Unless Greg runs back and tells you everything," Laurie echoed without believing it for one second. Her husband was adamant about his parents not knowing his marital business. How many times had they argued and fought on the way to his parents only to pull it together once the wheels of the van hit the driveway. Whatever Mrs. Wright was referring to was speculation.

"He doesn't have to tell me the details of your marriage in order for me to get an accurate read on your situation. You're the wife. You have more influence in your household than you're using. You think my husband got to where he is with me sitting back and letting him run the show? What you're looking at in this marriage is what I've crafted. I'm not ashamed to live well, because you better believe I've earned it, every penny. You can take my advice or not, but you and my son are headed for a great deal of heartache if you don't get a handle on your financial picture right now."

"We'll be fine because I have God on my side," she said, wanting, needing to believe her statement was true, but seeing no signs of change in Greg was making her wonder.

"Good, because you're going to need someone on your side if you don't get rid of that lazy attitude and get yourself a job. Maybe one day you can afford to be a kept woman, but it sure isn't today. My son never got the opportunity to provide for you and the boys in the kind of manner befitting a father and husband because you both started down this path of having back-to-back babies."

"We love our children and they don't have anything to do with this."

"The fact remains that you don't have the luxury of being a stay-at-home mom and at the same time struggling to put food on the table. Wake up, young lady, you're smart enough to figure out what has to be done."

"Mrs. Wright, I don't mean any disrespect, so I'm going to hang up now. Have a great day."

Chapter 11

Dealing with Greg's family became a high-impact sport that burned chunks of emotional calories. "They're too self-righteous for me," Laurie told her sister as they gobbled up the sunlight soaking the living room. The thirteen-inch TV in the corner wasn't working, which made the living room the perfect spot for talking. "I still don't know how you've put up with those boojee people all these years. Girlfriend, you are a better woman than me, clearly, because by now I would have kicked Mrs. Wright's—"

"Stop," Laurie interrupted before her sister could get too far down the vulgar path she was headed. "Don't even go there."

"I'm serious. Those people are a trip. I don't know how you put up with her. What is the deal with grown men and their mothers all up in their business?"

"I don't know," Laurie said, tucking her leg underneath her other thigh and pulling the tossed pillow into her chest. Sitting sideways she could face her sister who was at the other end of the tattered four-person sofa.

"Greg needs to put his mother in her place."

Amen. If only Greg had enough backbone to stand up to his mother, three years of lightweight needling and twelve years of pure torture could have been avoided. "He's not going to say anything to her."

"Why not?"

"I don't know. We've argued about it for years. I know he doesn't like the way she talks to me, or to him for that matter."

"More the reason why he should nip it in the bud."

"Girl, I gave up on him containing his mother years ago. Half the time she doesn't bother me. It's only sometimes that she really gets on my nerves. Those few times are when I get mad at Greg for not protecting me. I think he's afraid of disrespecting her."

"But it's okay for her to disrespect you. Please, he needs to get his head out of the sand and stop thinking his two women are going to play nice together in the sandbox. You don't get along, that's all there is to it, and he needs to step up and be a man about it."

Laurie stretched across the couch and hit her sister with the pillow.

"Okay, okay, I know, don't say anything about the great Greg Wright, love of your life. I know, I know. I'll leave your husband alone, but I still say Ms. Thang has some nerve telling you how to run your own household. She needs to mind her own business. That's what she needs to do. Humph, I wish she would get up in my face with some craziness about how I should handle my marriage. You need to get her told. Let my mother-in-law step to me like Mrs. Wright does with you. She'd get her feelings hurt real quick by this sister. I'd kick her so far from my house that when she looked back she wouldn't be able to see the block, let alone the house."

"What are you talking about, you don't have a mother-in-law? You're not even married."

"That's right, because I'm not ready to put up with the kind of crap you're putting up with. Stress is not my scene. Any man who marries me better have his act together."

"Nothing is going to be perfect in a marriage."

"I'm not talking about perfect. I'm talking about craziness, like some man putting his hands on you. I keep telling you, any man who gets as mad as Greg does is out of control, and with a mother and father like his, who can blame him. It's just a matter of time before he hits you."

"He gets mad, but he's never gone that far," she said, fidgeting.

"Trust me, he's capable of it. You better wake up, sis. Mama and Daddy didn't raise any fools. I'm cool with Greg so long as you're cool with him, but let it be known that if that Negro ever puts his hands on you, I'm telling you right now, it's on."

"We have our problems but nothing like that." She

cringed inside and wanted to repent on the spot but couldn't with Danielle sitting right there. There were a couple of times when she and Greg were fighting that she wanted to reach out and tell her sister and brother everything but ended up, each time, deciding against going that far. So long as he hadn't hit her, there was no reason to stir ill will between her husband and siblings. Each time they were at odds, eventually the storm passed and the glimmer of light in their relationship returned. It would be a shame to have everybody mad at Greg when her heart wasn't interested in leaving. She could get mad at him all day long but giving other people ammunition to put him down, even her sister, didn't set well. "Counseling really helped us."

"That was three or four years ago. You can't be talking about way back then. Did you start back recently?" Danielle asked.

"No, not yet."

"Why not? If it worked, you need to keep going. Do you have to lie on one of those couches and tell all of your business going back to when you were three years old?"

"See, you're trying to be funny. Counseling is serious. It was hard work. At first I didn't think Greg would go, but then I didn't think he'd complete the anger management classes last year either."

"What choice did he have? It was either anger management or lose his job. Sounds like a simple decision to me. You know good and well those people on his job weren't going to be comfortable with a black man over five feet tall running around there screaming at folks. He's lucky he didn't lose his job altogether—real lucky is all I can say."

"That wasn't luck, that was God's grace."

"Yeah, right, whatever, grace or luck, he better not act a fool up in there again, or you can bet his black behind will be out on the street looking for another job with a quickness. They're only going to let him get away one time with counseling, anger management, or whatever you want to call it. I still think he's out of control. Are you sure he's never hit you?"

"Ah, how many times do I have to tell you no?"

"Okay, okay, you don't have to convince me, but just remember what I told you. I'm cool with Greg. If you like him, I like him, as long as he never hits you. Because if he does, he's as good as dead."

"You are so melodramatic. You're about as capable of killing somebody as I am."

"Well, if Greg is as smart as you think he is, I won't have to prove myself, will I."

"You don't have to worry about me and Greg Wright. I have the Lord and that's all the protection I need."

"Here we go; it's Bible time. I know that's my cue to leave." She got up. "Drake has finally gotten to you. You sound just like him."

"What can I say, he's our only brother," Laurie responded. "Come on, why don't you stay, please?" she pleaded. "You don't have anything to do. You're off work all day today. Why don't you hang out with me for the afternoon? I don't have to pick up the kids from vacation Bible school until four, and Rick won't wake up from his nap for at least another hour."

"Un-huh, you know I love my little nephew, but he is too much of a handful. I'm definitely getting out of here before that ball of energy gets up."

"Come on, please, stay and talk a little longer."

"I'm sorry, sis. You know I love you. I'll call you later." Danielle was outside the door when she stopped and turned around. "Oh yeah, I almost forgot the main reason I came by." She pulled a ball of tightly rolled dollar bills from her petite purse, lifted the hand of her sister, shoved the money in, and closed her sister's fist around it.

"What are you doing?" Laurie asked.

"It's almost school time, and I want my nephews to be dressed in style."

"Here, take this back," Laurie said, extending her balled fist to Danielle. "We're fine. Besides, you know how funny Greg is about taking money from people."

"That's why I didn't give the money to Greg. I gave it to you, my sister. If I want to buy my nephews some clothes, you or Greg can't stop me. Now stop being hard-headed and take the money. Please, with six kids every dollar coming your way should be received with open arms, especially from your only sister."

Laurie initiated the hug. "I love you. Talk with you later." She stood in the doorway as her sister backed out the driveway. She opened her hand and stared at the wad of bills. Counting the gift out netted $400. She was consumed with glee. Greg crossed her mind. Marriage wasn't the place for secrets. Yet, some information was better left unsaid. She eased the money into her pants pocket and closed the door.

Chapter 12

Laurie wrapped the plate of spaghetti and a baked chicken breast with a piece of foil and set it in the middle of the stovetop. Mitchell and Junior stood next to her putting away the remaining plates and silverware taken from the dishwasher.

"When you finish with those dishes, don't forget to put your hampers in the basement so I can wash clothes tomorrow."

"Ma, I need three dollars for our pizza party tomorrow," Junior said.

"I need three dollars, too," Mitchell added.

The first half of the month was tough. After Greg paid the mortgage and bought groceries, not much money was left. Coming up with a few dollars here and there for the kids was a feat. Postdating a six-dollar check to the church wasn't a good idea. She'd only been a follower of Christ Jesus for two years and admittedly wasn't the most faithful in the area of stewardship, but it didn't take a high IQ to realize that cheating the church was like stealing from God. She could handle the wrath of Virginia Wright, but messing with God was on a totally different level. Danielle's money popped into her head, but she had to use the $400 sparingly, no sudden purchases so as not to alert Greg.

"Check with your father when he gets home." She looked at the round clock hanging above the sink. "He should be here any minute. He's never this late." She hit redial on the phone to call his work number again. She'd lost count of how many times she'd tried to get a hold of him since talking to his mother earlier in the afternoon. Every now and then he'd work late on a hot project but never past 6:00 PM. It was already 8:30 and no sign of him.

"What time is he getting here? We have to go to bed by 9:30 and I really need my money for tomorrow. If Daddy gets home after I go to bed, will you get the money for me?" Mitchell asked.

"You just finish those dishes and don't worry about the money. Don't we always make sure you have what you need?"

Laurie entered the living room and stood on her tiptoes to see over the hedge situated in front of the bay window. No headlights to be seen in the cul-de-sac. Where was he? Her heart was racing. Was he okay? How come he went to his mom instead of coming home if he had a problem at work? Maybe he was back at his parent's house. Laurie went back to the kitchen and picked up the phone. This was one of those rare times when she wished they could afford cell phones. The boys were finished and had gone upstairs. The kitchen was empty with only the waning sunlight poking in. She set the cordless phone back down on its base. She wanted to know if he was at his parents but didn't have enough heart to deal with Mrs. Wright again today. She could only pray that Greg was all right and on his way home with a perfectly good explanation for not calling. As mad as he made her most of the time, she still loved him. The image swirling in her head of him being hurt or in danger on the side of the road was too much to bear. Six kids and twelve years of marriage was enough reason to stick this marriage out. Besides, God didn't have to inform her of the basics. She'd been going to church long enough to know He wasn't in favor of divorce. But God couldn't be thrilled about her being miserable and unhappy in the marriage either. He had to help her figure this out, if there was to be any sign of real hope.

Chapter 13

Greg left the movie theater before the credits rolled. If he could at least remember the main character's name, then the ticket price, which was purchased with his last few dollars of gas money, was worth it. Ten-thirty was the latest he could recall staying out in years without Laurie or the kids. He wanted to go home, crawl into bed, and let sleep guide him to a place far from his troubles, but that wasn't going to happen. Laurie and the kids would be waiting for him and whatever peace he was looking for was sure to get drowned by his arrival. Instead, he crawled the faded Nissan Sentra hatchback to a secluded section of the City Park, bypassing the sign prominently displayed at the entrance: PARK CLOSES 1/2 HOUR AFTER SUNSET. Greg glimpsed at the notice and kept creeping through the darkness along the gravel road, looking for the right spot to do what had to be done.

He killed the engine, reclined his seat slightly, and rolled down the window. The muggy summer heat, which had held the city hostage earlier in the day, had been strangled into obedience. The hissing sound of the bugs that thrived after dark created an eerie sound around the car.

Would he ever be able to truly provide for his family the right way? What else could he do? Maybe that's just how it was. Happiness belonged to some men, not everybody, surely not him. Maybe Dad had been right all along—a loser of a son is all he was. A lifetime of decisions landed him here, in the black of night, alone, and no one cared.

He ran his open palm up and down his face, letting his thumb and middle finger massage his temples, rubbing out brooding tears. The moon hadn't reached the full brightness of the night. There were thousands of seconds separating the depths of this hour from daybreak, plenty of time for Greg to come to terms with a tough, life-changing decision that would impact his entire household. It wasn't his desire to bring such anguish to his family but what other choices did he have? Hopelessness darted in and out of his consciousness. He'd tried other avenues, each leading to a dead end. No luck. Maybe one of those Sunday morning prayers could help. But why call on God now? He hadn't at any other time. That was Laurie's new thing. If it worked for her, fine, so long as she didn't try to push it off on him. God the Father was too fuzzy of a concept. It was a hard enough struggle maintaining a relationship with his father who lived in town. How in the world could he manage one with a God who wasn't there? Having a second father, one who had the power to lump bigger coals on his head, wasn't enticing. Sterling Wright Sr. was enough father for any man to handle.

The crackling sound of the limbs overhead startled him.

Swirling emotions and random shots of his kids and Laurie danced through his mind. There was a slim possibility that someone did want him around. The boys, for sure. For them maybe it was worth him taking a chance on God. Might as well give him a shot. Nothing else had helped. Then again, his father went to church every Sunday like clockwork, in at nine and out at eleven, not a minute later. If church hadn't made Sterling Wright Sr. a better person, then there was no use in him going down that religious alley. Adding another desolate road of despair to his résumé of life's disappointments wasn't appealing. He stroked the pain reliever lying next to him. Thoughts popped in and out. He dug his buttocks into the seat and pushed his head back. He lifted his recliner lever all the way until he was resting on the back seat. His brother had a good life, but he wasn't any smarter. Life just came easy to Sterling. Why did everybody else get breaks but none came to him? What had he done that was so bad he deserved to suffer this kind of punishment? He couldn't shake the stack of bills from his head. A feeling of being in the middle of the ocean in a rowboat during a severe hurricane was rooted deep inside and spreading like metastasized cancer through his soul, devouring his existence like a ravenous dog. Reality was setting in. He wasn't getting promoted, not today, not tomorrow, not ever. He wasn't good enough to get the best of anything, especially his father's love.

He'd tried to pull it all together, to make everyone happy. His father wanted a successful son. Laurie wanted a dependable husband. The kids needed a loving father. The director wanted someone with more experience. Everybody wanted something. What did he want? Only one necessity pressed to the forefront at this point down the dark path—peace at any cost. Greg reached into the passenger seat and stroked the long, dark barrel of the gun he'd borrowed from his parents.

It would take a man, a real man, to pull this off. Sleeping his anguish away with the help of a few pills would be easier and less painful. But pills were for wimps, and he had to go out like a man. Maybe Dad would finally be proud of him. His son was giving up on something that hadn't paid off after years of effort. It was time to let go, no matter how difficult. The time had come. But what about a note? People always left one. He rummaged around the glove compartment but didn't find paper appropriate to capture his good-byes. He rocked his head back and forth on the seat. Of course, he snickered, why would Greg Wright have paper. That would be too reasonable. Better anyway to just go. Why ramble on when life had already written volumes for him.

He wrung his hands together and tilted his head up toward the open window, letting his glance fix on the carefree owl hooting above. The tears streaming down Greg's face glistened in the moonlight. He brushed the stream away roughly with the back of one hand and clung to the shotgun with the other. The combination of summer Georgia thickness, sweat beading on his forehead, and heat overriding the protection of his deodorant brewed a stench befitting the moment. Secure in the bowels of the night, he took a snip of comfort realizing no one would ever have to know until he was done.

Chapter 14

Tossing around the king-sized bed, Laurie jolted herself awake when she rolled onto the spot where Greg normally slept, slightly off the center, within an arm's length. The first four years of marriage, the full-sized bed was adequate since they slept sandwiched together. As the marriage aged, the bed widened. Acquiring the king-sized bed two years ago was working out, at least for her, and some nights for Baby Rick.

She felt around the bed. No Greg. She peeked at the alarm clock illuminating the room. 2:24. She got up and took a quick tour of the four-bedroom house, going from the top floor to the basement and checking the garage once before going back upstairs to the bedroom. Her heartbeats kicked up a notch. Eight years on his job and she could count the number of times on two hands when he hadn't been in the house by 5:30. One time was when the car broke down, another time he went to a happy hour with people from his job, which he never did again, and then there was last night. The rest of the instances were when he had to stay late to finish a project. That was it, the extent of his unaccounted evenings.

Visions and illicit thoughts were flooding her good sense. Even after she'd gained just shy of forty pounds, Laurie knew Greg still found her attractive. No need to go there. There was plenty of worry to go around without adding more. She sat up in the bed and turned on the light. Get up and go out and look for him. She whipped the covers back. Call his brother. He didn't have any other friends in the area. She stepped one foot on the floor and attempted to stand. Check with his parents? She dropped back down onto the bed and let herself go backward in a stiff-back free fall, landing square on the pillow. She rubbed her forehead with eyelids shut, hoping direction would manifest. *Lord,* she meditated, *where is he?* Two images shared equal billing: his lifeless body along the side of a road with the Nissan wheels spinning in the air, and his naked body lying in somebody's bed. Neither choice made his absence digestible.

Running out of options, she picked up the phone and began her phone search. First she called his office. He voluntarily worked an extra hour for free every day. Sporadically he had to work late, but not like this, and not without at least a call home. Something was wrong. She knew it. Her body chilled as she dialed 911 to find out the best way to locate Greg in the event something terrible had happened. She called the hospitals as instructed by 911 and was told there was no record of his admittance.

She pulled her bent knees up and tucked her chin on top, letting the cordless phone drop to the bed, near her feet. Her head hung as the two jockeying images intensified, bloodier, seductive. Where could he be that didn't have a phone? Raw concern flipped to anger as the cheating scenario gained a slight edge in the anxiety race, but not for long. Battered and beaten on the roadside eased back into the lead, and her fear resumed. She couldn't just sit there anymore while the man she loved was lying helpless somewhere. She stabilized her thumbs against her cheeks, letting her fingers move in and out like an accordion on her forehead. As much as she hated to involve his family, there was no way around it.

She dialed Sterling Jr.'s number and was about to hang up on the fourth ring when his sleepy voice answered. Laurie kept the greeting to the bare minimum, showered with an apology for calling so late or early, depending on how he viewed three o'clock in the morning. "Sterling, I really am sorry to bother you, but Greg hasn't come home yet and this isn't like him at all. I was wondering if you've seen him or talked to him."

What started off as a sleepy voice on the other end of the phone perked up instantly. "No," he stammered, "I haven't talked to him since we were at my parents on Sunday. I don't know what to tell you."

Laurie felt a rush of anguish surf through her body, ending with a lump in her throat and water building under her eyelids.

"Have you tried his cell phone?"

"He doesn't have one," she answered, permitting her index finger to take a slow drag along the bottom of her eyelid.

"I'm sure you've done this already, but have you tried him at work?"

"Yes, I've called him a ton of times and no answer." She gulped. "He's never been out this late without calling," she said, leaning forward far enough to read the clock. "I'm afraid something has happened to him," she said, gulping again.

Sterling said nothing.

"I've already called the police station and the hospitals."

"And?" he asked with reluctance in his voice.

She hesitated, not knowing if it was good or bad news that neither institution was able to help her figure out her husband's whereabouts. "They weren't aware of any accidents and neither the jail nor the hospital had any record of him."

"That's good to hear."

"I guess."

"Well at least we know he's not locked up or laid up."

"I don't know about the laid up part."

"What do you mean?"

"Maybe he's out with somebody," she suggested.

"Ah, no, no, I doubt that seriously. You know he's not like that. All he ever talks about is you and the kids. No, you don't have to worry about that."

Laurie wanted to believe her brother-in-law. His intentions were good, but his information might not be accurate.

"Yeah, I know, but I don't know what to think or even where to begin looking."

"What about his friends? Have you checked with them?"

She pondered for a moment. "He doesn't really have a lot of friends here in Augusta. Most of his friends from college live in Atlanta."

"Hmmm."

"He spends most of his time with our boys. So I don't have anybody else to call except you."

"And my parents."

Laurie shrieked. If Greg's disappearance wasn't due to some unthinkable tragedy and he had his behind lying or sitting up somewhere too ignorant to pick up the phone and call home, then he better not let his parents find out about it. There would be shaking going on in their family.

"I don't think we should bother them just yet," she said, although she remembered he was over there earlier in the day. But after giving it a little thought, there was no way he would have stayed there any longer than he had to, particularly if his father was home. Rest assured, he was not at his parents' house. She waited for Sterling's response, which didn't come rapid fire.

"Laurie, I think you should call them."

"What if Greg is okay and just acting a fool?"

"How often has he done this?"

"Never."

"Okay, there's your answer. It will be better for you to call them now than to wait and find out there was something they could have done."

"What can they do that we can't do?"

"I don't know, but you need to call them, Laurie. It's only right."

"All right, all right, I'll call them."

"In the meantime, I'll get dressed and come over."

The company would be good, but she didn't want to raise the flag to an all-out panic level prematurely. "No, Sterling, that's okay, but thanks for offering," she said, scratching her head.

"I don't mind. I might as well. I'll be worried anyway until we hear from him."

"I know. Me, too. But instead of coming over, maybe you can drive along the path he takes to work," she requested, then described Greg's routine route.

"I'll check it out and call you back. If you find out anything, call me on my cell." He rattled off the digits.

Good-byes terminated, Laurie held the phone in her hand dreading the call she'd promised to make. Which blade was sharper: Greg being missing, or having to tell his parents when she wasn't really sure if his absence was legitimate. She dialed so fast her mind didn't have time to interpret the signals going from brain to fingers. This was like swallowing castor oil, unpleasant enough to make you gag but necessary at times. A pause and then ringing, each second was an eternity. Then Mr. Wright answered in an intimidating voice that could have ruffled the feathers of a seasoned linebacker.

"Uh, Mr. Wright, this is Laurie, your daughter-in-law."

"Laurie, it's awfully late. What can I do for you?"

Spew it out and get off, that was her directive. "I'm sorry for calling so late," she said, pushing past her hesitancy, "but Sterling suggested I call you."

"Sterling," he said boldly. "What's wrong with Sterling?"

Laurie could hear Mrs. Wright in the background. "Nothing, nothing's wrong with Sterling. It's Greg."

"What's wrong with Greg?" he asked with the same boldness.

"I'm not sure. We can't find him, and I thought maybe you or Mrs. Wright might have seen him."

"What do you mean you can't find him?"

Laurie could hear the muffled conversation he was having with Mrs. Wright.

"He's not at work. I called the police station, the hospitals, and Sterling. No one has seen him this evening."

More muffled tones.

"Wait, Laurie, it sounds like Virginia spoke with him this afternoon," he said, continuing his pattern of talking with Laurie and then with his wife. "Apparently he had some trouble at work today, at least that's what he told his mother this afternoon."

"Yes, I know, she called me earlier." Laurie felt her head palpitating. She was still mad about him telling his mother before telling her, his wife. He might be a good father, but Greg was a lousy husband, more and more lately, keeping her confused. Embarrassment settled in and she moved to adjourn, not knowing any more about where he was than when she first called but refusing to let them know that she was clueless about her own husband's whereabouts.

She was preparing to end the call when Mrs. Wright got on the line.

"What did you say was going on with Greg?"

"I don't know." *You know more than I do,* is what she was thinking but dared not say. "Sterling is out looking for him. I've called the hospitals and he's not there. I even checked with the police to see if he'd been locked up."

"You two didn't get into a disagreement over money, did you?"

Laurie let her glance burn the ceiling. "No," she drilled into the phone, enunciating each letter.

"He's under a great deal of pressure trying to manage all of your bills."

Laurie let time and silence help her to retain a level of respect someone Mrs. Wright's age deserved.

Nobody said anything.

Finally, Laurie gave in. "When I find out something, I'll let you know."

Courtesies were extended and Laurie was set free. She held the phone and laid down, drifting in and out of sleep, stirring at every minuscule noise. The door pushing open popped her up like a jack-in-the-box.

Greg's silhouette stood in the doorway. He moved into the room in slow motion. A mound of meshed relief, anxiety, fear, anger, concern, and insecurity rolled into a tight ball and dove into her peace. Catatonic.

"You still up, huh?"

"Greg?" she asked, standing to her feet and lunging toward him with arms open. "We've been worried sick about you. I thought something had happened to you." She pressed her head into his chest as his arms enveloped her. Secure is what she was, a feeling that was not a frequent guest. If she could freeze this refuge, hang on tight, and not let the marriage slide from this place, they could rekindle the kind of passion and connection she longed to have, instead of the strained love lingering between them. "You've never been out this late. Where have you been?"

She felt him pull away. She didn't budge, watching him walk to the closet.

"I was out doing some thinking."

"You couldn't call?" she said, standing with her hand on her hip.

He glanced at her and looked away.

"Here I am calling the hospital, the jail."

He looked up again when she said "jail" but didn't interject.

"We thought you were in an accident or something worse."

"Who's we?"

"Sterling and your mom and dad."

"How did they get involved?"

"How else? I called them," she said with sharpness.

"Why did you call them? They don't need—" he started to say before Laurie jumped in.

"Need to know our business," she echoed without relaxing her tone. "I know all of that, but when you walk in here at four-thirty in the morning without an explanation, you should expect people to be worried."

"Laurie," he said, stepping from the closet in her direction, with eyes showing a flickering flame, "what's with the attitude?"

Code words. Her body processed his message and tensed before retreating to the safety of the bed.

"I have enough to worry about without my family breathing down my neck about why I'm out late at night. Thanks a lot, Laurie, for getting everybody involved in our affairs. I bet you called your sister and brother, too? Huh? Do they know I stayed out all night, too?"

Silence was safe.

"Geez, when are you going to help make life just a little bit easier for me? I bust my butt to take care of you and the boys and every opportunity you get to stick it to me, you do."

Oh boy, here he goes. Just like him to dash a bucket of cooldown on the rising affection she had rekindled for him. At least it's close to morning and the boys would be waking up soon. This storm had been heading inland since Sunday, really before that, and it was about to touch down, right there in the master bedroom. Whatever sleep she'd stolen during the night was all she'd be getting. Buckle down. Man the hatches. Hurricane Greg was in close proximity.

"I'm tired of struggling and then having to come home and put up with crap around here. I need a break sometime from somebody." He laid down on his side of the bed. "If I can't get help from my wife, who can I get it from?"

His hands locked behind his head, Greg lay flat on his back, staring at the ceiling.

"And we have to make some changes around here with our money. There's no reason I should be broke all the time when I'm working my behind off."

Laurie looked at the clock. Five o'clock. The money spiel would take twenty minutes, thirty-five if he was really having a bad day, and with any hope he would peter out by five-thirty and she would be asleep by five-forty, almost two hours before all of the boys got going. Before closing her eyelids, she would call Sterling and give him the news. Mr. and Mrs. Wright would have to hear from their own son directly regarding his missing episode. Enduring torture wasn't Laurie's strong suit.

Chapter 15

The morning breezed in like nothing had happened. No visible evidence to the world that his life was falling apart. He felt Laurie on the other side of the bed; a gorge was between them. He tried but couldn't remember the last topic they'd discussed before falling asleep earlier this morning. He couldn't forget his parents. "Why'd you have to call my father?" he tossed out, shifting his glance to Laurie and back to the ceiling. "Now I have to hear his mouth. Same old lines: You got a family to take care of. Why are you so irresponsible? Are you ever going to grow up?" One pop and it could have been over last night. Done. But courage wasn't there.

Laurie rested her elbow on top of her bent knees in the bed. Best to sit still and let the wind blow itself out of energy.

Greg rolled over, facing the window and away from Laurie. He pulled the cover tighter.

"Don't you think you should call your parents before you go to work this morning?" she asked.

Failure, failure, shouted from his bowels. How was he going to tell her? Please, no more looks of disappointment, words of frustration. He couldn't take it from her, too, but he couldn't escape the inevitable, short of getting up for the next thirty days and pretending like he was going to work. Lying wasn't his trait, and at 34 years old, developing the new habit wasn't appealing.

"I'm not going to work today."

"You're still sleepy?"

"No, that's not it," he said, swallowing hard. "I'll be off for the next thirty days."

"Thirty?" she questioned with a high pitch.

"Yep."

He could offer the information, spit it out quickly and move on, but it was more difficult than he anticipated. He wanted her to see him as a strong man who could provide for his family, but how could she when he was out of work and wondering where the next paycheck was coming from.

"Why so long?" she asked.

"Because," he said, stalling, "I'm on a month's suspension."

"For what?"

He could sense her intensity rising. "I didn't get the promotion, that's all."

"People don't get suspended just because they don't get promoted. There have been several times when you didn't get the promotion you thought you were getting, but you weren't suspended."

"You're right. I was suspended because I said what I had to say to Tom, and then other people complained about being scared, which is ridiculous. Anyway, without any opportunity to defend myself, I was suspended. I can't win at that place. I've had a tough time at work ever since I stood up for myself last year when that woman yelled at me. Manager or not, you yell at me, I'm yelling back."

There wasn't much he could say to win his wife's favor. She probably thought he deserved it. Maybe he did deserve some but not this much.

Chapter 16

Breakfast dishes lined the kitchen countertop. Jelly blobs and milk drops decorated the table. A skillet used to cook turkey sausage was pushed to the rear of the stove. Greg walked past the disarray in his pajama pants and poured a glass of juice from the refrigerator. He pulled up a chair, cleaned a small spot on the table, set down his juice, and let his body and mind relax, a feeling that was unfamiliar. Baby Rick was still asleep in his crib, thank goodness. Laurie had dropped off the rest of the boys at vacation Bible school.

Nine o'clock, the day was half gone. By now he would have read his e-mails and been close to finishing a couple of graphic layout drafts. Thirty minutes felt like a year. Thirty days would be eternity. On top of the job issue, he had to call his parents. He took a long drag of air and let it seep out. He clicked his thumb and index and ring fingers on the table in a rhythmic motion. Five after nine.

He paced the first floor. Ten after nine. He locked his fingers behind his head, standing in the middle of the living room. Take the punch to the gut—hard, fast, and over.

He dialed the cordless phone in the kitchen. If miracles were for him, his parents wouldn't be home and he could leave a message and be done with this unnecessary matter. Two rings and he hung up. He remembered the shotgun in his car. He had to get the gun back to his parents before they realized it was gone. Best not to alert his parents when he wasn't quite sure where his head was. No guarantees he wouldn't have to use it. He took the stairs three at a time. He snatched his pants and shirt from the closet door and jumped into them. He smeared a strip of toothpaste on his brush, a few strokes and he was rinsing. His face was the proud recipient of the only water gracing his body this morning. He pulled a sheet from the linen closet. The ringing phone was probably his parents, but he wasn't going to answer. He hustled out the door and put one foot on the step and stopped. Baby Rick, what was he going to do with him? He didn't feel right having his son ride in the backseat while the shotgun rode alongside him in the front. A miracle, Laurie was back. He could hear her downstairs. He dipped down the stairs in a swoop and darted through the kitchen past Laurie, who was surveying the train wreck in her house. He grabbed his keys from the counter hook, not losing steam.

"I have to go."

"Where are you going?" she asked, looking bewildered.

"I'll be back," he said, slamming the back door and opening the garage.

Out late two times in one week and leaving without explanation. He knew she was probably suspicious, but what could he tell her in his defense. He was trying to cope, barely hanging on.

Greg drove rapidly but safe. He couldn't get pulled over. Worse, he couldn't let his parents know what he had.

He made it. The Mercedes and the Cadillac were sitting in front of the other set of garages. There was hope that they were both still inside. If not they probably hadn't gone into the leisure garage where the boat, tools, and hobby items were stored.

He eased the car quietly and close to the garage door. Without belaboring the deed, he hopped out, ran around the back of the car, threw the sheet on top of the gun, and whisked inside. Invisible. He didn't breathe, look around, or do anything that might cause him to think. He just kept moving.

The shotgun was back in its place, mounted, loaded, and ready for use, was how the judge kept his assortment of firearms. Greg brushed off his pants along with the stress associated with remaining undetected. He strolled to the house, preparing to take his medicine.

Lily opened the door and called out to his parents. He watched her retreat in the direction of the kitchen after greetings were extended.

His mom came running into the foyer. She didn't stop until Greg was in her arms. "Where in the world were you last night? You had us worried to death."

He tried to interject but couldn't wedge into the conversation with a shoehorn.

"What's wrong with you staying out and not calling?" she continued. "Are you okay?" she asked, finally releasing him but hanging on to his arms, near the bicep area.

"I'm fine," he said, leading the way to the great room.

"Was that you who called and hung up a few minutes ago?" she asked.

"No," he said, hesitating. "Didn't the name come up on the caller ID?"

"It was unavailable," she said with voice trailing off at the end. "Anyway, back to you. Where were you?"

"I needed time to think about my situation with the job and everything. I just needed some space."

The air stopped circulating. Birds ceased chirping. Free-flowing love halted. Mr. Wright was entering the great room. "When you're a father and a husband, you don't get the luxury of feeling sorry for yourself. You have mouths to feed and responsibilities to handle. The least you could have done was pick up the phone and call to let one of us know you were okay. Sometimes your behavior doesn't make any sense."

"Sterling, leave the boy alone. You see something is bothering him."

"Humph, his only problem is that you're treating him like a baby. He's a man, Virginia. Let him act like one."

"Maybe if he had more of an example, he would."

Didn't they see him standing there? Greg kept quiet. A part of him wanted to defend himself and protect his mother but words and motion didn't gel. He wasn't the little boy hiding in his room anymore, afraid to stop his father. Dad could say whatever he wanted to him, but the days of putting a hand on his mother were over. Sterling Wright Sr. was going to see a side of his son he wasn't going to like, if Greg could muster the guts. He wouldn't need to call the police like he did one time when he was little. He would take care of it himself this time. His father was still mad at him about the call. Cut off from his father's affection at eight had been his fate. After twenty-six years, it wasn't like he could cause any more damage to their relationship anyway.

"Virginia, it's too early in the morning to start." He threw his hands in the air. "I'm scheduled to tee off at ten-thirty. I'm leaving."

"But, Dad, I was hoping to talk with you about my job."

"What about your job?"

"I need legal advice." He paused, collecting his thoughts. "I was suspended for thirty days without pay and I want to know what my options are legally."

"Suspended?" Mom shouted and clasped her hands over her mouth.

"What did you do to get suspended?" Dad demanded.

"I had an argument with my manager and it was blown out of proportion. That's all."

"That can't be all if you were suspended," Judge Wright responded.

"Sterling, let him tell us what happened," Mom defended.

"I know what happened."

"How do you know?" she snipped. "He was the one there. I wasn't there and you weren't either."

"That's okay, Mom. Don't worry about it. I was hoping you might be able to give me some advice on what to do, Dad, but that's okay. You can't help me. What's new?"

"See, that's your problem right there. Your smart mouth has already gotten you suspended off the one paycheck you had coming into the house. As little as it was, you did have something. Now you don't have anything coming in, and don't think for one second I'm giving you a handout."

"Did I ask you for anything?" he shouted, taking a step in his father's direction, arms outstretched, up and back down, swift.

"Wait." His mother jumped between them, her usual position.

"Did I? Did I ask you for any money?" Greg shouted again, walking around his mother.

"Virginia, you don't need to stand between me and Greg. He knows better than to approach me."

"Stop this. What in the world are you doing? This is absurd. Let's sit down calmly and figure out how we can get through this situation."

"The two of you can sit down and cry into your water

glasses. I'm heading to the golf course." The judge slithered out of the room, down the hallway, stopping at the front door. "He made his bed, now let him be man enough to lie in it," he hurled down the hallway.

Their son deserved better. Greg was here, a living, breathing son. It wasn't Greg's fault she got pregnant while Sterling Sr. was in law school, but her husband seemed determined to hold it against her and the baby forever. Not getting his father's namesake was only the beginning of the punishment Sterling Sr. had generously dished upon his oldest son. So what if Senior was trapped into marriage. After thirty-five years, he needed to get over it. That was his problem. She ran out behind Sterling and caught him on the walkway, heading in a direction opposite to where Greg's car was parked. Turning back, she saw Greg standing at a distance, closer to the door.

"You can't help your son, not even once?"

"He doesn't need my help. He created this situation. Let him fix it," Sterling echoed not breaking his stride.

"If Junior was in this kind of mess, you'd bend over backward to help him, even if it meant prosecuting the company all the way to the Supreme Court, wouldn't you?"

"Junior wouldn't get himself into anything like this. Junior wouldn't make the same kind of stupid mistakes Greg keeps making. One bad decision after another."

"And you won't forgive him for the first one."

"What's that supposed to mean?" he said, bracing the car door and throwing his gaze her way.

"You know as well as I do. We don't need to go there," she said.

"Correct, let's not. I'll be back this evening," Sterling said.

"Are you going to spend your entire week off golfing?"

"Why not, if that's what I want to do?"

"I really don't care what you do so long as you respect the rules," she told him.

"And what would those be, Virginia?" he said, slamming the trunk of the Cadillac.

"Keep your business away from me."

He opened the car door with no response. She saw Greg going to his car on the other side of the driveway a few minutes earlier and now he was waving bye as he drove past.

"The hang up calls have started back and I won't tolerate it, not this time. You keep your mess in the street. Don't bring it to me. You understand me, Sterling?"

He stepped toward her.

"If you slip up, you'll regret the day you ever laid eyes on this woman. I promise you that. I've worked too hard to get us to where we are."

"You've worked hard." He snickered, then let it roll into full laughter. He got into the car and started it up. "That's funny, Virginia. You've worked hard," he said, still laughing.

She backed away from the car as he put it into reverse. She remained in the driveway until he disappeared. Thirty-five years of marriage, nothing would be lost. She closed the heavy wooden door behind her, the shield blocking out elements of the uncontrollable world. She ascended up one side of the wide oak curved double staircase. At the top of the landing, she gained composure, strength building as she passed the bedroom of Sterling Sr. on the right. At the end of the hallway she opened the double doors to her kingdom where reality was whatever she deemed appropriate. She entered her bedroom of solitude, letting the doors and the craziness close behind.

Chapter 17

The kids were out of the house. Why couldn't he be gone, too? There was laundry, dinner, dusting, and scrubbing to be done. She sprayed the furniture polish on the table and wiped around Greg's feet, which were relaxed on the makeshift ottoman. Next task, she ran the vacuum back and forth, bumping the coffee table legs, behind the entertainment center, around Greg's feet, which had relocated closer to the couch. *Get out of the way* is what she wanted to howl from the top of her lungs. Keep vacuuming. He'll move. She bumped his foot again.

"Huh." He sighed.

She pushed the vacuum forcefully, mumbling under her breath.

Ten-thirty and the living room was clean. The kitchen was next. The dishes were stacked and the table was dirty. She rinsed the dishes with the spray hose and loaded them into the dishwasher. This time, she was the one giving the sigh. Greg looked up from his magazine. "You want to help me clean the kitchen since you're sitting here?" she asked.

"No, not really, you seem to have it under control."

"What about checking the boys' rooms and making up the bed in our room?"

"The boys are supposed to clean their own rooms. They know the rules. We shouldn't be doing the work for them," he said.

"They do clean their own rooms the best they can, but they can't vacuum yet. Goodness, we're talking about a four year old, a five year old, and a toddler. We can't expect them to do everything."

"Why not? I do."

"Well, what about making the bed in our room and cleaning the bathroom?" she asked.

"Oh, nah, you agreed to make the bed every morning so I can get to work on time. Right?"

"But you're not working, remember?"

"That's true, but I'll be going back pretty soon and it doesn't make sense for us to change the way we do things around here. What you're doing with the house seems to work for all of us."

"Oh, really," she said, wrapping the cord around the hook on the vacuum cleaner, pulling it, and stretching it tight until all of the slack was eliminated.

"I think so. You know I don't have time to help with housework. I go in early and get home late."

Hello, could he hear himself yapping? He was sitting his unemployed behind in the way. If he wasn't going to help, the least he could do was move so she could do the work. She smeared the table, swiftly, brushing against Greg inadvertently. She brushed against him. He lifted his glance from the periodical and directed it toward her. Greg rubbed her back. "You know, we're here all alone," he told her, grinning.

Without warning he had swooped in and was rubbing her back.

"Rick is upstairs."

"True, but he's sleep," he responded.

She wiggled out of his loose clutch and tossed the towel into the sink.

Greg reached for her. "Did you hear me?"

"Yes, I heard you, but I'm too busy cleaning this nasty house to think about what else I could be doing to eat up my time."

"Too busy," he said, letting his head roll around his neck. "I should have known."

If he wanted affection, how about putting his lazy hand on a broom and sweeping the kitchen floor. His effort would be awfully romantic, but she didn't have to worry about him going too far and actually lifting a finger. Slaving around the house was her job, at least that's how he felt and made sure she knew it time and time again. Looking at him made her emotions churn. She loved him, really she did, but liking him was a whole different discussion. How long could she realistically live in this murky relationship where she couldn't see the end turning out positive? Divorce wasn't for someone like her who wanted to please God, but misery in the marriage wasn't a suitable alternative either. There had to be another option.

"I helped the boys get dressed this morning, that's enough. I did my share for the day," he said.

"But I drove them to vacation Bible school. You could have driven them."

He pondered that. "You're right, I could have. Tell you what, I'll take them tomorrow if it will help you out."

Wow, don't do me any favors. Those are your sons, too. It was true that she never had to ask for his help when it came to dressing, bathing, or reading to the boys. Greg saw it as his job and did it without fail, but since he was off work, there were other chores he could help with around the house, which would make her life easier for the next thirty days.

Greg finally stood up. Good, he would be out of the way and she could finish the kitchen. Two major rooms spotless.

"I'm sleepy. I think I'm going back to bed for a quick nap. You want to go, too?" he said, letting his grin widen, slowly.

"Greg," she said, holding the broom, "I told you, I'm busy."

"What is it with you, this not wanting to be with me? You're seeing someone, aren't you?"

"Oh," she gasped without shifting her gaze from the

motion she was making on the floor with the broom. Not this again. The question didn't dignify an answer.

"What, you don't hear me?"

"What," she said in a firm but not brazen tone, "what are you talking about? I have six children to take care of every day, all day. When do you think I have time to sneak around to see anybody?" She resumed sweeping the same spot over and over. "I can't believe you can even ask me something like that." She paused. "I should be asking you the question. You're the one who's been out late twice in the last week with no real explanation."

"Shew." He sighed. "I gave you an explanation. I can't help it if you don't want to accept it, but you know in your heart I could never cheat on you, never."

"Oh, but I could? I'm offended."

"I'm not trying to offend you, but there's a problem somewhere." He inched toward her with arms ready to embrace. "You never want to be with me. I'm a man. I have my needs and you don't seem to love me like you did when we first got married." He hugged her.

"Greg"—she laughed—"we have six boys now. I don't have time to lie around all day with you like I did when we were twenty years old. I have to finish cleaning, wash a few loads, and cook dinner before the boys get home this afternoon. You're off work. You don't have anything to do but sit around and wait for your thirty days to pass."

He pushed back.

"So what, we have sons. I want to be able to spend time

with my wife, too. I don't have to choose between one or the other. I want both," he spoke softly, sealing it with a kiss on her cheek.

Laurie figured her task list would take most of the day. Unless she gave in and got Greg out of the way, she'd have to hide around him all day. There were times when she wanted affection, but between the kids and the house, the times when her desire and energy coincided were at best once a month. Today wasn't one of those days. Spending the day with him wasn't in her plans. If only Greg knew how terrified she was of getting pregnant again. She loved her boys but six was enough, more than she ever expected or wanted. Her options for avoiding pregnancy were limited. Since Greg's health insurance no longer covered birth control pills, the monthly charge was a luxury her budget couldn't afford. Besides, she still hadn't gotten a straight answer from anybody at church on whether the pills were okay with God. With unanswered questions and limited resources, for now she had to restrict Greg's opportunity. Although this would have been the perfect time to be with him while the kids were in school, money, pregnancy, and the residuals of his latest tirade put a damper on her would-be flickering romantic flame. Why should today be any different than all of the rest? Reality was setting in. If God was in the middle of this marriage, she couldn't tell. All she needed was for Greg to change and they could be happy. Maybe it was time she stopped asking God for help and came up with her own plan for Greg. After all, no one knew him better than she did.

Chapter 18

Defeat rested in the kitchen chair next to Greg. Paperwork, bills, and junk mail laced the table. The batteries were good, but the calculator didn't have the juice necessary to balance out the column of income versus expenses. He'd added, subtracted, and even tossed in a prayer, or at least it was kind of like a prayer: "Help me please, God." The baby prayer was the best he could do for a Saturday. He was sure the effort counted a little bit. The TV evangelist said call on Jesus when you need him, and this was a time of need. Hopefully Jesus was in the office and taking early morning requests because Mr. Electric and Sir Gas weren't going to wait much longer. Their cousins Cable and Water were hovering around the nickels left in the checking account, too. But Big Daddy mortgage was elbowing at the front of the line. The grace period was exactly five days away and his check had come and gone last week. No other reinforcements were in sight. The savings account was collecting mothballs.

The boys were roughhousing on the stairs. "Stop playing on those stairs," he spewed out. Instant silence flooded the house. Floorboards didn't dare creak. Greg leaned his arm on the table and scratched frantically across his forehead, following with a slow fingertip rub.

Where was the money coming from? He remembered the $1,000 check his mother offered, but it didn't swallow well. No matter how tough times had gotten over the years financially, he was proud knowing they'd always made it through mostly without outside help. His mother made a routine of asking. She was coming to expect the answer no by now, except for those two times when the answer was yes: when the rotors, brake pads, thermostat, and radiator went out on the van all at the same time; and when Jason was born, he took an extra two weeks off without pay to take care of Junior and Mitchell while Laurie recovered. Mom would come through, but he didn't want to go to her. There was always the chance his dad would find out and wail on him until blood oozed from his emotional knuckles. Foreclosure sounded better than the judge's mouth.

Greg closed his eyes and pounded his palms into both sides of his head. Options were fleeting. The savings account was as empty as a gigolo's heart. The credit card was a few hundred dollars short of maxing out. Dirt was falling on his head, dark, fast. He couldn't catch his breath.

The threat of fear had subsided and the boys were back at play. A thud came from the steps and chatter from a few of the boys.

"I said get off those stairs," Greg hollered loud enough for the dog down the street to hear and bark in response. He screeched the chair from the table. "Didn't you hear me the first time?" Before Greg could grace the stairway, feet could be heard scattering. "If I have to come up those stairs, I'm going to whoop everything in sight."

Laurie felt the whirlwind as the boys hustled past her, ducking for cover in their rooms. She couldn't be bothered with Greg's ranting this morning. She had her own problems, or potential ones. She wasn't fond of her monthly visitor, but after six pregnancies, what was a burden for others was a welcomed sight to her. Where was her visitor this month? She had six good reasons why it was late in the past. Adding a seventh was out of the question. Block out the thought. God had to be merciful. There was no way another child could squeeze into their household or into her schedule. Holding the family and the house together with eight people already required a miracle. She descended the stairs, bypassing Tornado Greg. After two weeks off, he was getting on her nerves. *Go to work* is what she wanted to tell him. Please.

He went back to the table and let his body rest on his stiff arms, his gaze locked on the mounds of stress. He'd been brewing over the bills for two days, and his attitude was getting worse by the hour. She could pray for good weather. The worst storms had an eye, that time of superficial peace, quiet, and safety. Greg's storm had been raging for two weeks. The Wright Island was due an eye.

"Look at these bills." He slapped a few down on the table.

"I have to turn in my twenty-dollar deposit for the women's retreat tomorrow. It's the last day."

"Do I look like I have twenty dollars? I'm trying to pay the mortgage for August and you're talking about a church retreat in March of next year." He laughed and cut it abruptly. "You must be joking. I can't believe you can stand there and ask me some mess like that."

Laurie didn't budge. The pressure cooker was cranking and the log she threw on the fire may be the one to send it percolating.

"Don't you realize what trouble we're in?" He shook his head. "You don't seem to care about how hard I struggle around here to pay the bills. All you care about is getting your funky twenty-five dollars for church and another twenty dollars for the retreat. Not one time have you asked if I needed any help with the bills."

"That's because you know I'm not good with money."

"So what, you think that gives you enough reason to leave all this on me?" he asked.

"What do you want me to do, Greg?" He was the one who couldn't control his temper and got kicked off his job. *Why do I have to pay for his mistake?* she thought but didn't consider letting the words reach the airways. Riding it out and keeping her words to a minimum was her best bet.

"I don't have to tell you what to do, Laurie. Come on, you see these bills. What do you think you can do to help me?"

"I don't know, Greg, seriously."

"Have you ever thought about getting a part-time job, just to help out for a few months?" he asked.

This man was crazy. In the beginning she had wanted a job, had pleaded with him to let her work and help out. He wouldn't hear of it; he had been determined to be the breadwinner. The kids started coming and her desire died. Asking her to get a job now was ridiculous. Taking care of his six sons and his grown behind was equivalent to two jobs, and he wanted more juice from a piece of dried fruit. "Are you serious?" she asked, holding back the hurt. "You want me to get a job and still take care of the housework, the kids, cook, and give you affection," she said curtly, not caring about the consequences. When would this torture of a marriage get better or end? A week ago, the marriage kind of mattered, before she gave up on God being the one to fix Greg. Two years ago, staying married was important, but each day was like water streaming over a mound of dirt without divine intervention or a sign of improvement; eventually her resolve would be washed away. She wasn't actually seeking divorce; it still didn't feel right. Besides, how could she leave with six kids? But some kind of change had to come. She couldn't take the torment anymore.

Laurie heard creaking on the stairs. Instinctively she knew it was Junior. Like a stalking fan, he was lurking nearby whenever there was a heated argument going on between her and Greg.

"I'm not asking you to take a full-time job and work until retirement. I'm asking you to get a job for right now and help me out of this jam."

"If I'm getting a job, are you getting one, too?" she asked.

His back had been to her throughout most of the conversation. He turned around, deliberate, and hurled at her, "I already have a job. What do I look like going down to McDonald's or Burger King and working for two weeks? That's stupid."

"But it's okay for me?"

"What do you want me to do, Laurie? Huh? What do you want me to do?" he asked, jumping in her face.

"Greg, you better not hit me."

"I'm not going to hit you." He pounded his fist into the cabinet behind her. "Why do you keep saying not to hit you? I've never hit you, have I?" he bellowed in her face.

"You better not because I wouldn't take it. I'm telling you now, you'd just have to whoop my behind because I will fight you back."

"What, what?" he screamed in her ear.

Junior got off the stairs and walked into the kitchen.

"Junior, go back upstairs," Laurie demanded.

Greg turned and saw Junior planted by the table with gaze piercing and fists balled up by his side. "Ah, I'm out of here. If you need me, I'll be at my brother's."

"For what?"

"I have to get some help from somewhere. You don't seem to want to help us, and I'm definitely not going to ask my father. That's like asking you for affection. I might as well cut off my left arm if I have to wait for you and my father to help me stop the bleeding."

Watching him leave was a relief. Even if she wanted to rekindle her passion for Greg, his volatile tirades continuously wore down her love. Fear kept her in the relationship, not fear of personal injury, but fear of being on her own—a single mother with six children with no skills, no degree, no money, and worst of all, no plan. Ten years ago, no one could have told her that she'd still be in love with Greg but wouldn't like being around him very much.

Chapter 19

The end of the third week was approaching and the torrential downpour hadn't let up. The mortgage, association fee, and utilities were crossed off the monthly budget. Sterling Jr. wouldn't hear of it, but his brother was getting his $1,500 back as soon as a few extra dollars came into the house. Greg tucked the unemployment letter underneath his stack, which read in big, bold letters, CLAIM DENIED. Laurie would get a paycheck next week. She started last Thursday. It wouldn't be a full week, but she got four hours in on Thursday and Friday and a full eight on Saturday. At $7 an hour, she would get about $112. After taxes, he figured she'd bring home roughly $90. He ran the pen through the word INSURANCE. Credit card, food, gas, cable, and phone were crying out for attention, but triage had them at the bottom of the list. He put a checkmark next to the phone and cable. One by one they were getting paid. It was a miracle.

Greg pulled away from his kitchen office to answer the ringing phone. His mother was on the line.

"How are you making it without any income?" she asked, foregoing greeting courtesies.

"We're fine." He hoped his brother hadn't mentioned the loan to their parents. It was his business and the multitude didn't need to know.

"I have some money I want you to come and get. Bring the kids over for something to eat, too."

"What about Laurie, Mom?"

"Of course she's invited, too, but wouldn't her time be better spent looking for a little job that could help bring some money into the house?"

He needed the help from his mother and from Laurie, but it sickened him to be reduced to a place of having women take care of him. What else could he do? He could tell his mother about the telemarketing job he'd found for Laurie online, but he wasn't prepared for his father's mouth. The job would last three months. There would be other opportunities to announce the news once he was back to work.

"All you need is a little bit of help right now. You'll be back on your feet in no time. Don't forget that I'm here for you."

Greg got his keys, gave the call for the boys to load the wagon, and set off for the rescue squad, Virginia Wright. He wasn't sure about the check, but the food would fill a few crevices.

* * *

Laurie flicked on the kitchen light and anger stirred. She missed midweek church service tonight because of the new job, which was only slightly disappointing now that she'd stop relying totally on God for her happiness in the marriage; but to come home and find a mess in the kitchen with a house full of men upstairs made her flesh ignite. Enduring cramps added to her disposition.

She zoomed past the clutter, up the stairs, and bounced between the rooms of her two oldest sons. "Junior, Mitchell, get downstairs," she yelled from the doorways. Baby Rick turned over but didn't wake up. Tonight he would have to cry himself back to sleep.

She went back down to the kitchen. "Now," she continued.

Feet were running behind her.

"Okay, Mom," Mitchell called out.

"Why are these dishes sitting on the counter? You know you're supposed to rinse them and put them in the dishwasher. What have you been doing all night?" Her shoe stepped in a red glob. "Look at this mess on the floor. What is that?"

"Spaghetti sauce," Junior answered.

"Who made spaghetti?"

"Grandma Wright."

"Your grandmother came over here?"

"We went to her house and she gave us a whole lot of food to bring home. We left some spaghetti for you in the refrigerator."

"Oh you did. Well, get this kitchen cleaned and get yourselves into bed. It's almost ten-thirty."

She hauled her body back upstairs for the last time that evening. Going back to work was an adjustment. If she had to stretch her physical limitations to help out around the house, then so did everybody else over the age of eight.

Greg asleep, what a dream that would be. She opened the master bedroom door. He was spread across the bed, half asleep. She could breathe easier.

He heard Laurie enter the room and sat up, groggy. "Hey, you're home. How was work?"

"Work was work. I'm tired and ready to hop in the bed."

He flung the covers back on her side. "Jump in." They were struggling, but thank goodness, the mortgage was paid, utilities were on, food was in the boys' bellies, and his wife was home.

"I can't believe you let the boys go to bed without cleaning the kitchen." She undressed in a flurry. "The kitchen is a mess and everybody's in bed like they don't have a care in the world."

Can't she just come home without complaining? He was sick of hearing it. So what if the kitchen was dirty. It could be cleaned tomorrow. "I've been waiting up for you. I've been thinking about another baby, a girl this time." No doubt, times were tight, but one more mouth wouldn't make a difference, the last two hadn't. No matter what happened on the other side of those doors, having his family secure under his roof was the only part of life that kept him going. They were all that mattered. The more children the better, never enough. Laurie didn't agree, but he'd convinced her before, maybe this time, too.

She probably wanted to say something like "look around here, how many more babies do we need," but she harnessed her tongue. "Did you hear me? I want another baby."

"Greg, I'm not ready for another baby. I've been pregnant and raising babies almost our entire twelve years together. I need a break."

"What does that mean? You don't want to be a mother?"

"You know that's not what I'm saying."

"That's what it sounds like to me. I guess Junior, Jason, Mitchell, Keith, Larry, and Rick were all mistakes."

Laurie took a deep deep breath and let the air out rough.

He's the one with the college degree. Didn't he know the man carries the little Y chromosome, the one that dictates the sex of the child, not her? If he could get his manhood on track, it wouldn't take a hundred pregnancies to net one daughter. Practice was over.

"I miss having you here at night."

"Uhn-hmm."

"That's all you can say."

"That's all I want to say." The sharpness in her tone drilled deep.

Reaching out to her and getting nothing but attitude back was insulting. She wasn't the only one putting up with a tough situation. *Keep my wits. Don't push. If she doesn't want to be affectionate, that's the way it is.*

"You know, Greg, I can't work a job every night and come home to a dirty house. I'm working here all day and night. I need a break." She slid the nightshirt over her head. "You've been sitting around here for almost three weeks doing nothing," she said, letting nothing linger in the midst.

"What do you mean, nothing? I'm paying the bills and taking care of the boys during the day. I get them dressed and make sure their clothes are washed and clean."

"Helping out is all well and good and I'm glad you are, but I'm working a job, too, which means I have less time to do work around here."

"So what, you're working a little telemarketing job. Don't act like you're running some company downtown."

"Whatever I'm doing is bringing in a bigger paycheck than you are this week. How's that for you, Mr. Big-Time Man?"

How could she reduce him to a paycheck? She was talking over him. Not listening. Not feeling his pain. He needed to be heard. She had to know where he was coming from. He wanted to rip her head open and scream directly into her brain, *I'm doing the best I can.* She didn't know the crap he put up with every day on his job—a black man trying to get ahead in a conservative town. He heard the lectures, putdowns, and digs from Judge Wright. He couldn't take it from her, too. The walls were closing in. Where was the respect, the love due him as a husband? Before reason could catch up and overtake action, he had Laurie in his clutches and was shaking her. "Who do you think you are to put me down like that? Who do you think you are?" he howled, getting louder and louder.

"Let me go," she hollered, but his grip wouldn't loosen.

Mitchell and Junior darkened the doorway. "Go back to your rooms," he demanded, flinging her to the bed and jumping up to slam the door.

Laurie huddled on the bed, sobbing and clinging to the covers.

Greg saw the red line-in-use light brighten on the telephone from the corner of his eye, but the distraction wasn't great enough to draw him from the battle in progress.

"Don't you ever talk to me like I'm your child. Do you hear me?"

Sobs substituted for a response.

"Do you hear me?"

"Yes, I hear you, but you can't make me do anything," she hurled at him like a woman going mad.

She lunged at him and he instinctively flung his arm in the air for protection and caught her on the chin, pushing her teeth into her lip. A little blood spurted, then stopped.

"Laurie, I didn't mean to—"

"Don't you say a word to me," she hissed, crying and screaming. "Don't touch me."

Greg looked down on his wife. He'd let the beast out and getting control back in was going to be a monster.

A faint, familiar sound was heard at a distance but was getting closer. Sirens. "Police, who called the police?" He wanted to duck into the closet and hide like a kid. They couldn't be coming to their house. His mind charged around the room. Think. Think. What would he say?

Banging on the door was heard all the way upstairs. Confirmation, it was the police.

Greg rushed into the hallway. Two cops were coming up the stairs, led by Junior. "There he is."

"Mr. Gregory Wright."

"Yes."

"We received a call about a disturbance. Is everything okay?"

"Everything's fine."

Junior slipped into the master bedroom.

"Where is Mrs. Wright?"

"In the bedroom," Greg said, pointing to the door behind him.

"We'd like to speak with her."

Greg beckoned for them to go in.

Laurie was sitting on the bed with knees bent and Junior glued to her. Tears flowed without interruption.

Both officers, with guns strapped, entered the bedroom. Greg followed.

"Mrs. Wright, are you okay?"

"Yes," she gasped, "I'm okay."

"Can you tell me what happened here tonight?"

Continuously gasping, she tried to speak. "We had a disagreement, that's all."

"Are you okay, do you need an ambulance?" one officer asked.

They had a little tiff, but come on. She wasn't injured, Greg thought. They made it sound like he'd really beaten her. Actually, she threw the first punch.

"Mr. Wright, will you please step into the hallway? I'd like to speak with you," one officer asked.

Greg acquiesced without resistance.

"Mr. Wright, can you tell me what happened?"

"We had a disagreement and the argument got out of hand."

"Did you physically attack her?"

The way he said it sounded so criminal. The argument hadn't been dire. He pushed her. She hit him. That was all there was to it; a family matter didn't require the police.

"I didn't hit her on purpose if that's what you mean."

"Sir, your wife has been visibly shaken up. Her lip is cut."

"I know, but it's not what you think." He couldn't believe how cliché his own words sounded. He couldn't imagine what the officer was thinking. "I admit that I pushed her. Then she attacked me and I put my hand up to defend myself and it caught her lip."

"The situation seems to be calm now, but I need to talk with the other officer to get Mrs. Wright's side of the story. This shouldn't take but a minute."

The officer went to the doorway and beckoned for the other officer.

Standing in the hallway while his wife and son were sequestered in the room with two police officers made him feel like a gnat, the pesky little bug that no one wanted around, the one that seemed to have insignificant worth in the ecological picture. Greg took a few steps toward Junior's door. He would close all three doors to the boys' rooms.

"Mr. Wright, please stop," the officer stated firmly, unlatching his holster.

"Wait, wait, wait, wow, I'm just closing the doors to my sons' rooms. I don't want them to be afraid. That's all I was doing."

The officer snapped his holster back into place and gave Greg the okay. He closed the third door in sync with the officers' ruling.

"Okay, Mr. Wright, it sounds like your story checks out and your wife doesn't know if she wants to press charges. But by your own admission you shoved and pushed your wife. When we come out for a domestic call such as this and see visible signs of a physical altercation, we are obligated by law to make an arrest."

"What?"

"We're going to have to take you in, Mr. Wright. We'll book you and you'll probably be out by tomorrow morning on your own recognizance. But for now, you're going to have to go with us."

Junior clung to the doorpost as the cop put on the cuffs. There had been low periods, but nothing as low as tonight, knowing his son was enduring exactly what he had twenty-some years ago. He'd tried, using every fiber in his body, not to be the man and so-called father that Judge Wright was. Descending the stairs, down, down, down deeper, he felt defeated, unable to break the cycle that a generation before him had created and a generation after him would now have to suffer.

Chapter 20

Shhh. Listen, the blistering sound of silence, nothing. No shouting, no fear. She rolled over to face Greg's side of the bed. Emptiness. She was tired. Tired of being scared. Tired of being taken for granted. Tired of living like a slave in good clothes. The marital train hauling a load of distress had careened out of control once again last night and was temporarily derailed for servicing. If she wanted to leave the locomotive of unhappiness, this would be the jumping off point—the time when Greg was out of the house and she was out of his reach. Perhaps she'd been unrealistic thinking the marriage would get better, that Greg would get over his bouts of anger. She'd tried everything: patience, yelling back, giving in to his whims, and up until recently, praying for the marriage to work out. Two years down the I-can't-take-it-anymore-please-God-save-this-marriage tract and she was still feeling zero improvement. As a matter of fact, the tension was worse. Making the decision to handle her own marriage, without God's help, had probably been best seeing that His perfect will didn't include divorce. Truth was, she still didn't want a divorce, but circumstances dictated that she leave all options open. Continuing in a state of confusion, in and out, up and down in the marriage wasn't working. Any change had to be better; it couldn't get worse.

She pulled herself together and got the kids stirring. Regular routine was best.

"Where's Daddy?" Larry asked. "I want him to fix my racing car because it doesn't work anymore."

"Daddy's in jail," Junior told him.

"Where's jail, Mommy?"

Junior didn't wait for his mother. He jumped in. "It's a place where mean people go."

"Uhn-uhn," Larry cried out, clinging to his mother's leg. "Mommy, Daddy's not in jail, is he?"

Chastising Junior with a look wasn't enough, but she couldn't deal with him right now. "Honey," she said, bending down, "Daddy is gone for a little while. He'll be back later. Okay?"

He wrapped his little arms around her neck in approval.

Pulling away, he said to Junior, "See, I told you he wasn't in a mean place." He sealed his commentary by sticking out his tongue at Junior and darting into his room, slamming the door.

The hallway was clear of the other boys. Only Junior remained. She put her hand on his shoulder. "Did you call the police last night?"

His gaze dropped to the floor. She took her finger and lifted his chin. "You did the right thing." Needles and daggers would be easier to endure than watching her twelve-year-old son have to make an adult decision that could change the tide of an already drowning family. What could she do to ease the blend of his guilt and anger? She absorbed him in her arms, hoping to preserve his ounce of remaining innocence.

"You boys have to get dressed. Can you check on everybody and get them going? Help Rick, too," she told Junior. Laurie remained standing in a fog. "I don't know what I'm going to do with all of you today."

"It's school today, our first day back."

She gasped; her head dropped back and her eyes closed briefly. "Oh, that's right. Oh my gosh. Well, let's get moving."

She didn't tell Junior since he was so excited about going back, but the fact was, she couldn't worry about school at the moment. Greg could get out at any minute and would probably be mad. She needed to hustle and get the boys to dry land. Laurie pulled out an outfit that she'd worn four times in two weeks. Finding something to wear to church every week was challenging enough without factoring work clothes into the mix. She was doing the best she could. Her wardrobe was sparse but clean. She dressed while weaving a plan of attack. She could pick up her check, which would be short, but $90 was a start. A hotel was an option. That way no one would have to find out what happened. She wouldn't have to listen to anyone's mouth about what she should and shouldn't do. She needed to figure this out on her own, without Greg, the Wright's, Danielle, or her brother. On the other hand, she wasn't expecting a multiroom suite for a string of nights with $90. Making sardines out of the six boys in a cramped hotel room wasn't the recipe for her sanity restoration. Who did that leave?

She splashed water on her face and combed through her kinky-at-the-roots hair. She looked around the room to see what she'd need. She grabbed a few shirts, a couple pairs of pants, underclothes, sanitary pads, and a toiletry bag. She closed the bottom drawer with her foot, juggling the armful of clothes, causing the family photo positioned in the center of her dresser to topple over. She saw the picture fall and left it where it landed. Gathering what she needed for a few days, she plopped the goodies on the bed. She pried a tote bag from the jumble on the closet floor and stuffed in her belongings. Keep moving. Get the boys packed and out of the house before eight was the goal. Greg couldn't get out that early. They were in good shape.

Churning and bubbling, her emotions were in turmoil. She was barreling ahead like her actions were concrete, methodical. She put one foot in front of the other, wishing last night had never happened, like other days and nights that looked and felt just like it.

She knocked on Junior's door, then entered to find Baby Rick dressed and playing in the corner. Junior was on the computer. She went about packing for the baby and instructed Junior to get his clothes together for a few days. He didn't ask any questions. She made her rounds, ducking into the rooms of the other boys, and tossed a few items into a bag for them.

"Where are we going?" Mitchell asked.

"I don't know yet, probably to your Uncle Drake's."

"Why are we going there? What about school?" Mitchell questioned.

"Where's Daddy? Is he coming?" Larry asked.

"Boys, you are always asking too many questions. Get your bag zipped and get downstairs. Take your little brothers with you."

"I'm hungry. Can I eat before we go?" Mitchell asked.

She hadn't factored in the morning necessities. Ten minutes to eight. She hesitated, looking at him and back at her watch a few times. "Yes, go ahead and help Larry with his cereal. Jason and Keith can fix their own. But hurry, we have to go."

Eat, clean, and out in twenty minutes wasn't a hope, it was a necessity.

Chapter 21

The new school year was kicking off and the boys were excited to be back. Laurie was fuming. She carted Baby Rick a few steps before letting him down to walk.

"Aren't you taking us to school?" Junior asked.

"No," Laurie barked.

"Why not?" Junior responded in a similarly aggressive tone. "It's our orientation day at school, and I'm supposed to get my computer ID and locker today. I don't want to be the last one to get mine. I have to get to school today."

"Well, you're not going," she snipped, trying to balance her carry-on bag, purse, and Baby Rick's hand. The pain felt like a pendulum with a fifty-pound weight attached, which was swinging back and forth and using her head as a stopper. She rang the doorbell, leaning into it for a dab of relief.

"Everything's always messed up for us," Junior said.

"Where's Daddy? Is he coming over here?" Larry asked.

"No," Junior griped at his four year-old brother, "it's his fault that I'm missing school anyway."

Larry hit Junior's leg. "It's not. Stop saying that," Larry wailed amongst a heap of tears.

The house door opened, framing the six-foot-one, coconut-colored brother with a medium-sized stature accented with thin-rimmed glasses. He wore a stiff-collared, dark blue and white-striped dress Polo shirt with dress pants. "What are you doing here at nine o'clock in the morning on a weekday with all my nephews?"

"Hi, Uncle Drake," Jason said.

Larry forced his uncle to sway side to side as Larry, Mitchell, and Keith dashed inside the playground of a house.

Baby Rick broke away and ran behind his brothers. He was on the loose, running ahead of his legs, like a magnet drawn to the Mikasa crystal vase adorning the marble and mahogany coffee table.

"Get him," Laurie belted to anyone with feet.

"Oh hey, little man. Watch out," Drake called out, giving chase to his nephew. He caught him in mid-reach, snatched him up, and twirled him in the air. "Uncle loves you, but if you break my vase, you're going to be in big trouble." Baby Rick laughed and laughed. Laurie hoped her baby wouldn't laugh up his breakfast on her brother.

Laurie ushered the rest of the tribe inside. Each boy went his own way. Junior shot for the loft upstairs that overlooked the living room. "Can I use the computer, Uncle Drake?"

"You live on that computer, Junior. You're not going into the chat rooms or any other place where you're not supposed to be, are you?"

Junior grinned and darted up the stairs with Baby Rick in pursuit.

"Junior, watch your brother up there."

"I know, I know."

Mitchell detoured to the kitchen first, and if his pattern remained consistent, he would follow Junior upstairs. Jason and his younger brother Keith flipped on the TV in the den and pulled out the electronic game set. Larry ran behind them. Preschoolers didn't get to play when bigger brothers hogged the machine.

"Larry, do you still know how to color?"

He nodded his head in affirmation.

"Can you color some pictures for Uncle Drake? I would like to have a few new ones from you."

Larry's face lit up. His slow nod energized. His head bobbed up and down like a little toy dog rocking in the back window of a car.

The boys were settled for now. She would leave the suitcases in the car until Drake gave her the okay to stay.

"I didn't hear you answer yet," Drake said.

"What?"

"You know what. Why are you and my nephews

ringing my doorbell at nine AM on a Thursday morning? What's wrong?"

Telling Drake could lead to Danielle finding out, and Laurie wasn't ready to get into the details of last night with a sister who wouldn't rest until Greg was hurt. Drake's was the best place to be. There she was out of the clutches of danger and drama. Rest for her soul was what she needed, without a round of interrogation. Drake was a man who didn't just preach about how great God was, he lived it. If there was peace on earth, she was going to find it at her brother's house, since she wasn't sure God had been by her place. Drake was the one person who wouldn't judge her situation. Even when he didn't agree, he never made her feel stupid. However, her brother wasn't an idiot. She had to toss him some kind of bone before he figured out what was really going on.

"I need a break." Drake didn't respond. She knew more explanation would have to be sacrificed before he retreated. "Ever since Greg got suspended he's been hard to live with."

"It's been like a week or two, right?"

"No, actually, it's been three weeks."

"You're kidding. Three weeks already. He should be going to work soon," Drake commented.

"Another week," she said, doing cartwheels in her head.

Larry blanketed the dining room table with his colored pages. "I'm going to make one for Daddy, too, so he can have one for jail," he said.

She wanted to drill through the floor straight to the basement. Laurie doubled over inside. She let her gaze roam the room, anywhere it wanted to go so long as it didn't stop at her brother's burning stare. She could feel his look. She let her weight free fall into the Victorian chair in the family room. Drake swooped in next to her.

"What is he talking about?"

Laurie had to give up the goods. Drake was a pit bull unwilling to release her until she acquiesced. "Greg was arrested last night, but it's no big deal."

"People don't go to jail…oh, on second thought, what am I thinking? A brother is bound to have at least one run-in with the law. What happened to Greg? Is he still scaring those people on his job?"

"Nope," she said, making a clicking sound at the end of the word.

"Then why is he in jail?" Drake asked with his voice deepening.

Laurie twiddled her fingers. "We had an argument and Junior called the police."

"What?"

"See, that's why I wasn't going to say anything. I didn't want you to draw conclusions without hearing what happened."

"What happened?" He stood to his feet. "Come out front."

"Why do we have to go outside?"

"I want to talk without the boys hearing us," he whispered. "Come on."

The fresh air slowed the pendulum to barely a tap. "What did he do to you?" Drake asked, his frame towering over her.

"He didn't do anything, not really. We just had an argument, that's all. It was blown out of proportion."

"Right, that's why you and six boys are on my doorstep at the crack of dawn."

What could she say?

"Did he hit you?"

Laurie fought back the water filling her eyelids.

"He did, didn't he?"

She didn't respond. Less was more.

"Oooo," he shouted like a hooting owl. "I knew it," he said, gritting his teeth and pounding his fist into the other hand. "This brother just can't get it together."

"No, no," she said, digging into his arm with her grip. "He didn't hit me, not really."

"Did he, or didn't he?"

"Yes, but it was by accident."

"Accident? So if someone kicks him up and down the street, it will be by accident, too."

"I don't want anyone to do that."

"How do you think I should react? Let him hit my sister and not do anything about it?" Drake paced the sidewalk in front of his house. "He has to deal with a man. You understand that."

"No, I don't. That's crazy."

"What's crazy is hitting my sister."

She grabbed her brother's arm again, bringing him

around to face her. "What about my children? How are they going to feel if Uncle Drake hurts their father or ends up in jail, too?"

"Oooo," he said, shaking his head. "You're putting me in an awkward situation, Laurie. What do you expect me to do?" Drake huffed. "Lord, what do I do? I want to do the right thing in your eyes, but my flesh is crying out, no, more like wailing for justice. You have to help me, Lord."

Drake knew God better than she did. Maybe God would hear Drake, but she'd given up on the religious path of help.

"What should I do?" Drake asked.

"Nothing. It's bad enough that he was arrested. I just want to let the situation die down and figure out what to do later." Drake stared at her with no reaction. "I'm hoping you'll let me and the boys stay with you for a few days until I can sort out my situation."

"You know you can stay here for as long as you need to." He pulled out his key chain and twisted a key around the loop. "I hope you're not planning to go back there for a while?"

She hadn't taken time to exhale, let alone make real decisions about what to do next. Actually, now that she was thinking about it, she didn't have a plan. Getting out of the house before he came home angry was her number one objective. Goal accomplished. What came next for her and the boys was fuzzy. "I'm tired and I just need some space away from Greg. That's all."

Drake enveloped Laurie in his embrace. “Whatever you need, you got it.”

“Oh, and can you do me one more favor?”

“You got it.”

“Please, don’t tell Danielle that Greg went to jail. She will make this worse than it is.”

“I won’t tell her, but she’s no dummy. How are you going to explain being over here with the boys for who knows how long?”

He was right, but she’d deal with Danielle later, after she’d had a moment to breathe.

Chapter 22

Packing in haste, she was bound to forget essentials. Half came with toothbrushes, the rest didn't. She shuffled back and forth between the three bedrooms Drake had relinquished to her tribe, excluding his from the rotation.

The boys were dressing for school.

"Can we stay home again today?" Mitchell asked.

"Yeah, can we?" his roommate asked, too.

Laurie dug inside the duffle bag. "No, you cannot," she said without hesitation. "You already missed the half-day yesterday. You're going to school today." She extracted a medium-sized children's shirt from the jumble and shook it out, hoping at least one or two wrinkles would show mercy and run. "Put this on," she said, handing the shirt to Keith.

"I don't like this shirt," he said, pouting.

Laurie shoved the shirt into his hand. "Put this on and

don't give me any lip." He accepted the shirt with a scrunched face. "You have way too much mouth for a six-year-old little boy. Get that shirt on and put on the same pants you had on yesterday." One day out of her house and laundry needed to be done already. She gritted her teeth. This was Greg's fault. She and the boys were uprooted for no reason. He should be the one living out of a bag, not her six babies. "You finish getting dressed, too, Mitchell. You need to be downstairs in five minutes for breakfast."

She ducked into the next bedroom to find Junior and Jason practically dressed. "Downstairs in five minutes for breakfast you two."

"Okay," Jason responded.

Junior didn't say a word. "You hear me, Junior?"

"Yeah, I heard you."

"Well, speak up when you hear me talking to you." She reinforced her rule and wasn't waiting around for a rebuttal.

Laurie heard the phone ringing downstairs but didn't dash to answer the call since Drake was still home. There was a good chance she knew who it was anyway, call number twelve in less than sixteen hours. She was crossing the hall going back to her room, the one shared with Baby Rick and Larry, when Drake called up the stairs, "Laurie, it's Greg again." She went to the top of the stairs in eye view of her brother. "Do you want me to keep telling him that you don't want to talk?"

She didn't know what to say.

"He's going to keep calling until you talk with him," Drake said.

Hot and cold couldn't dwell in the same place without generating a lukewarm result. No matter how embarrassing or irrational, deep, deep inside she missed Greg, or maybe it was the concept of having a husband that she missed. Whichever it was, a part of her was reminded that Greg was the man she'd spent more than a decade building a family with. Still, the other half of her felt better living out of a bag in her brother's house than sleeping in the same bed, night after night, with a maniac who didn't know how to keep his rages under control. How much longer could she realistically tolerate him without going crazy? Sure, her kids needed their father, but she needed peace. Would it ever come? Only God knew, and He didn't seem to be telling.

At this moment, the boys weren't in their own beds, but they were safe. So was she.

"Is that Daddy?" Keith asked, overhearing the conversation from the hallway. "Can I talk to him?"

"Go back in the room and get your pants on," Laurie demanded. He stood still. "Get in the room, now," she demanded, with temples pulsating.

"I'll tell Greg you don't want to talk," Drake interjected.

"No," she told Drake, "I'll talk to him." Before descending the stairs, she yelled out for everyone to get downstairs. "Junior and Mitchell, make sure Baby Rick and Larry are dressed and downstairs in five minutes."

Acknowledgments rebounded from the respective rooms.

Drake extended the phone to her. "Are you sure, because you don't have to?"

Her head bobbed up and down in affirmation. "I'm going to have to talk to him eventually. It might as well be now."

"It's on mute," Drake said, handing her the phone and walking away.

She held the phone, composed her thoughts, and pushed the MUTE button.

"Hello," she uttered in a raspy voice, taking a seat on the bottom step.

"Hi," was all Greg could give back.

Silence choked the line until finally Laurie jump-started the conversation. "How are you?"

"I've been better."

"I know the feeling." She rubbed strands of carpet between her fingers.

"Laurie, I'm sorry about the way things went down the other night. I'm sorry."

"Uh-hmmm," she said as a herd of boys came barreling down the stairs. She squished close to the wall and waved them on. Baby Rick plopped down on the steps next to her.

"You've heard it before, I know, but this time I really mean it."

"Uh-hmmm," she said, reaching under her oversized shirt to pluck her waistband, which was cutting into her stomach.

“You have to believe me, Laurie. I’m sorry.”

“I definitely believe you’re sorry. You always are.” How could a man she once loved so much with all of her heart be so despicable at the same time? Ideally she wanted to continue loving him as her husband, but with almost identical passion she hated him for the man he’d become. He hadn’t intentionally hit her the other night, but he always lured the fear over her head. He didn’t let her love him freely. Their love was a roller coaster driven by unpredictable mood swings. Freedom was what she longed to have, with or without Greg.

“I want you and the boys to come home.” She heard his sniffles. Years ago, his crying moved her. A two-ton Dumpster stuffed with *I’m sorrys* and baseball-sized tears didn’t have the same weight.

“I’m not sure, Greg.” Baby Rick wrestled free and ran into the kitchen.

“Why not? I miss you so much. I want all of you to come home.” He paused. “This is Labor Day weekend. I want us to spend it together, as a family.”

The boys were ready to go home. Uncle Drake was wonderful but couldn’t compare with Daddy when it came to their affection. Her mind floated upstairs to the bags of clothes that had been stuffed in disarray. Her sons deserved better. They shouldn’t have to incur the cost of their parents’ marital woes. They should be in their own beds. “Let me get the boys off to school and we can talk after that.”

“You want me to come pick them up?”

"No, I'll drop them off at school and then I'll stop by the house later on this morning," she said, lowering her volume and covering the mouthpiece with her hand. He created this mess, and as a result, she had to be undercover talking to her own husband. She wanted to ask him why of all the places in the universe did he call Danielle yesterday looking for her and the boys. Staying at Drake's was intentional, partly to eliminate the chance of Danielle finding out and wailing into her. Thanks to Greg's big mouth, her plan failed.

"What time should I expect you, Laurie?"

"As soon as I drop off the boys. I'll be by the house before nine-thirty."

She might as well consider going home. Where else could she go, and who would want her with six children and forty pounds of extra body weight? They couldn't stay at Drake's house forever. Running away every time she and Greg had an argument wasn't the answer. The decisions she had to make were like a bowl of goulash, too much confusion. She wanted to tell the Lord that the only way she was going to be able to survive in this marriage was through His rescue, but pride mixed with her resentment, for what she believed was two years of His silence, kept her from reaching out to Him.

Chapter 23

Filtered light swept into the office den, comfortably able to fight off the impending dusk, which wasn't scheduled to arrive for another three hours. It was 4:15 on Friday afternoon. Drake would be home sometime during the next hour. She owed him at least a good-bye. Clothes were packed and already in the suitcases. Laurie was glued to the computer, drawn back into her new world like a suction cup. The Internet ship was sailing, evolving, and she'd never bothered to jump on board, until yesterday. Junior lived on the computer. Now she had a sense of why. Adventure. Education. Something new. Logging on was exciting. Going where she'd never gone before. Yesterday Drake and Junior had shown her how to use the e-mail feature. Drake also showed her the search engine thing and whatever they were called. She pondered before remembering they were called *chat rooms.* Those were harder to remember. One step at a time. For now, mastering e-mail would be an accomplishment.

Navigation complete. She stared at a blank message page. Drake, Danielle, Greg, and Junior, the extent of her e-mail address book. She'd sent her brother and sister four messages each, for the practice. Junior got twice as many. There wasn't anyone else left. She tapped on the mouse trying to think of somebody she could contact. Names didn't flash across the screen. Her circle was tiny and shrinking. Then it dawned on her, Rachel Matthews. She sat up tall in her seat and typed out a note to her old friend.

> Hi Rachel.
> Guess who? Can you believe I'm on e-mail? I can't believe it either. How's Chicago? How's your family, including Mr. Neal, Ken, and your grandmother? As for Greg and me, well, that's a long story. Now that I'm using the computer, we can keep in touch more often. Don't worry, you'll still get your annual Christmas card around Thanksgiving. How many years have I sent you that card?—a bunch. Can't break that tradition. Anyway, I have to run to work soon. Yes, shock #2, I'm working a job. Can you imagine? You know the last time I worked was when I worked for you, so long ago. I miss talking with you so much. But e-mail is going to work well for me. We have a computer at home, and if I

can just get Junior off it, I'll be able to write you often. You're like my only friend outside of Danielle and Drake. You remember them, my sister and brother. Okay, I'm definitely going now before I write you a whole book in my first e-mail.

Bye, Rachel, and I hope to hear from you soon.

Laurie typed in the subject line and prepared to send the message before realizing she didn't have Rachel's address with her. A perfectly good message, her masterpiece thus far, was going to be wasted. She clicked around looking for a way to save the message before aborting her search prematurely, afraid that the entire note would get lost or deleted. Old-fashioned techniques weren't passé. She scrounged through the top drawer of the desk in hunt of a pen and piece of paper. The message could be scribed and sent later, once she got home.

"Laurie, are you here?" Drake called out.

"Up here," she responded, jotting down the last few words.

Within a minute Drake was upstairs and sticking his head into the loft.

"I should have known." He came into the room. "You're hooked, aren't you? You have the Internet bug."

"It's fun."

"Which chat rooms did you go into?" he asked.

"None, I couldn't remember how to get there so I just practiced on e-mail. Don't worry," she said, returning the pen to its rightful place in the drawer, "I'll get to the chat rooms. Give me time, but you or Junior might have to show me how one more time."

"You better let me show you. You don't want Junior becoming too familiar with chat rooms unless you're monitoring him."

"Why, what's the big deal?"

"Let's just say the Internet can be fun, but it can also be dangerous. There are a lot of sick, perverted people on the Internet looking for easy prey. Children are prime candidates."

Keeping six boys out of harm's way kept her busy. Expanding their world with the Internet could be overwhelming. In the best of all worlds, she'd lock the boys away and keep them safe, acknowledging that reality and desires didn't always have to agree.

"You want me to show you how to get into the chat rooms?" Drake asked, commandeering the mouse and leaning over his sister's head.

"I won't have time. I need to get to work. I was just waiting for you to get home."

"Where are the boys?"

Laurie didn't expect a lecture from Drake but still wanted to delay the inevitable for as long as she could. She had to leave in thirty minutes if there was any chance of stopping home and getting to work on time. If this did turn out to be the one time he elected to give a dissertation on her decision to go home, time wasn't on his side.

"They're at home."

"Home, as in your home?" he said, straightening his back.

"That's the one," she said, rising from the chair, hoping to whiz out untarnished.

"You're not going home, too, are you?"

Quiet answered loudly.

"I can't stay here forever."

"You can stay here as long as you like, Laurie. You know that. At least be honest; you don't have to go home this soon. You want to go home, don't you?"

"Okay, yes, I want to go home. Your place is nice, but I want to be in my own bed, with my own clothes. My boys need their own space. I'm sorry, Drake, for letting you down, but I have to go home. Nobody can solve our problems but us."

"Laurie, I'm not telling you what to do. It wouldn't matter anyway. Grown people always do what they want to do, but I'm wondering if you've allowed enough time for the air to clear?" He bit his lip. "But I'm sure you know what you're doing. I'll support you in whatever you decide to do." He wrapped his arms around her and held still. "Understand, though, supporting you doesn't mean that I'm going to sit back with my Bible in the corner and let Greg hurt you. If he ever hits you—"

"He won't," she interrupted, pushing back, too embarrassed to hear the words spoken out loud. "I know that he won't. He's agreed to start going to church again." She was going, too, with a better attitude, but Drake didn't need to know about her recommitment. Keeping the spotlight on Greg was more productive.

"Great, but"—she tried to interrupt again, but Drake kept talking—"if he does hit you or comes close, I'm going to have to deal with him man to man."

"What does that mean?" she asked, leaning on the corner of the desk.

"Don't worry about the details. Just know that I'm serious. Greg has to be accountable as a man for the welfare of my sister, bottom line." Not a blink, flinch, or grin daunted his demeanor.

"But, Drake, you're not a violent person. That's our sister's thing, got to love her, but that's not you."

"Who's talking about violence? I'm not taking an eye for an eye. Greg has to answer to God for his behavior, just like we do. But I can deal with Greg without any violence. I keep telling you it's just a man-to-man thing. Don't worry about it, little sister."

"I don't want you to get caught up in my drama." She tightened the grip on her brother's hand. "You're the main reason I'm in church today, because of how you live and how much faith you have. I wish I could have faith like you. My life would be so different." She let her glance fall. "Regardless, I don't want you worrying about my problems."

"Laurie, remember I'm here for you, always. I love you and I'm proud of you. I'm not going to tell you to leave Greg. I never will."

"Other people would," she admitted. "And actually, I

understand where other people are coming from. I would probably tell somebody in my situation to leave, too; but it's different when you're the one living it. Walking away isn't easy." Her voice lowered. "Mostly, I'm tired of God letting me stay so confused. If I'm going to stay, I want to be happy. If I go, I want peace in knowing that me and the boys will be okay."

"Laurie, God is not the cause of your confusion."

"Maybe not, but He hasn't answered any of my prayers about what to do, and I've been asking ever since I started going back to church two years ago. I was practically living in the church, and what good did it do?"

"First of all, just going to church isn't enough. You have to spend time with Him through prayer, meditation, and reading the Bible. You have to get to know Him. Sounds like the only time you're in touch with Him is when you're asking for something. That's a one-sided relationship. Who wants a friend like that?" he said, nudging her. "You have to learn how to speak to Him and learn how to hear Him. That's going to make the difference for you. He's not always going to shout like you do," he said, grinning.

"Well, at least I'm going to church. That's a start."

"True."

"And all I got from living at the church all the time was more confusion. I'm trying to live right, but it's not easy with a man who doesn't go to church and half the time doesn't want me to go. That's why I need God to tell me something."

"The church isn't the problem. They have it going on over that Beulah. I think the problem is that you're really looking to the Lord for help. Maybe a part of you really wants to leave, so you've been cautious with God. Exactly what have you been asking Him for?"

"Simple really, I've asked God to change Greg. It's not like I've asked God to help me get divorced. That's like asking Him to help me steal. I know better than that, but still, I need something more than church folks telling me to stay because God doesn't approve of divorce while most of them are in miserable marriages, and then there's Danielle telling me to get divorced because God doesn't want me to be unhappy and living in fear. Which is it? If it was just me, that would be one thing, but I have children." She closed her eyes briefly, shaking her head.

"That's one of the problems, letting people both in and outside the church, including our sister, tell you how to live your life. You also have to stop blaming God for the choices you and Greg have made. Don't get me wrong, I love you and you know I'm not judging you, but let's keep it real. You want God to fix your marriage overnight, but it took years for the two of you to break it. You want God to do all the work, but are you willing to make tough choices?"

"Like what? Greg's the one with the problem, not me."

"See, that's what I'm talking about. You're not ready to make the serious kind of changes necessary to move forward."

"Are you talking about divorce? You think I should get divorced?"

"I don't know. I can't tell you what to do. You don't need to be living in fear, that much I do know. Other than that, you, Greg, and God have the final say. I'm just here to support you."

"I'm surprised you're not trying to tell me what to do like everybody else."

"Why would I? You're a grown woman. No matter what I say, you're going to do what you want to anyway, as it should be."

"But I could use some advice, especially since I've stopped asking God to change Greg."

"What about you?"

"What about me?"

"We both know Greg has issues, it goes without saying, but my dear, you're a player in the marriage, too. You can't just pray for changes in Greg."

"But he's the real problem. The only time we really fight is when he gets into one of those mood swings."

"Maybe, but you need to let God work on both of you."

"Greg is the main one who needs to start going to church."

"Don't worry about him, just take care of Laurie for the moment."

"Are you defending him?"

"No, just giving you the advice a brother should."

"Advice is good, but I need a miracle if I'm going to be happy."

"What you need is for me to tell you the truth, not sugarcoating what you want to hear."

"You're right," she said, grabbing his shoulder. "I'm so glad you're my brother."

"You have to get out of here for work. So I won't get into the long conversation now, although you need to hear what I have to say."

She glanced at her watch. It was 4:50, but she wasn't ready to leave. As long as she left by 5:30, getting to work wouldn't be an issue. She just wouldn't be able to stop by the house first as originally planned. "I have time."

"Okay, Ms. Businesswoman."

She giggled.

"Seriously, I respect you as an intelligent woman. You know what you want to do, and if you don't, this is a good time for you to turn back to the Lord for direction."

"People think somebody in an abusive kind of situation, not that I'm in a really bad situation or anything close, but anyway, people think abused people should leave," she said. "If I really was getting beat up or something serious, what does the Bible say about leaving?"

"I don't know, Laurie."

"I'm surprised," she said, "I thought you knew the whole Bible."

"Only God knows the whole Bible, but what you're asking isn't just a Bible question. You have to seek God for your own interpretation and direction. The decision you make about your marriage will be a reflection of where your relationship is in the Lord and how much faith you have in His guidance. Everybody's situation and solution are different."

She sat down and he pulled up a chair. No one else had come close to making sense about her up-and-down relationship with Greg and the Lord. At times she loved her husband and wanted to stay. Other times she wanted to run away from that man. Like a seesaw, her marriage was almost level most of the time; but more and more, discontent was claiming the edge. So long as the marriage could at least stay balanced, she had it in her to stay, but the seesaw was teetering.

"Like I said, nobody can tell you to leave a marriage that you already had the Lord sanction. Separation and divorce, no matter what your justification, is not God's best for your life. On the other hand, you're not supposed to live in fear in your own house from the man who promised before God and witnesses to love and honor you. Where is the victory in a miserable marriage? Here's the deal, sis, you can't say you're staying for the kids if all they see is fear and fighting. If you and Greg don't end up in counseling, it's just a matter of time before the kids will."

"We don't fight all the time, and he's not really abusive. I can honestly say he's never hit me."

"You're talking semantics. Abuse and intimidation are close enough. To be honest, abuse isn't an issue if a man is right before God."

"Why do you say that?" she asked.

"Because abuse wouldn't happen if men understood

Ephesians five, verse twenty-five, which says 'Husbands, love your wives, just as Christ loved the church and gave himself up for her,' instead of trying to strong-arm a woman into submission."

Greg had gotten better over the years about not harping, like a broken record, on being the man of the house. She knew who he was. Why didn't he?

"And verse twenty-eight," Drake continued, "says 'husbands ought to love their wives as their own bodies. He who loves his wife loves himself.' If a man truly loves his wife, not just lip service, the kind of love God has established in a husband, then we wouldn't be having this conversation, because people don't hurt those they truly love."

"So are you saying Greg doesn't love me?"

"Let me put it this way: I believe the brother wants to love you. I just don't think he knows how to love based on what you've told me about his parents and from what I know personally about Judge Wright."

"What do you know about his father?"

"Don't worry about the judge. Let's stick with you. From what I know about Greg's family, he has probably never experienced unconditional love and doesn't know how to give it in return. He didn't grow up with parents like ours."

"I know Mom and Dad are one of the main reasons I'm trying to stick this marriage out. Seeing them together, happy until they died, was wonderful for us to see. I want the same for me and Greg and our children."

"Greg has probably never experienced the kind of love you're talking about."

"His mother loves him," Laurie said. "She doesn't care much for me, but that's a different story. She thinks I trapped Greg and ruined his chance for the good life. His father is always mean to him. I don't know what to say about him. Thank God their issue didn't rub off on his relationship with our sons. He's great with the boys, and they love their father to pieces. Sometimes I feel like they can get by without me, but their father, no way."

Drake chuckled. "Those boys adore you, all six of them. Mothers, you don't usually have to worry about a mother when it comes to loving her child. I guess God knew some of our men wouldn't be the best fathers. So, as the ultimate backup, He became a father for everyone."

"I've never thought about God like a real father, but I guess you could. Wow."

"You see, that's why you have to talk to God for yourself."

"I'm still not convinced He can help me."

"Don't lose faith. Just wait. In the meantime, if Greg needs more time to mature into his manly responsibility, then he can send you home."

"Home, where's that? Mom and Dad are gone."

"Since they're gone and I'm the oldest, that makes home right here with me."

"Yeah, right, with six children."

"That's right, six children and all. You're welcome here any day, any time. Don't ever feel like you're trapped and that you don't have a way out. I love you."

They rose to their feet and hugged. Acceptance without judgment felt like a warm cup of hot chocolate on a cold winter night, sweet, soothing.

"At least our sister isn't here."

"I know," Laurie said, wiping away her tears with her hand. "She spends way too much time trying to live both my life and hers."

"She was ready to beat your husband down last night and wanted me to go with her."

"Oh my goodness. I don't want to hear her mouth tonight. I have to go to work. I can't miss another night. When she gets on her tirade, she's as bad as Greg."

"After throwing her fit over here last night, she's probably too tired to start up on you again, but you better get on out of here before she gets off work. You know she's coming, huffing and puffing, ready to blow my house down if she gets wind of you going back home."

The siblings laughed, wiping out any semblance of despair.

Every problem in the Wright household hadn't been solved, but the sun was peeking into her soul and life was brightening. Was Drake right? Was there hope? Maybe she'd given up on God too quickly. Laurie scurried home, bopping to the radio. The unfiltered chime of "Memory Lane" spewed from the speakers as Laurie waited for Minnie Riperton to hit that infamous note, which was so high it knocked on the gates of heaven taking Laurie along for the ride.

Chapter 24

Back to normal, like nothing had happened. Shake the adversity off the heel of his shoe, straighten up, put on the family face, and get on with life. The van, filled with his family, was on autopilot trudging toward judgment. Today could land him an extra kick in the spine if a sniff of this latest indiscretion with the law and Laurie roused the nostrils of his parents. Never having savored the best end of a bad situation, he didn't dare rest on the side of confidence. The legal bowl was the size of a pinhead in their town. Mountain-high hope would be required to believe the mighty judge wasn't informed about his son's latest shortcoming. Greg squeaked past the gates as he'd done countless times. Like the strike of Big Ben, precise without fail, Sterling Jr. had already arrived; at least the presence of his two-seater sports car said so.

Routine offered a dose of reassurance. Greg parked in his normal spot, a car length beyond the heavy wooden doors that blocked out all light, which found its way into the mausoleum. Swallow hard and fast. With stern direction and little tolerance, Greg had Laurie and the boys standing at the door in record time, waiting for the sacred invitation to enter. Hopefully Mom would answer and delay his amputation by a few moments. When she opened the door, glee danced inside. At least one iota of favor had fallen his way. Sunday afternoon was looking up. Maybe he should consider taking his family to church more often, instead of his attendance being more of a peace offering for what happened more than two weeks ago. Laurie was kind of serious this time about not wanting to come home. Promises had to be made to get his family back under his roof. Whatever he had to do had to be done. Laurie and the boys didn't belong anywhere else, except with him, the man who loved all of them more than anyone else in the world. Church three Sundays in a row was a small price to pay.

"My, my, well if it isn't my prodigal son and his wife," Mom said, with arms outstretched for him. Hugging her back was a welcomed gesture. Sincerity, intensity, and frequency of her outward expression of love weren't factors. Right now was all that counted.

"It's only been three weeks."

"I don't know which is worse, you working or being off work. I don't see you anymore either way," she said, easing something that felt like a check into his pocket.

The boys were getting jittery. Laurie was planted still with a sharp-edged grin.

"You're not pregnant again, are you?" Mom asked.

Laurie sucked her blossoming stomach in and pulled her shirt down tight, as close to her thighs as it would go. "No, I'm not pregnant. We are plenty happy with our six sons. We're not looking to have any more."

"Never know," Greg teased.

"I do know," Laurie spit out.

"I see you have a working woman now, son. Those days of having a doting housewife are over. A career woman is in the making," Mom said.

Laurie corralled the boys as close together as possible. "I'm taking them to the kitchen before they get out of hand standing here."

"Wait," Greg said, "I want them to go into the dining room and say hello to their grandfather and their Uncle Junior first." Perform every action perfectly; leave no room for criticism.

"Ah, boy, I'm hungry," Mitchell whined.

"Boy, you better straighten up," Greg told his son. "You know better."

Mom strolled ahead like the engine of a train steaming toward the dining room with Laurie bringing up the caboose and the boys filling in the middle. "When both parents have to work, the children are the first ones to suffer. Pretty much raise themselves, poor things," Mom barked.

"There's nothing wrong with my children," Laurie hissed in retaliation.

Usually the fire was on his feet. Having Laurie get burned in his place didn't make him feel any better. Character attacks were painful for him and those he loved. His attention shifted to a larger tool of destruction. Greg braced himself for Sterling Sr., sure that his father was brewing on the other side of the French double doors that led into the dining room. Interesting term, *dining room*—the only element consistently devoured with pleasure in this section of the house was Greg's pride, typically two Sundays per month. But today life was wonderful. Hope was alive. Going to church with his family felt right. Why, he didn't know. It just did. Nothing the judge said this day would penetrate. The armor of love and hope were solid. Mom opened the door and on his throne was the judge, sitting at the head of the Wright table. Where else would he be?

The boys cowered around their parents until they saw Uncle Junior. Greg wished one day his sons could show the same level of excitement with seeing his family as they did when Drake and Danielle came around. It could happen. If he was attending church regularly and liking it, then truly any request in life was possible. The greetings weren't free flowing, and Dad didn't help the process. With a bit of prodding, the courtesies were extended and normalcy was back in place. Mom and Laurie ushered the boys to the kitchen for their special meal, whereas Greg was left behind to drop a wet rag on the festive atmosphere Sterling Jr. and Dad had so easily generated.

* * *

"Get out of my way," Larry howled at Baby Rick in the kitchen, pushing him to the floor and sending his brother into an instant crying fit.

"Young man, you stop that," Mrs. Wright said, getting to Larry first and grabbing him by the collar, then helping Baby Rick to his feet.

Laurie was next in line to snatch him back into reality.

"Why did you do that?" Mrs. Wright asked him, bending down and staring into his face.

"My daddy yells at my mommy all the time and I want to be just like my daddy," Larry said, beaming with pride.

Laurie wanted to hide under the floorboards. Greg was worried about her telling the family secrets. Now that the boys were getting older, his worries were increasing sixfold.

"Yelling is mean, and you don't want to be mean, do you?" his grandmother asked.

Larry's face shrunk, and he shook his head with lips poked out.

"Now tell your brother you're sorry before I have to get your father in here," Laurie demanded.

Greg had an idea. Why let the space in the dining room go to waste? The air should be bottled and sold in lieu of insulation, thick, stuffy, and hot.

"How's it feel being back to the grind?" his brother asked.

"Man, I had no idea how good it would feel to be back

on the job. I thought I'd be bored to death with so much free time," Greg said, taking a drink from his crystal water goblet. He waited on a remark from his father but none was offered.

"We need to get you on the golf course. I can't imagine having an entire month off. I'd golf every day."

"Don't worry, son, with the amount of money you're dumping into the stock market at your age, you'll be retired by the time you're forty-five." He rolled up the sports section of the paper and took off his reading glasses, which were hooked on a chain that hung around his neck. "A man like your brother will be working all of his life, probably up until he's eighty years old or so. Fellows like him never get ahead."

Laurie and Mom returned. Good timing, because he had no intention of responding to the comment made by a man who had everything except peace. Greg took another sip of water and pulled the chair out for his wife, full stomach and all. Whatever relationship his parents had, Greg didn't want. Broke and happy didn't look any worse than wealthy and miserable.

"When are we eating?" Greg asked in a bold tone. "I'm hungry."

Chapter 25

Laurie placed the glasses and remaining silverware into the dishwasher while Greg wiped the table.

"I forgot to ask you how work was today?"

"It was okay."

"Nothing special?"

"No, nothing special. No matter how you cut it, the Features Department is not as challenging or as interesting as my old department," he said with volume lowering. He tossed the dishcloth into the sink. "But, what can I say, it's a job and I'm glad to have it. Until something better comes along in the company, I'm going to take my happy behind in there every day. I just smile and say very little to anybody. That way I can't get into any trouble. I'm keeping this job. Whatever I have to do, I'm doing. That's the bottom line." He wrapped his arms around her. "Not everybody loves their job like you do."

"The people I work with are nice," she told him. It wasn't so much the job that kept her smiling. Having her own sense of accomplishment, and to be honest, being away from the boys and Greg for a blip of time was the source of her joy. Greg didn't understand when she used to spend so much time at church. She didn't expect him to understand her glee about getting out, even if it was for work. Being seen as only a mom and his wife hadn't mattered before, but now that she'd gotten a taste of freedom, she couldn't help wondering how much she'd missed out on over the last twelve years by giving up her interests and living purely for Greg and the kids. She wasn't sure when it happened, but somewhere along the way she lost herself and no one seemed to care, especially Greg. Maybe he needed to know how she really felt. On second thought, best not to tell him the total truth, only what he could handle. "I'm glad to have a paycheck coming into the house. We need all the help we can get."

"Wait a minute now," Greg said, pulling away. "I'm still the man around here. It's my job to provide. The Features Department may be boring, but the pay is still good, and it's still enough to take care of our household."

"I know, I know." Diffuse and keep rolling. The marriage was in a state of bliss; she needed to avoid derailing at all costs. "But the little money I make will help us get your brother paid back quicker." He didn't know she was also aware of the checks his mom had given to him. She'd seen one for a thousand dollars back in

August and another one for a thousand dollars almost two weeks ago. Whether he'd cashed it was questionable and unlikely. Mrs. Wright often tossed money his way, but Greg didn't like taking handouts unless it was an emergency he couldn't handle, and those circumstances could be counted on one hand. He was a provider, always had been. No one could deny it, except his father, who denied Greg everything anyway. So Mr. Wright didn't count.

"That's true, and you know how much I want to get Sterling paid off. Once we have the money paid back, you can quit. The sooner the better. I don't want my father to have anything to say about my taking money from Sterling." He leaned back into Laurie. "Isn't it a crying shame, a grown man like me is still afraid of his father? What's he going to do, whoop my behind?" he said, laughing heartily. He kissed Laurie on the cheek and said, "I'll run upstairs and get the boys ready to go."

"Perfect, that will give me a few minutes to go online."

"You really are into the computer now. How bizarre. Before you never showed any interest. Now you've moved the computer out of Junior's room and into the family room. What a drastic change. I hope you don't change too much on me. New job, Internet-savvy, what's next?" he said, tapping her size eighteen back end, which was attached to her size sixteen body.

"Don't forget their book bags, because I doubt if Mitchell and Jason have finished their homework."

"Got it covered," Greg said, careening around the

kitchen table and heading for the stairs. "The sooner we get to counseling, the sooner we get back home," he teased, arching his eyelids and letting his gaze comb her eyes.

She closed the dishwasher door and pressed the buttons to get the cleaning under way. A sound byte from the song they sang at church two days ago was still mulling around. "It's only a test" was the line she remembered. She could hum the tune but the words were fleeting.

Missing work every other Tuesday was the only downside to counseling. Court, which came when summer was taking its last spin earlier in the month, was uneventful. Greg humbled himself before the family court judge. He looked so much like the man she'd fallen in love with and dreamed of marrying years ago. The judge asked, "Mrs. Wright, I've read the complaint. Do you want to press charges?" The answer leaped out. *No.* The judge ordered both of them to attend counseling; otherwise, Greg would sit in jail for thirty days. Three sessions beat thirty days. After tonight, one down, two to go. Six weeks would fly by and they'd be done by the end of October. She wasn't convinced that Drake was completely correct with his comment about where the marriage ended up was contingent upon where her relationship was with the Lord? Against her initial decision, she had continued praying for a few days after talking with Drake. She even found time to skim the Scriptures a few times, particularly Ephesians chapter five about marriage and Acts chapter fourteen about enduring hardships; but all in all, the Wright household was doing okay. She didn't need to rely on God so much to fix the marriage this time around. She was leaning on her own efforts and it was working. Laurie was thrilled to see the change in Greg. She wasn't ashamed of her decision to stay. Miracles were flowing their way.

The song wouldn't go away. What was the next line, something about your storm? She hummed and wiped the countertop. Greg had already cleaned the table and swept the floor. Dry clothes on a damp night. Her prayers were finally being answered; this was too good to be true. The two of them were clicking in every way. Having him chip in with the housework was the help she needed. Great for him, too, because by bedtime she wasn't as worn-out as she used to be when she was the only one doing all the housework, taking care of the kids, running errands, cooking the meals, and working her part-time job. There used to be no energy or time left for even the *a* in the word *affection*. What a huge difference a little help around the house made, and Greg sure wasn't complaining. These times, moments of raw love and affection, were the elements that kept her in the marriage. As much as she'd like to say the marriage was on an upswing because of the Bible and her prayers, the truth was she hadn't spent enough time with either to know, not consistently. Better to take credit herself.

She pulled up the chair to the computer desk and hopped online to check her e-mail messages. There was sure to be one from Rachel. They were chatting at least twice a week. Having Drake show her how to set up a free e-mail account on Yahoo was smart. A small bit of privacy in a house with seven males was a blessing. Her short window of opportunity wasn't wide enough to get into her favorite chat room. She'd wait until tomorrow morning for her adventure, ten to noon, like every other weekday. The extra hour, which she added last week, was essential if she was going to be a regular participant in the Georgia chat room.

Chapter 26

The sweet taste of fulfillment, a feeling that didn't make a habit of dwelling in or around Greg Wright, was lingering, with no sign of dissipating in the foreseeable future. Sterling Jr. probably felt like this most of the time, hopeful, like life was going his way. Knowing he was exceptional. Greg held Laurie's hand as they walked into the five-story building that was filled with an array of medical, legal, and business offices. He read the board and found the Wade Family Counseling Center on the fourth floor. Hand in hand they boarded the elevator and made their way to the office.

Greg winced at the fun part of today's outing, filling out insurance papers and scheduling the next appointment two weeks from today. He needed to get through the first session, then he'd be free until the middle of October, when they'd return for the next shock treatment. The hardest part of counseling was getting started, the time when they had to dump all of their problems onto the floor, and then the counselor would sort through them and pick out her favorite, the issue with the most potential, like picking out a puppy from the pet store. He completed the questionnaire, providing as little history as possible, and handed the clipboard back to the receptionist, ready to take his treatment. A short five-minute wait and they were summoned. Greg jumped to his feet. Bring it on. The toughest counselor wouldn't be able to destroy him. Judge Wright had tried for years with no significant success. Three sessions with a rookie was like candy.

"Mr. and Mrs. Wright, I'm Katherine Harrington, but I'd prefer for you to call me Katherine. If it's okay with the two of you, I'd also like to start out on a first-name basis."

"Sure," Greg responded, knowing Laurie was fine with the informality, too.

The insurance company covered three visits and didn't give a choice on the counselor. They got whoever had a time slot available. A female counselor again. The privacy brochure Greg read in the waiting room claimed that knowledge of the counseling sessions and their content was confidential and not accessible to the patient's employer. He wondered if the claim was true. Greg squirmed in his seat, with hands clasped together in his lap.

Laurie looked relaxed. Why not? She didn't have anything to worry about. The last time they went to counseling the session wailed on him as an angry man who terrorized his co-workers. They never got around to Laurie's issues. With three sessions to go at fifty minutes each, there was a good chance they wouldn't get to her this time either. Beat up on Greg. Might as well get started and get this over.

The counselor perused the one-page questionnaires that both he and Laurie completed before the session. It felt like pins were sticking out of the chair. Greg kept moving around in search of a comfortable position.

"Okay," Katherine said, "I see you've had some form of counseling before."

"Yes, we have," he said with pride. She didn't need to know the previous counseling was completed several years ago as a peace offering to his wife and the anger management session last year was required in order to keep his job. A stranger who didn't really care about his life beyond fifty minutes didn't need to know all of his business. His plan was to tell only what was absolutely necessary to complete the court order. None of this counseling stuff mattered anyway. He was convinced their marital issues could be resolved if both he and Laurie put their minds to it. They didn't need some woman, an outsider, who was probably single, gay, divorced, or a man-hater telling him how to live a happily married life. Nope, she wasn't getting into his head, and if there was mercy on earth, Laurie wouldn't use this as an opportunity to spill her guts either.

"How did the counseling work for you?"

Laurie and Greg looked at one another, and Laurie finally answered. "I thought it helped."

"What about you, Greg, how did it work for you?"

He shifted his weight in the chair again and propped his elbow on the arm of the chair. "I didn't," he stammered, "get anything out of it." His rebuttal was drafted prior to coming and was ready for articulation.

"It didn't work for you. So what brings you back?"

Laurie let her glance graze the floor. The response was on him.

"We had a disagreement, minor, very minor. There was a big misunderstanding. The police got involved and here we are."

"You were charged with domestic violence?"

Greg propped the other elbow on the chair and leaned in its direction. "I wasn't charged with anything," he said, his voice cracking, requiring him to clear his throat before apologizing for the noise.

"You didn't press charges?" Katherine directed to Laurie.

Before Laurie could answer, Greg jumped in. "There wasn't any reason to press charges. I didn't do anything. I mean, I did, but not what the police were making it out to be."

"Greg, wait a minute. Understand, the purpose of this session is not to point out all of your flaws. The purpose is to identify where the challenge points are in your relationship and discuss tools that might help you to work through your problems. Let me warn you that the situation will most likely get worse before it gets better, but I believe counseling can be life changing for your relationship if you're committed to the hard work."

"We've tried counseling and it didn't help, not at all."

"It takes time."

"My insurance only covers three sessions, and we can't afford to pay one hundred dollars for extra sessions."

"Let's not worry about additional sessions. Let's not even worry about your second and third sessions. I would like for us to concentrate on this session." She looked at the clock on the wall. "For our remaining forty minutes, I'd like to talk a little bit about your support groups."

"Aren't we here to talk about our marriage? We only have three sessions and I'd like to get something out of them. Might as well, we're here," he commented.

"We will get to the marriage. But, Greg and Laurie, you will be amazed to know that many problems couples encounter originate long before they get married. Reality says we don't live in isolation. Every experience, conversation, and feeling helps to make us who we are. The spouse you become is often defined through your backgrounds, going all the way back to your childhoods."

She made sense, but if there was truth in her assessment, then three sessions definitely would not be enough if they were going to weigh down the sessions with his family. Gnawing off his toe and swallowing it whole would be more palatable than squeezing Sterling

Sr. and Virginia Wright into his marital counseling session. No, three sessions wouldn't cut it. Three years might be getting close, but no guarantees.

Chapter 27

Eight hours a day was about six too many for the handful of work generated from the Features Department daily. Greg was accustomed to chomping at tree-high stacks of graphic requests that required his attention from sun up to sun down. He used to get in early and stay an extra hour each night in the Advertising Division. No longer. Getting through the day without being bored out of his mind was a miracle. He toyed with the pumpkin icon bouncing around on the computer. In less than ten days, October would be over. Hopefully the company was going to be around long enough for him to get redemption and be moved back to a full-sized office with daylight. With the drastic drop in company earnings, which everybody was talking about in the cafeteria at lunchtime, nothing was guaranteed. The best source of comfort for Greg was his eight years of seniority. Many bodies would be swinging out the doors before him. He was surfing around the corporate site to see if there was an update from the CEO on the state of the company when the group manager stepped into the cubicle, the one Greg shared with another coworker.

"Greg, how's it going?" the manager asked, letting his buttocks rest on the absent employee's desk.

"Going well," Greg said, spinning his chair fully around to face the manager.

The manager rubbed his open palm up and down his stubbled chin. "Got a minute? I need to speak with you."

Greg's heart palpitated. He was safely squished into the corner of the dungeon, away from all of the good citizens of the company who might feel intimidated by his presence. He wracked his brain, trying to remember anyone he might have bumped, sneezed on, made eye contact with, or merely came close to infringing upon their space. "Sure," he stammered.

"Great, we can meet in the director's office."

Greg felt a hot flash rush his body. "Any particular reason?"

"I'd rather wait and let the director speak with you."

The message was sent from his brain telling his legs to stand, but they weren't budging. Greg felt woozy and took a deep breath to gain composure. He hadn't attacked, yelled, or even so much as traded glances with anyone since he'd been back to work for the past six weeks. How could he? Only those who were lost ended up in Features. Not even daylight frequented the place.

Greg schlepped behind his manager, hoping by some divine act the boulder attached to his ankle would be broken, freeing him to walk without the burden of the weight.

They finally made it to the execution chamber. Greg stood by the doorway, afraid to go inside. The director beckoned for him to enter, along with the manager. "Have a seat," the director offered.

Greg sat. The chair seemed to overpower him. He felt like a tiny cartoon character, the size of a miniature candle sitting on the big chair, barely visible to those in charge.

"Greg, I realize you have work to do, so I want to keep this meeting brief."

He would have responded, but there was nothing to say. Wait and see was his approach.

"As you know, we had a great second quarter this year, but," the director said, rearing back in his chair with his gray hair blending in with his pale skin, "third quarter didn't do as well."

So far the director wasn't telling Greg anything he didn't already know. Any employee in the company with access to the intranet, which was everybody, knew about the drop in numbers. What did this have to do with him?

"In order to stay viable in this dynamic marketplace, we're going to have to make changes, tough changes," he said, bringing his arms back to the desk.

Here it comes, Greg thought, he was getting demoted again. Where else was there to go, in the furnace?

"As you know, we've spent the past three weeks assessing each department and identifying areas that have to be modified."

Greg rocked in his seat slightly.

"We've determined that Features can be absorbed by the Advertising Division, effective immediately."

"Really." *Yeah,* he wanted to scream. They were finally moving him back upstairs. It was about time. Nobody on the third floor could push out quality graphics like he could, and it was high time they acknowledged him. He sat tall in his seat waiting for them to ask the big question, did he mind going back upstairs. His eyelid twinkled.

"This means everybody in the department, with the exception of Mark here, will have their job eliminated."

"What?" Greg felt a jolt hit his body. It was a nightmare. "Are you saying that I'm"—he hesitated, refusing to give the words feet—"I'm fired?"

"No," the Director of Marketing immediately jumped in. "Your entire department is being downsized, effective today. Human Resources will meet with you this afternoon to discuss the details, but overall each employee will get one month of pay for each year they've been with the company up to eighteen months." The director scrolled down a sheet of paper with his finger while putting on his reading glasses with his free hand. "It looks like you've been here eight and a half years. So, you're entitled to eight and a half months plus medical benefits for one full year. You can elect to receive your severance in a lump sum or continuous biweekly payments. The decision will be totally up to you."

How kind. They're actually letting him make a decision in this execution. Greg shrugged in his soul but remained steadfast in the face of the director.

"You're also entitled to four weeks at an outplacement service. You will receive your normal salary for the first two weeks. The fee for your four weeks at the outplacement service, should you need the entire time, is of course covered in its entirety by the company. I don't have all of the specifics about the service, but HR will provide those details for you. My objective is to make sure my direct reports hear about the downsizing from me. I want you to understand just how important it is to the leadership of this company that we make your transition as smooth as possible. You've been an asset to this company."

Oh, please, Greg wanted to say. Cut the words. Issue the lethal dose and get this fiasco over.

"Also, I have to reiterate. You will receive your salary for the first two weeks, but not for the last two weeks of outplacement. Your severance will kick in at that point."

Greg couldn't move. The words were flying around the room, and every now and then one would pluck him on the head, but none were entering his ear or filtering to his brain. This was a nightmare. When would he wake up?

Chapter 28

The Sentra sputtered along, dodging the potholes, both known and unknown. An inch too far to the left or right and he was sure to be swallowed by the holes of despair lining the path home. Greg drove along the slow, winding road leading from town. He meant to turn three lights ago and take the long scenic route home but didn't notice the street as he drove past in a haze. The car moved down the road, practically driving itself. He wanted to go home and hide under a mound of pillows, but Laurie and the boys would be there. How could he face her without a job, again?

Failure ran alongside the car, trying to jump in when he slowed to a crawl, but every time he felt it getting close, he pressed on the gas. If he could keep Failure and its running buddy, Shame, off his back for at least twenty-four hours, then he could think straight and come up with a plan. Laurie and the boys deserved to have a man they could count on. It wasn't an experience he had growing up, but that didn't mean he couldn't set the precedent for the Wright men going forward.

He swung off the road into a strip mall parking lot, causing cars behind him to slam on their brakes. The honking drivers slid off his back. They had some nerve getting bent out of shape over his minor quick turn. Didn't they know his world was falling apart, again? He was almost thirty-five and this year wasn't any better than last year or the year before that. As a matter of fact, each year seemed to bring more problems. He wasn't progressing. He was retreating. Loser hopped in the passenger side of the car and strapped in. Greg didn't try to fight him off. He rested his head on his hands, which were clutching the steering wheel. If life wasn't getting any better, regardless of how hard he tried, then what was the point of continuing. Maybe this was one of those come-to-Jesus moments he'd heard people talk about, the time where hope was gone and there was no way out. But every time he got an inkling to pray, the image of his father sitting at the head of the table chanting his thirty-year-old line left him empty. He pounded his head repeatedly, softly, into his hands.

He fought to clear out remnants of Judge Wright and save his brain cells for a thought worthwhile, because all the judge was good for right now was supplying his son with a shotgun and a few shells. The haze returned. Why did he always have to be on the short end of life? The judge wasn't a better man, nowhere near. Mean, nasty, some kind of father; maybe he was worth something to Sterling Jr. but not much to him. He dug into the wheel, firmer. How could he love a man who he hated so much? Love or not, the judge didn't deserve to be so blessed and so successful when he could care less about the amount of pain he'd caused his oldest son. It was just a matter of time until Greg would get the courage to use the shotgun and create his own peace. Wrongs had to be made right. Everybody knew sins were bound to catch up with you sooner or later, and sinners had to pay the price. He had, and so would the judge.

Greg glanced at his watch. 5:27. He wouldn't get home in time to meet Laurie before she left for work. By now she'd probably figured out he was running late and dropped the kids at Danielle's house. He looked around the perimeter of the parking lot for a pay phone. He could call Laurie and let her know he was coming home later. A little more thought led to the conclusion that he shouldn't call. She would badger him about his whereabouts and a lecture was all he needed to push him over the hundred-foot cliff. He was hanging on by a thin thread, which was threatening to snap at the slightest nudge.

Six o'clock came and went in the parking lot. He had to keep moving. He jerked the Sentra back onto the main road, letting the car go where it pleased. He drove aimlessly around town. His first choice was the park, but he wasn't equipped for the task. He ended up in his driveway at 8:30, sitting with the car running, unable to get out. The house lights were off, which meant the boys were with Danielle or Drake. He could hobble inside and lock himself in the bedroom, letting sleep usher him to a better place, but he was reminded that sleep only lasted for a season, whereas his misery was enduring. He shifted the car into reverse, took his foot off the brake, and let the car roll into the street. He moved with the speed of a ninety-year-old driving at night with cataracts. He had nowhere to go, except deeper into his pain.

Hours were lost. The gas icon located next to the speedometer on the dashboard came on for a few seconds when he went uphill and dimmed as the car leveled off. He journeyed back home, not wanting to refill the gas and hoping that running out wasn't going to be added to his long list of woes.

The clock over the sink displayed 12:40. He maneuvered through the dark. The best scenario was that everyone, including Laurie, was asleep. He could drift into oblivion too and start again tomorrow. Today was gone and so was his tolerance. He glided up the stairs, avoiding the creaking spots. He eased into the bedroom and migrated to his closet. So far he was in the clear, not a creature stirring. Home free, for once. He heard the light switch click on outside the closet door, shattering his hope of going to bed without interrogation. He could stay in the closet until she went back to sleep, but there was every reason to believe that wasn't going to work either. Might as well go out, face her, get it over, and go to bed demanding a better day. Tomorrow couldn't be any worse. Shoulders square in his pajamas, he emerged.

"Where have you been?" Laurie blurted.

Her anger had always been a spark for him. When she was mad and jumped him with an attitude, before he could arrange his thoughts right in his head, his anger was usually jumping up front and retaliating. He sucked in his pride and lay down as close to the edge of the bed as possible, trying to ignore Laurie, who was sitting up and hollering.

"Don't you hear me? Say something."

He dug into the bed but kept quiet.

"Say something, you hear me? Where were you? You knew I had to go to work tonight, and I don't like being late."

"I don't care about your job. Quit if you need to." He rose up and drilled her with his eyes. "We don't need that funky seven dollars an hour you're making anyway. It's a waste of time," he said, yanking the covers from her side of the bed.

Her body seemed to tense. "I like my job, and my seven dollars an hour helped pay the bills when your black behind was out of work last month. You didn't seem to have a problem with my job then."

Before he could say "hold up," his feet were on the floor, body stretched across the bed, braced with one hand on the mattress and the other free to point a finger an eighth of an inch from her nose. "You think you're big time now because you have a job." She winced, but he didn't acquiesce. His demons were raging and the moment was out of his hands. "Who do you think you are? Yeah, so what if I was off work for a few weeks last month. I still make the money and pay the bills in this house. What, do you think you're the man around here now just because you've spent a few months begging people on the phone to buy stuff that nobody wants? I want you to quit the job if this is what it does to you, to us."

The floor creaked outside their closed bedroom door, causing Greg to pull back from Laurie as she scrunched her knees in tight to her chest, shaking. "I'm not going to let you keep talking to me like I'm some kind of child."

Tears rolling, she fumbled for the phone sitting on the nightstand next to the bed, dropping it first before securing her grip.

"Who are you going to call? Huh? The police?" The floor outside the door creaked again. "If I open that door and find anybody who's not in their bed, asleep, they're going to be in big trouble," he howled.

Laurie trembled but maintained her death grip on the phone.

"Go ahead, call them if you want to. I didn't touch you and you know it, church lady."

"I'm not calling the police," she screamed.

"Who else you going to call, your big mouth sister? Go ahead, what's she going to do? Beat me up?" he mimicked, punctuating the comment with a sneer. "Oh, oh, no, I got it, you're calling your big bad brother. That's it, right? What's the gay boy going to do, come and scare me away?" He laughed. "Oh, before you even say anything, I know, he's not gay," he mimicked again. "But any man who doesn't plan to have sex before marriage has something wrong with him, simple as that. So go ahead, call gay boy, because if he comes over here trying to preach up in my business, he will get dealt with. So by all means, call your family if you want them to get their feelings hurt." He lay back in his space and pulled the covers up to his chest. "Next time, don't start an argument you can't finish."

There wasn't anyone else to call, besides the police, who had the power to make Greg treat her right. She could try God, but His timing wasn't the same as hers. She couldn't think of anyone on earth who commanded such respect from her husband. Forget about him. She dialed Danielle's, pressing the buttons aimlessly, hoping the numbers were punched correctly. She put the receiver to her ear and hung up on the first ring, tossing the phone between her and Greg. She sniffed and wiped her eyes with the palm of her hand while he lay calm, resting without concern. She wanted to bang the phone against his head, into eternity, over, done. He would be out of her hair for good. No more fear. No more confusion. No more wishing and hoping for the fairy tale marriage, which wasn't coming by any means. She could do it. There wasn't anyone to stop her, except that pricking sensation in her spirit saying no. She wanted to block the rumbling out, but God wouldn't go away. She knew it was Him, although they hadn't really talked in a while, not since working the job and keeping afloat became a priority. But she still recognized His voice. She hadn't asked Him to come but sure was glad to have Him there. No one else had a chance with Greg.

The phone rang, startling him awake since it was next to his ear. Before Laurie could grab the phone, Greg reached behind his head and snatched it. He glanced at the clock reading 2:15. "Somebody better be dead or in the hospital." He pressed the TALK button. "Hello."

"Let me speak with Laurie."

"Who is this calling my house this late?"

"Put Laurie on the phone."

"Danielle, who do you think you are calling my house and disrespecting me?"

Laurie reached for the phone, but Greg didn't release.

"Put Laurie on the phone," she said with more force. "You better remember I'm not Laurie. I don't care jack about you. Don't forget that, Mr. Greg. Don't pull your crap on me, Mr. Man. I'm not taking it, and you better not be doing anything to my sister over there. Do you understand me? Because I'm only twenty minutes off your behind."

"Whatever happens between me and Laurie doesn't have anything to do with you, and I'd appreciate it if you'd stay out of our business."

"That's your problem, you need to get some business."

Laurie reached for the phone again, without success.

"I haven't done anything to your sister," he said, unwilling to let her know how aggravated she had made him.

"Let her tell me. Now, I'm not going to ask you again, put my sister on the phone before I—" was the part she got out before he tossed the phone back to the middle of the bed. "It's your big-mouth sister. Keep it short. I have to get up for work in a few hours," he said and rolled over. The last thought he recalled before slipping off was the feeling of Laurie staring into the back of his head, hot, blistering hot like a madwoman who was bent on being heard. He could apologize tomorrow, but as for tonight, it was settled and what needed to be said had been said.

Chapter 29

Greg turned on his tabletop lamp and sat on the side of the bed, massaging his scalp. Laurie didn't budge, showing no sign of life. Hopefully he would get up and get out. A long day of chores and slave labor around the house culminating with four hours at work was more desirable than spending five more minutes in the presence of this man.

"Laurie, you up?" he asked.

No, and leave me alone would be her response of choice, but she didn't feel like resuming the fight from last night. She stifled her attitude and said what he wanted to hear. Didn't matter, he would be on his way to work in less than an hour. "Yes, I'm awake."

He twisted his body around, laying one knee sideways on the bed and resting his weight on the arm stretched out behind him. "I have to tell you something," he muttered.

She didn't say anything.

"Can you hear me?" he asked softly.

"I'm listening," she responded with a distinctive edge, although she really was trying to keep her festering contempt under control.

Turtles with broken legs moved faster. She wanted him to get to the point, get dressed, and get out. Please.

He wouldn't turn and face her; instead, he kept his back between them. "I found out yesterday that I was..." he said and stopped, clapping his hands together. He had her attention, attitude cast aside. Something serious was coming. She braced. "I was downsized yesterday."

"What do you mean?" she said, unable to prevent anger from converting into worry.

"I lost my job yesterday."

"What, are you kidding me?" she said, slamming the heel of her palms against her forehead, concluding with thumb and finger caressing her temples. "What happened? Don't tell me you got into another fight with somebody at work again?"

"No," he answered immediately with a tone of sincerity, then turned to face her. "I didn't do anything."

"So what happened?"

"The company had a slump in revenue last quarter and my new department was totally cut, not just me, but all twenty-five people, everybody except the manager. Features wasn't the only department cut. Other areas in the company were cut, too."

"What are we going to do if you don't have a job? The

money I'm making is a help, but it can't take care of our entire household."

"I get paid for another two weeks, and then I'll get eight and a half more months of severance pay plus benefits. Don't get me wrong, I'd rather have my job, but at least it's something. Don't worry," he said, drawing closer to her. "I'm going to take care of you and the boys," he told her, landing a kiss on her cheek. Instinctively she pulled away, igniting an equal reaction from him. "I see you're still mad about last night. I'm sorry," he said, standing to his feet en route to the bathroom.

"Uhm-hmmm." Promises, promises, he had made one to love, honor, and cherish her too but hadn't. There was no reason to believe he'd keep this promise either. She sat up in the bed, stern, feeling strength rising from below. She looked around the room. Eight years in the same place, the same furniture, the same man, and the same mind-set. She closed her eyes and saw last year looking just like the current one, several nights four years ago was identical to last night, nothing new in the Wright household. How had she gone from the loving wife, excited about a happily-ever-after future with Greg nearly thirteen years ago, to this woman, scared of her own shadow. There was more to life, and she was going to find it. Greg had spewed his last venom her way. No more. The remaining drops, which had snuck into her space, were swatted away, sending a message of discouragement to any other tears, which might be contemplating the journey. Her spirit cried out. She wasn't a victim. She was young, smart, a nice person, and she had a job. She could take care of herself even if Greg couldn't. That much she was beginning to believe. The darkness which had been strangling light from the room was loosening its grip. She got up and opened the blinds, setting hope free. She vowed to herself and her soul that her next five years would not be like her former five. Only death would come between her and happiness; and at this time, if that's what it took, so be it, because living with bitterness and fear day after day was death.

Chapter 30

Greg could continue sitting around the house boo-hooing if he wanted to. It didn't bother Laurie in the least bit. A few hours in the chat room earlier accented her day. At 5:15, she was ready for work.

"What are we going to eat for dinner?" he asked, watching her close the coat closet.

"I don't know, I guess whatever you cook."

"You know I can't cook."

"Then I guess you'll be eating Boston Market again."

"We've eaten that four nights in a row."

"I know. Isn't it great that they have chicken, turkey, meatloaf, steak and even ham? Variety is always good," she said, continuously moving.

He smirked. "You just don't care about me and the boys, do you?"

"You know that's not true. You know how much I love them."

"Oh, them but not me, huh, okay. I get it."

"Greg, look, you're a grown man with car keys and money. You'll find something to eat. I'm not worried about you or the boys starving. Now let me get out of here before I'm late."

"How are you going to be late?" he said, scowling. "You get to work twenty minutes early every night. Are you so eager to get out of here?"

No sense responding to a question that already had the correct answer.

He made his move, approaching, holding. He whispered into her ear, "Why don't you quit this little job? We don't need the money anymore. My severance pay starts this week."

"And?" she said, wiggling free, inching for the door.

"And you don't need to work. You can stay home with me until I get a job."

"You've already been out of work for three weeks and you haven't had one interview yet."

"I know, but you know how hard I'm looking. My company is one of the biggest employers in the area. There aren't a lot of graphic design jobs in the area, and I'm not willing to commute back and forth to Atlanta every day. That's two hours each way. I can't do that, but I'm going to get a job."

She stood with arms folded, peering into his eyes. "In the meantime, I need to keep this job. Every little bit helps." When she took the job back in the middle of August, at Greg's insistence, the motivation was money.

Nearly three months, a promotion to senior telemarketer, and five $100 bonuses later, her desire to stay had nothing to do with compensation. It was about her sense of independence and choosing her path that was separate from Greg and the boys. The job was for her, and she enjoyed every minute at work.

From the garage, she told him, "Since we have so much money, why don't we pay for more counseling sessions?"

Greg shrugged his shoulders, standing at the steps in his bare feet, sliding his hands into his pockets. "It's a waste of money. A counselor can't help us. All we have to do is spend more time together and we can fix our own problems. That's one of the reasons I want you to quit this job. It's not helping our marriage."

Laurie didn't bother to respond. Ignore the insinuation and move on to a topic that made a difference. "I want to continue counseling, Greg. We're just getting to our real issues. We shouldn't stop again."

"Three sessions is all the insurance covers. We're done," he said, hiding behind a smug grin.

"The church has free marital counseling," she suggested, although she hadn't been to Beulah Grove much lately.

"Oh, no," he said, dancing around on his bare feet. "I definitely don't want those church folks trying to give me advice. With my luck, I'd probably get assigned to Judge Wright. Now wouldn't that be a joke, the biggest hypocrite in town trying to counsel me on how to treat my wife. The whole concept is laughable."

Laurie wasn't laughing. If he only knew how close she was to calling it quits, laughter wouldn't be his first reaction. If they were staying together, a miracle would be the only solution. Each time she found her way back to Greg, back to a place of heartfelt love and respect, back to his warm hardworking arms, he would go off on an unannounced bitter rampage and singe her connection to him. After a countless number of burns, grabbing hold to the marriage wasn't so easy, not without coaxing. This was the end of the roller coaster ride. Counseling might be a dead issue with him, but it was alive and well as far as she was concerned. Maybe the only hope left.

"Got to go. I'll see you tonight. Don't forget that Youth Night ends at seven. The boys will be looking for you to pick them up."

"I'll be there. I love you, Laurie."

"See you tonight" is all she could sincerely offer in return as she closed her car door.

Chapter 31

The decision to take charge of her life was going easier than she anticipated, with the exception of Greg plaguing the house all afternoon begging for affection instead of going to the outplacement service like he should. She understood that getting fired, downsized, or whatever the nice-sounding term was could lead a person to depression, but he needed to get over it. Greg had six children, a wife, and a mortgage. He didn't have time to wait for Mr. Job to come knocking on the door. He had to go find him and wrestle him to the ground, refusing to let him loose until his W-4 was signed and direct deposit activated. She couldn't rely on Greg to take care of this job-finding business. She didn't have a four-year degree under her belt, but her certificate in Business Administration from community college, which she'd earned before getting married, gave her enough impetus to run circles around Greg's motivation level.

Laurie fired up the computer and hopped online. With Baby Rick and Greg out of the house, both for at least two more hours, she could probably find him a job and have him working next week. Peace had a price, and sacrificing a morning online in order to find Greg a job and get him out of the house was worth it.

First stop, advice from her mentor. If there was a systematic way to finding a job, Rachel could tell her. Laurie sent the e-mail message.

> Hi Rachel. Guess who. J This time I'm writing about something serious, a JOB—not for me though. It's for Greg. Remember I told you about him getting downsized. Well, he hasn't found any graphic artist jobs at all, and I'm getting worried. I want to go online and help him look for job listings. How do I do that? Help.—L.

Rachel responded in what seemed like a blink of time.

> Is he willing to relocate?

Leaving Augusta had never been discussed, not even in jest. If worse came to worse, he would have to consider moving, but Laurie wasn't convinced Greg had exhausted the possibilities in Augusta, Atlanta, or Georgia yet.

> I don't know, I guess if he had to. Maybe to Atlanta, I guess.

Laurie was surprised by Rachel's response.

> What about Chicago?

Chicago! Leaving Georgia would be huge. Atlanta was a big enough move. Going all the way to Illinois wasn't a consideration. Rachel continued.

> I'm asking because we started a new Creatives Department in-house to handle our graphics needs. We have a temporary manager filling in to get the department operating, but we need an assistant manager with a strong graphics background and someone we can groom to take over the manager's position in six to eighteen months. Do you think Greg would be interested? Starting salary is sixty with a jump to seventy-five plus bonus and stock options upon promotion to manager. With as much as you've told me about his graphic talent and his degree, I think he'd be a viable candidate. The fact that I'm director doesn't hurt his chances either.

How could he not be interested, a manager's position paying twenty thousand more than he was making now? Chicago was far away, but there wasn't any other job on the table.

> Wow, I'm sure he'd be interested. What does he have to do?

Whatever Rachel asked, Greg could do.

> Have him send me his résumé and you call me, so we can really talk. E-mail is fine, especially since the novelty hasn't worn off for you, but, girlfriend, there is nothing like the phone. ☺

Laurie wasn't quite as proficient on the computer as she wanted to be. Better not attempt to find Greg's résumé on the computer and mail it to Rachel without at least talking to him first. She read the rest of Rachel's message.

> P.S. Neal and my grandmother told me to tell you hello. Big Mama still refers to you as the blessed woman with a houseful of God's little ones. You know how my grandmother feels about children—however they get here, they're one of the biggest blessings you can get from God. I have to go before I start crying thinking about my twins. You know they weren't born under the best circumstances or at the most ideal time, but Big Mama was right, they are a blessing from God and definitely not a mistake.

I look forward to hearing from Greg soon. I'm off to a meeting. Talk with you later.

Laurie felt encouraged. Maybe God hadn't completely abandoned her, although she'd given up on him, too afraid of what He might say, words she no longer wanted to hear. Greg had issues, but at least her sons had their father. There was something special about a boy having his own dad around, a gift worth her sacrifice.

Chapter 32

Greg held the offer letter in his hand, as he'd done practically since it arrived via overnight delivery on Saturday. He read the most important portion over and over:

Assistant Manager position at a rate of $60,000 (sixty) plus a $5,000 (five) signing bonus to be paid in four increments: $2,000 upon acceptance, $1,000 after thirty days of employment, and $1,000 each after six months and one year. Bonus payable annually in the amount of no less than 10% (ten) of base salary and not to exceed 50% (fifty) based on company earnings. Three weeks vacation, five personal holidays, and benefits as outlined on the attached Exhibits A and B. Employee's relocation package will include: The transportation of the employee's household items and/or vehicles from Augusta, GA, to Chicago, IL, via a *company-hired van line; twelve round-trip tickets from Illinois to Georgia for a total of three months; accommodations for the employee for a time frame of three months, to cover room, board, and reasonable local transportation to and from the company location. The company will provide assistance with the selling of your primary home upon request. Terms of employment contingent upon successful completion of a drug test, background search, and credit check.*

Drugs and credit weren't a problem, but the background check had made him restless over the weekend. What if his domestic violence incident had shown up? Not only would he have lost the job, he could never show his face in front of Laurie's friend Rachel. Thank goodness his background and other tests came back clean yesterday, probably because Laurie hadn't pressed charges.

Laurie walked into the kitchen for a glass of juice. "What have you decided to do about the job offer?" she asked, taking a seat at the table.

"I don't know."

She sipped some juice. "What do you mean you don't know? The decision seems pretty obvious to me."

"Really?"

"Yes, really. Your outplacement runs out in three days, and you don't have any other offers. Shoot, you don't have any other prospects."

She was right. The job market wasn't as fruitful as he'd

hoped. A lot of not right nows were piling up next to his bills.

"It's a good job," he said, reading the letter again. "And it would give me the opportunity I've been looking for. It's perfect when you think about it, with the exception of being in Chicago. That's a big move for you and the boys."

"Sure is."

"But like you said, what other offers do we have," he said, bouncing the letter on the table. "Maybe this is a blessing in disguise. Maybe that's exactly what we need as a family, a fresh start in a new city away from everything familiar. Chicago will be new for both of us. Although it's the middle of November, I saw on the Weather Channel this morning that the temperature is already down in the thirties. We're going to freeze our behinds off." He snickered, attempting to lift the serious flare in the room. "If you can stand the cold, so can I," he said, caressing her hand and hoping she would give him the last boost of encouragement he needed to accept the offer and get preparations to move under way. "What do you think, are we moving to Chicago?"

"I think you should take the job. It could make such a difference for us. You could be making money and we'll still get your severance for another eight months. We could really get ahead."

"But what about moving, are you okay with Chicago?"

"It doesn't matter how I feel about Chicago. How do you feel? You're the one who has to work there," she reminded him.

She seemed to be dancing around the topic, but he didn't want to push too hard. Leaving her sister and brother was a bigger deal than him leaving his relatives. He could pack up this afternoon and be on the first highway or runway blazing out of town if he was sure Laurie and the boys were packing up, too.

"We can make Chicago work. Just take the job. You can go there first, without us, and let's deal with the rest later."

"I'd miss you and the boys like crazy. It almost sounds like a separation, me being over a thousand miles away."

"It does, doesn't it," she said, with a jingle in her voice. "Let's call Rachel and tell her you're taking the job. She can probably pull a few strings and have you working tomorrow."

"Nobody starts a job on a Thursday. Geez, give me time to pack and at least a day or two to get myself together."

"Okay," she said, skipping along, "no later than Monday then." He could hear her pecking away on the computer keyboard and followed the trail to the family room.

"Things are looking up for us."

"They sure are," she said with a jubilant look, bright enough to light up the old Fulton County Stadium on a dark night. He was happy to have a job, too, but she seemed ecstatic. "Did you call Rachel yet? Don't wait too late. I know she'll be happy you've accepted. Excuse me for a moment," she said, still typing on the computer, "I need to go online."

"Oh, okay. When you finish with the phone line, I'll call Rachel. Then," he said, leaving the family room, "we can pick up the boys and celebrate."

"Not me, remember? I have to work tonight, but don't worry about me. Have a great time with the boys. They'll love going out somewhere special with their daddy." Words poured out of her mouth, but her fingers didn't break their stride. "There you go," she said logging off the computer. "The phone line is all yours."

He could hear the joy in her voice. This job was a miracle. They might not celebrate his new job tonight as a whole family, but there would be plenty of time. First steps first. He would call Rachel and officially accept the offer. They'd flown him to Chicago last Friday for a full day of interviews and would probably bring him back out to get his paperwork done this week or early next. Whenever they wanted him to start, he would be ready. He would get to Chicago, bring Laurie out in a few weekends to look for a house and get on with life. It was time to leave Augusta and the shackles that so many times had tried to beat him down and bury his hopes. The company was allowing three months for relocation, but from his best guess, if plans went his way, Laurie and the boys wouldn't have to wait until February. He would do everything in his power to get them to Chicago by early January, during the children's winter break. Skipping must have been contagious in the Wright household, because his feet felt light too and for good reason.

Chapter 33

The boys were at school and Baby Rick was in daycare. Laurie thought she heard the ants crawling across the sidewalk outside. Then again, maybe the sound wasn't from the ants, but it was so quiet in the house she could hear every movement. The ambience was weird and the silence was suffocating. When Greg used to be in town, he was at the office all day. She only saw him evenings and weekends. With him working in Chicago, somehow her freedom seemed to multiply exponentially. What would she do all day? Since he was finally out of the house, and out from under her skin, she thought it would feel more exciting. As long as he was gone, from Monday morning beginning at nine AM to Friday evening around eight PM, she was in charge of the castle. His absence was kind of like a separation but without the label. One burden she no longer had to carry was the carefully orchestrated act of walking gingerly around the house, trying to dodge Greg's mood swings and prowl for affection. The less he was around, the less chance of another pregnancy. She finally had the money to buy birth control pills, but why bother now. Distance was better than the pill. She perked up. Boredom was lurking, but she had something in store for it, too.

She loosened the drawstring on her favorite pair of lounge pants, the comfortable ones she had bought from the men's section of Wal-Mart. The maternity-looking top wasn't attractive, but after six rounds, it was broken in and hung like a tent without direction.

Laurie sipped her glass of hot Lipton tea, hoping to eliminate her mild cramping sensation without having to resort to pain relievers. Three months ago, when she'd taken her first ride around the Internet, logging on and getting to where she was going took nearly an hour. Three months ago, she was still reading the Bible in her free time. A sea of change. She jumped online and was into her Yahoo e-mail account, jmjklr6. Another reason not to have any more children, she'd have to change her e-mail address. In less than two minutes she was online. The only delay was the slow dial-up. Once their savings account was over $5,000, and they were able to pay off a few bills, then extra money would be flowing and high-speed DSL would be hers.

Nine-thirty Georgia time was only eight-thirty in Chicago. Rachel probably wasn't in yet, but she wanted to check anyway, just in case. Greg was probably in the office, but why spoil the moment.

> Hi Rachel, guess who? I was hoping that you might be in early on this bright Tuesday morn ing. Are you?

Laurie hit the SEND button hoping for a response. She waited for a few minutes, surfing around the chat room directories in the interim. "Forging New Friendships" sounded interesting. She clicked on the profile. The description read "Are you a fun-loving person who's always eager to make new friends? If this is you, then join us. Please complete a profile and you're on your way to making a host of new friends." Ah, Rachel, she remembered and clicked back to her e-mail box. No new messages.

> Rachel, I guess you're not in yet, but since you're the Director of Finance, I guess you can come in whenever you want. I'm so proud to have you as my friend. Hopefully we can talk soon about some personal things. I've always valued your opinion. By the way, if I haven't said it enough, thank you so much for giving Greg the job. Our boys miss him so much, but what can we do. He needed a good job, finally. You have no idea what a blessing his new job is to our family, and it came at such a critical

> time in Greg's career and in our marriage, but I'll tell you about that some other time. This is only his second week and I haven't seen him this happy about work in over five years. Thanks again.—Laurie

Back to the profile page and "Forging New Friendships." She combed the questionnaire, cringing when she got to the section asking for a photo. Her self-esteem wanted to hide under the rug, but she refused to let it escape. She relaxed when the tiny word *optional* printed under the box came into focus. Unless she used her senior prom picture from fourteen years ago, her photo spot would remain a mystery to any would-be new friends. Personality is all she could offer comfortably at the moment. She progressed line by line. Name would be Friendly Mama. Description would remain blank. For the three choices under gender, she put an X next to female. She put another X in the age section, next to the 30–40 years old choice. She filled in the state box. Georgia was large enough for her to feel safe. It wasn't like someone could come and knock on her door based on the sparse information she was providing. The final question asked if she wanted to use an optional photo. She clicked on the female link and was tickled when the selection appeared: Wilma Flintstone, Betty Boop, Olive Oil, Minnie Mouse, Catwoman, and Foxy Brown. She clicked on Foxy Brown, afro and all. Done. She submitted the profile and followed the instructions for entering the chat room.

Her fingers felt sweaty. Why, she didn't know. Meeting new friends was good. So much of her life was centered on Greg and the kids. She didn't have many friends; Drake, Danielle, and Rachel, her sister, brother, and long-distance friend in Chicago. How pathetic. She didn't have anyone else nearby. That's why taking a job that paid barely above minimum wage was a joy. The chance to be around other adults who could hold a real conversation without argument or wanting affection was a dream, an absolute dream.

As a first timer in the chat room, the information extracted from her profile was implanted into a two-paragraph form letter and popped up when she entered. She couldn't contain her amusement looking at the picture of Foxy Brown. Believe it or not, there was a time when her body was as tight as Foxy's. Six kids later, the only tightness she had was the elastic around her waist, which was tight because it was too small. She was hanging with the size sixteen, but a few more cookies this week and eighteen was swooping in. The humor she basked in a few seconds ago was gobbled up by one of the many rolls around her midsection. "Enough," she said, jumping out of the chat room and surfing to Yahoo! Search. She typed in *weight loss program* and thought about ways to narrow her search since the Web site hits were over five million. She could be another fifty pounds heavier if time was wasted on even contemplating the idea of trudging through most of those sites. For the short term, she was going to the Y. Good old-fashioned exercise was a sound place to start. She grabbed her purse from the table and didn't stop until the van was en route to her new beginning.

Chapter 34

The laid-back weekends where the boys burned off energy, mostly outside with their father while she relaxed inside, were long gone since Greg began commuting. Family activities, which used to spread over seven days, were crammed into two and a half, a hundred miles an hour. She loaded the dishwasher, still in her loungewear. The clock hanging above the sink confirmed that her period of relaxation would soon be over. Greg and the boys were due home from church around one o'clock. One of these Sundays she'd have to squeeze church in and go, too. An hour and a half on a mild December morning was enough time to soak in her Jacuzzi and get dressed or take a quick shower and spend the remaining hour and twenty minutes online. Not a comparison, she stripped her clothes while running up the stairs and hopped into the shower.

Having high-speed DSL installed last week was a gem.

They hadn't reached their nest egg goal of having $5,000 saved before wasting money, but why put off what was attainable today. She could move around the Web with ease and speed. Why in the world had they stayed with dial-up so long? She hopped into her favorite FNF chat room. For someone with no friends three weeks ago, she was quite the social bee. Friends galore, well not quite like real friends, the blood-flowing kind, not people she could actually meet for dinner or go to a movie with, but they were probably coming her way, too. At this point in her social debut, she was satisfied with any and all cyber friends, whose basic criteria for acceptance into her circle was that they could crawl, type, or speak online.

A snippet of someone else's profile scrolled across the bottom of the page. From what she could tell, one other person was in the chat room.

> Who else is playing hooky from church today?

She missed out on years of Internet life but was determined to make up for lost time.

> Where have you been, my love? I've been in love with you for over thirty years.

Who is this and how do they know me? Her pulse quickened. Was it a he or she? Did they know her address? Was this some prankster? What had she gotten into?

> Do I know you?

Whoever this was would have met her at two years old if they'd truly known her for thirty years. Then it dawned on her, none of her really personal information was divulged on the profile or anywhere else in the chat room. She submitted generic information for a reason. So, she took a breath, nothing to worry about. Back to why she got online in the first place, to have a good time and meet new friends. She read what they had to say.

> Sure I know you, Foxy Brown. You were mine and every other man's heartthrob back in the seventies.

Foxy Brown? Oh yeah, that's right. She still wasn't as shapely as Foxy Brown, but a few more months at the Y and who knows. She'd already shed five pounds. The loose elastic around her waist was both a reminder of what she'd accomplished and an encouragement to keep going. If only she'd known that sending Greg out of town would be her impetus to finally shed the pounds after nine years of being overweight. She keyed a few more words.

> To be honest, Foxy Brown was a little before my time, but my brother was in the group of young boys who covered his bedroom wall with her picture. Since I didn't want to use my own photo (smile), Foxy Brown was the next best choice given the options I had.

Periodically she glanced at the clock on the VCR to keep perspective. Greg and the boys would be home in less than forty-five minutes.

> Any woman who is gutsy enough to use Foxy Brown's photo has to be a special lady.

She couldn't see the gentleman on the other end of the dialogue, but he had color rushing to her cheeks. Two lines and he was able to do what Greg hadn't in years, well, maybe not years, but definitely months and a whole lot of them.

> Instead of Foxy Brown, you can call me Ms. Friendly.

Maybe she wasn't supposed to let her guard down so easily but he felt interesting, more like intriguing, curious, alluring, and dangerous meshed together. There was a tiny pricking sensation in the back of her mind, or perhaps it was deeper? Maybe it was in her soul. Wherever the feeling of discomfort or dishonesty was stemming from, it was being squashed by the warm sentiments showering her body. She felt like a schoolgirl, having fun, uninhibited. Her growth in the Lord, which she'd become so proud of months ago but not recently, was trying to have an opinion, too, but she was able to drown out the voice of judgment with loud singing in her head. Being online and making new friends was good, she reminded herself, refusing to hear anything to the contrary. Nobody could tell her different. If someone, anyone, made her feel better about herself, then it had to be a good situation overall.

Hello, Ms. Friendly. I'm Deep.

She snuck a look at the clock; she was still in good shape.

What kind of a user name is Deep?

She didn't expect a real answer, but make-believe was fun, too.

You'll have to get to know me in order to find out, won't you?

They shared another thirty minutes of dialogue back and forth. Where did the time go? Two other people entered the chat room, but she and Deep ignored them.

Ms. Friendly (aka Foxy), let's find some privacy. I'll send you an IM.

Laurie knew about instant messages but wasn't as proficient with them as she'd become with basic e-mailing and surfing the Net. If Deep was willing to exercise a little patience, she was sure to master the process.

Sounds good to me. You can use my new e-mail address: hotmama6@yahoo.com

It was almost five minutes to one. She logged out of the room and sure enough, up popped a message from Mr. Deep. Shoot, if she only had another ten minutes. The garage door would be rising any minute. She had to say her good-byes, save his e-mail address, and log off. He was only a friend, a cyber friend at that, not an actual living and breathing entity. She could even tell Greg about her Foxy Brown fan. Perhaps all three of them could form a friendship. Then again, Greg didn't have to be involved in every single aspect of her life. She'd been alone for so long. Even when Greg was living at home, she was alone. Making her own friends, both men and women, was a positive step. Life was looking up and she had Yahoo to thank for it.

Like clockwork, the garage door chimed and the van rolled in. She put on her mommy and wife cap, willing to relinquish her independent-woman scarf until 9:00 AM tomorrow when Greg would be on the airport shuttle, taking the first plane out of town by 10:15, leaving a jubilant wife behind. Her only sadness came from seeing her sons cry every Monday when it was time for their father to leave. As far as she was concerned, it was too bad the company didn't require him to fly in Sunday night. Patience. It was a new job; he was just getting settled. Maybe in another month or two he could leave early, or better yet, stay in Chicago over the weekend every now and then. As long as direct deposit worked and the bills were paid, Greg Wright's presence in Georgia wasn't required on a regular basis. She patted herself on the back having finally figured out what it took to make the marriage last, distance both physically and emotionally.

The boys skipped into the house, clinging to their father and bearing gifts, drawings, and various crude art projects.

Greg gave her a kiss on the cheek. "Mrs. Williams and Pastor both said to tell you hello and they hope you feel better."

"Thanks," she said, resisting the guilt that came with lying about her reason for not going to church. She wasn't actually feeling badly this morning or the last three Sundays either, more like tired or something.

"Mrs. Williams wants you to call her."

Oh no, Laurie thought. She would be a fool to call Mrs. Williams for another dose of the same lashing imparted on her not more than two weeks ago about backsliding. Mrs. Williams didn't play when it came to God and holiness with words of correction destined for those who chose to live with one foot in the church and the other one on the outside. Laurie wasn't opposed to going to church, but life was finally enjoyable, thanks to her own efforts, rendering church not as critical as it once was. She was doing just fine without it.

"Are you going to my parents?"

"I don't know. I'm still a little tired."

"I have an idea," he said, rubbing her shoulders. "Why don't I pick up a meal from Boston Market and you relax. I'll call my parents and let them know we're not coming. We'll see them next weekend."

"Are you sure?"

"Positive. We need time to talk about the move to Chicago anyway," he said.

"I thought we agreed to move during winter break next month if the job worked out?"

"Oh, it's definitely working out. My job is wonderful. I can see myself staying with this company until retirement."

What was the hurry in moving? Money from the new job, the signing bonus, severance from the old job, and her working was unbelievable. Financial pressure was nonexistent. She was stable, so were the boys. "We might want to think about waiting for the sake of the boys and school."

"Uh-uhn," Mitchell rudely interjected. "I want us to go to Chicago with Daddy."

"Yeah, can we?" Jason and Keith joined in.

"You boys stay out of this. This is an adult discussion for me and your mom." Greg grabbed his keys from the table. "We can talk later. There's a lot to consider. We have to put the house up for sale and make arrangements with the moving service, although the company will cover all of the expenses. As a matter of fact, they have some kind of program where they'll buy the house if it doesn't sell in a certain number of days. This job is great. I am thankful to God for this chance to do right by you and my boys." He leaned down and kissed Laurie on the lips, slow this time. "Be right back. I'm going to pick up the food."

"I'm going, too," Mitchell yelled with his brothers following suit, including Baby Rick.

"You don't want to stay with Mommy?" she asked. He shook his head and wrestled free of her grip, trotting behind his father.

"What about you, Junior?" Greg asked. "Are you staying or going?"

He looked at the computer, and then at her. "Can I use the computer, Mom?"

Now what was she going to say, no? He'd publicized his request in front of six witnesses. "Boy, you know you can use the computer. You don't have to ask me something like that," she said low and clear, sure that Greg heard the conversation, even if he was stepping into the garage. She had to make a note to check out computer prices. The boys needed their own computer because she was savvy and beyond sharing.

"I'm staying, Daddy," Junior decided and went to the computer, preparing to waste time online, precious time she could be using to handle important business like making new friends around the world.

Chapter 35

The van buzzed down the road, purring into his parent's driveway. A few more months and his family would be riding in a brand-new Suburban with so much room they could add a couple more car seats without blinking. He hadn't given up on having a daughter and completing their family. It could happen; his dream could come true. Everything else was going well. This was finally his time to taste the sweetness of life. Greg floated to the wooden doors, which didn't seem as huge as they normally did. The middle of December and Georgia was chilly, but the satisfaction he felt inside his soul was burning logs at a record pace, not giving any coldhearted gestures or comments a chance, which were sure to come from Dad.

No surprises. The kids fidgeted before Mom opened the door. Laurie stood back waiting on Mom's cynical greeting. Mom gave her oldest son the customary hug and tried to slide a check into his coat pocket. Not this time. He caught her hand in midstride and folded her fingers over, delicately, with check clasped inside. "I'm doing really well, Mom, I really am." She let her eyes give acknowledgment but wouldn't release a smile. Perhaps too much joy was foreign to her as well. After all, she did live under the same roof he'd grown up in.

Laurie helped the boys take off their coats and Greg helped her.

"My, my, look at you," Mom said to Laurie. "You don't look pregnant."

"Neither do you," Laurie said, cutting a grin as Mom scowled. Laurie did look terrific. The eight pounds she'd lost showed. She'd gone shopping yesterday, coming home with a bag of size fourteen clothes, a size she hadn't seen in over three years.

It was finally their hour to shine as a family. The coats were put away. The boys were on their best behavior, and Greg held his head high, strolling with pride toward the dining room.

The door opened and there was the judge and Sterling Jr. too. "Say hello, boys." The customary greetings were extended and Greg said, "I'll be back, Mom. Laurie and I are taking the boys to the kitchen."

Within a puff, the boys were safely deposited into the care of Lily. He and Laurie joined the adults in the formal dining room. The armor was polished, impenetrable. Dad couldn't touch him today.

"So, how's the job, man? Haven't seen you in weeks. What's going on?" Sterling Jr. asked.

"Let's say grace, and then we can eat while you get the details on Greg's new den of destruction," Dad flung around the table.

"Yes, let's pray," Greg offered, extending his hand to Laurie and Mom.

"This is my house. I'll do the praying."

"By all means, Judge." His father peered over his reading glasses without comment. The prayer was spoken, short and repetitious, just like it had been for over thirty years. Greg hadn't gone to church regularly until the last few months. He had an excuse for being weak on the prayer circuit, but what could the Judge say, a man who sat in church every Sunday, whether he needed it or not.

The bowl of field greens in lime vinaigrette circulated, followed by roasted garlic potatoes, honey wheat mini-loaves of piping hot bread, baby asparagus, and baked chicken doused with herbs.

"So, tell me about the job, big brother," Sterling Jr. said, forcing his lettuce onto the fork with his knife.

"It's great, man. I'm Assistant Manager of a Creatives Department."

"That's great."

"Yeah, and what's so good about it is that in a year at the most I automatically get promoted to a full manager's position."

"Titles don't mean anything. You can't spend a title at the store."

"Sure can't, Dad, but my two thousand dollar a month increase does, with more to come when I get promoted." His father peered at him again, with no retort.

"Two thousand," his mother reinforced. "That's wonderful, son."

"And I'm still getting my severance checks every two weeks for about seven more months."

"You're finally getting your chance to define your own career path. I'm proud of you," Mom said.

"Two thousand dollars and a handful of corporate welfare checks don't go far when you're running two households and living in a big city like Chicago."

"Actually," Greg said, swallowing his lettuce, "I'm staying at one of the company's executive apartments."

"But you're not an executive. Last time I checked, an assistant is at best second in charge. What do you have to do, wait for the manager to die before they take you out of the booster seat?"

"Sterling, please, can we enjoy our dinner as a family for a change?" Mom said, standing and clearing the salad plates. "Can you help me, please?" she asked Laurie.

"No, it's okay, Mom. Dad has a right to his opinion, even if it is wrong." He took a sip of water, expecting a reaction, and his father didn't disappoint.

The women left the room carrying five plates and the large salad bowl.

"You watch your manners in my house, boy. I don't care what kind of executive, overseer, sharecropper, or stately mansion you stay in out there in Chicago. In this house, I demand respect, or get out."

Greg hadn't quite expected as much as Dad gave. The logs on the inside were going out. Dad had managed to squelch the flame, and Greg's air balloon of glee was crashing to the floor.

"I'm never good enough for you, am I?" Greg said, springing to his feet and tossing his napkin on the table.

Mom and Laurie reentered with two dishes each and made room on the table.

"What's going on?" Mom asked, sliding items around on the table.

"Ask your beloved husband." Greg grabbed his wife's hand before she sat down. "We're leaving."

"What?" his mom said with a look of bewilderment.

"Let him go, Virginia. He's a grown man. He can leave if he wants to. Nobody's going to stop him."

"I am," she retorted. "Please stay," she begged, latching on to his arm. "I just brought the main course out. This is way too much food for me, your father, and your brother."

"Mom, it will be better for us to go. I've managed to lose my appetite, which isn't unusual in this place."

The boys were collected and the van pulled out of the driveway with a thud. The ride home was solemn with the exception of an occasional seed of small talk. They stopped at a local diner and ate a not-so-filling meal. But bad food digested outside of his father's house was like eating the best meal he'd ever had. Afterward, they proceeded home. Once inside the comforts of his kingdom, Greg sighed, watching his family disperse to their dominions. The only person needing help was Baby Rick and Junior had him.

Greg and Laurie went to their room. "I want us out of Georgia," he told Laurie, leaving her looking confused. "The next four weeks can't come fast enough for me. We'll all be in Chicago, together, like a real family. No more Sunday charades. That alone is worth the move," he said, trying to laugh away his disdain.

"I need to talk to you about moving," she said.

"You have some ideas about the movers?"

"No, I have an idea about when we should move," she said, entering the closet.

"As opposed to next month?" he asked.

She didn't answer right away. "I was thinking that January is the middle of winter. As cold as Chicago gets, I think we should move during spring break."

"When is spring break this year?" he said with a tone of sadness.

"April, only three months later than we originally planned. But if we move in April, the boys will have completed most of the school year and won't lose out on much of their studies when we get to Chicago. The house will sell better in the spring than in the winter, too."

Her points were legitimate. However, three more months would feel like an eternity on top of a one-month life sentence, at least that's what being away from Laurie and the boys felt like. Commuting home the past five weekends was starting to wear thin. The sooner his family was in Chicago, the more he could concentrate on his job and his inevitable promotion. Maybe moving in the winter wasn't the best short-term solution, but from a long-term perspective, the family would benefit more by sticking to the plan and getting them moved next month. Laurie might not agree right away, but she would come around. "I'm sorry, honey, but we need to stick to the plan."

She emerged from the closet. "I'm not moving before April," she said sternly, almost bordering on belligerence.

"What's with the attitude?" Laurie and his father in the same afternoon were heavy. He wanted to keep floating but the ground was coming into focus.

"It's not an attitude, Greg. I'm telling you, I won't move in the winter."

"What choice do you have?"

"I always have choices," she said, sliding her slippers on and then looking up. " I might not elect to use all of them, but trust me, I have options."

"What is up with you? Aren't things going well for us? What's with this mood of yours?"

"It's not a mood. We're having a discussion and I want to make it clear, I'm not ready to move next month. April, okay, but not January. That's all there is to it."

"I don't believe this," he snapped. "I finally get a job that can take care of this family in the right way and you don't want to support me. What a trip," he said, flailing his arms in the air. "I can't win with you. You're the most ungrateful woman I know," he heaved at her and snatched the door open.

One night's sleep didn't calm the choppy waters. Before catching his shuttle to the airport, he tried to broach the subject one more time. "Will you at least consider moving next month?"

"Nope," she responded, putting on her exercise gear, "April is the earliest."

"I guess that's that," he said and left. No sense trying to change her mind with only five minutes before the shuttle pulled up to the front door. Weight wasn't the only attribute she was losing in his absence. If he could just get her and the boys to Chicago, everything would be all right. Maybe he would talk to Rachel and see if she could convince Laurie to move sooner than later. He was desperate and time was running out. He could feel it in his soul.

Chapter 36

Monday mornings were hectic. Two months into Greg commuting back and forth to Chicago, the Wright family knew the routine. Greg's shuttle arrived at the front door precisely at 9:00 AM, allowing plenty of time for him to drop the boys off at school, which the little ones—Larry, Jason, and Keith—demanded. Mitchell and Junior took the bus, and Baby Rick was left for Mom.

Laurie kissed the boys and Greg good-bye, then tossed on a pair of sweatpants and a sweatshirt. She dressed Baby Rick in warm attire. Christmas had come and gone last month but winter was in business. En route to the gym, she dropped her son off at the daycare. Birds were chirping and her life was singing in rhythm to Whitney Houston as the van hummed down the road.

Restoration flashed across her heart. She reflected on the minister's message yesterday during one of her rare visits to church. He said something like God was able to make good out of a bad situation. She dwelled on his words, "Praying is like planting seeds. The fruit of the prayer might not manifest immediately, but in due season, when the time is right, God will spring forth the answer in such abundance that it will be hard to believe the result was associated with the original request." She'd given up on prayer months ago and resorted to her own energy, which seemed to be working, at least a little. Happiness wasn't dashing in and out of the house like it had for years. Since she started putting effort into the marriage, peace had actually unpacked its bags and taken a seat with feet solid on the ottoman. She'd prayed for her marriage with Greg to get better for several years, believing that's what she wanted. Now a smear of happiness was surfacing and she wasn't ready. Maybe she didn't want the blissful marriage, at least not right now. The timing was wrong. Greg shouldn't have life so easy. He needed to feel the pain she'd suffered at his doing for years. Uneasiness seeped into her conscience. She clutched the wheel and wouldn't let up. God had finally answered her prayers, but why was she still feeling an inkling toward John? It still seemed weird calling him John, instead of Deep. A ball of yarn, twisted, tight, and dysfunctional. How had she let herself get into such a predicament?

Conviction cut like a machete a month ago when she'd told Greg straight out that moving so abruptly wasn't for her. She tried but couldn't block out his look of betrayal. In those subsequent days, she had been overcome with guilt and elected to be more supportive. She decided to give the marriage more attention, setting aside her Deep distraction but keeping in mind that continually gluing a broken vase was a waste and eventually an eyesore, useful to no one and more trouble than it was worth.

She parked the van and let her worries fall along the path to the gym door. A workout on the treadmill would help her make sense of the chaos. Wednesday she would go back to weight lifting. Forty minutes later, Laurie emerged sweaty and still confused. It was evident that she needed more advice than the treadmill could offer. But who could she go to? Surely she couldn't ask God to help her decide whether to stay with Greg or venture out and blaze a new trail. The thought of God knowing caused her to duck down in the driver's seat. The weight of a dual relationship was growing too heavy. She rattled her emotions and swept them under her rug of secrecy.

Into the safety of her home, she locked the dead bolt behind her, shutting out the ghost of conviction. She lingered up the stairs to her room, stripped down, and lavished in the shower, letting the warm water wash away her dirtiness.

Chapter 37

The mirror couldn't be lying. For the past ten years, her image had been consistently brutally honest, reminding her of the forty pounds she'd gained. She locked her hands on her hips and twisted slightly to the left, then to the right, never taking her gaze off the mirror. Twenty pounds was like losing a case of bottled water. She pulled the side zipper the remaining inch and did the button. Stretch pants and elastic waists were gone. She smoothed the cotton material down across her size ten thighs and checked out the image one more time. Satisfaction inside was too intense to contain, so it spilled out, illuminating the room.

She couldn't help the thoughts ravaging her mind. What would John think? Was a size ten big or small to him? Lord, she knew Greg should be the one on her mind, but he wasn't. She wanted so desperately to feel good about herself, the weight loss, and the marriage all in the same moment, but only two out of three seemed to dwell in the same space at any given time.

The clock on the nightstand displayed 12:30. Exercising at the Y in the morning was working out. She had time to come home, get dressed, do a few chores around the house, and run a few errands if necessary. Laurie dragged the basket of clothes from her closet and set out to attack the boys' rooms. She started in Mitchell and Jason's room, forming a pile in the middle of the floor. She moved to Keith and Larry's doing the same. Last was Baby Rick and Junior's room. She separated the colors from the whites but couldn't stay focused. Toss a shirt on the pile, look up at the computer, shirt, computer, pants, computer. She plopped her behind on the floor, wrapping her arms around her bent knees. Give the urge time to pass. Don't give in. It's not right. God will know. Arguments from both sides of the moral divide took a position, wrestling for center stage. Good ole-fashioned conversation. That's all. Nothing serious. She hadn't even met John. Surely there couldn't be any harm in encouraging someone while being encouraged. As a matter of fact, if she really thought about it, John was helping her to be a better wife for Greg. If talking with John made her happy, Greg was bound to benefit. Hold the sentiment and scream it over and over in her mind, ensuring that it drowned out the other voice, which was saying, "This is wrong in the eyes of God and your husband."

Like a sweet-aholic without a candy or cake fix for

three days, Laurie was jittery and second guessing the promise she'd made during her pilgrimage to church last month, which was to pull back on her communication with John. Before she could filter action through her reason censor one final time, the computer was booting up. No time to run downstairs and use her own computer in the family room. She needed the fix right now. The candy bar wrapper was off for the addict. She bypassed the chat room prompt, going directly to her Yahoo e-mail account. Using her private e-mail account, which didn't require her to use Junior's message box, was brilliant. Greg didn't use the boys' computer but anything was possible. The very time she slipped and forgot to delete one of John's e-mails from both the received and sent boxes, her newly crafted world of joy and fulfillment would come crashing down. Protecting her investment was critical.

She would instant message him first to see if he was online.

> Hi John,
> It's been almost three weeks since we were in touch. I hope you're not mad at me for pulling back. I was starting to feel a little confused about our relationship.

She stopped. Relationship, what a big word, with even huger ramifications. Relationship wasn't the right word. It gave the wrong impression. She hit the backspace until the nasty little word was erased and began typing something more settling.

> friendship. You've been on my mind and I'm wondering how everything's going for you? Are you still looking for another house? I know that was taking up a lot of your time. Well, I don't know if you're around today, but at any rate, I wanted to say hello and to let you know I miss you.

Her fingers lingered on the keys, digesting. She was having difficulty swallowing "I miss you" and decided to delete those words. She didn't know where the friendship was headed, but certain phrases would stir her down a road she wasn't willing to travel just yet. She pressed the SEND button using the mouse. Finished. There was tingling in her abdomen. Blood rushed through her veins. She waited for a few minutes. No response. A few more minutes. Nothing. She perched her lips and gazed around the room, landing at the pile of clothes. It was after one and she needed to at least get the laundry and dinner started before picking up Baby Rick between 3:00 and 3:30 from daycare. Taking him on Mondays, Wednesdays, and Fridays had been a godsend, thanks to Greg's surplus funds. Having the extra time was a perk.

She stood up and was almost back to reality when the new message indicator activated. Her legs went limp and the chair drew her back. Emotions were simmering. She caressed the mouse without double-clicking to open the message. She needed time. Her emotions were boiling. What would he say? What if he didn't want to talk to her anymore? What was he thinking? Her emotions were erupting. She clicked the mouse and opened the message.

> Well, well, well, Ms. Beautiful has returned. I've missed you terribly. So many times I've wanted to e-mail you, especially two weeks ago for Valentine's Day, but I was determined to respect your wishes. I never want to pressure you into doing anything you don't want to do, but you must know that it was killing me not to be able to talk to you about the house, my job, and just my life in general. You make me happy. I hope I'm not laying it on too thick, but you have to know how drawn I am to you.

She wanted to giggle like a giddy schoolgirl. If she could close her eyes and let these be Greg's words, the world would be perfect. But it wasn't; this was John. Greg would be home by 8:00 if his 7:30 flight landed on time. Forget about Greg for the moment. This was John's time.

> You embarrass me with such flattery. I don't know what to say.

His responses were rapid fire. She liked not having to wait for his admiration.

> Say that you've changed your mind and you're willing to meet me in person.

The fluttering in her abdomen resumed. Her sweaty palm blanketed the mouse. Secretly meeting online was manageable, on her terms. The interaction was friendly, harmless. Meeting face-to-face was going to a different level. She didn't know how to respond. She thought about the twenty-five pounds. At least she was physically ready, but emotionally she was questionable. She tapped the mouse for what seemed like hours, even though the clock counted less than five minutes.

> Are you still there, beautiful?

She didn't want this feeling to go away.

> Yes, I'm still here. I'm just thinking about

She stopped. Did she hear running up the stairs? Laurie was scared; she couldn't move. Who was in her house during the middle of the day? The boys were at school. She was about to panic when an unexpected voice called out to her. *Oh my goodness, it's Greg.* She was in a tailspin. Disarray racked her mind. She pushed the OFF button without logging off. Turning the computer off was all she could concentrate on. Greg called out again.

"I'm in here," she responded once the computer powered down.

Greg stuck his head in the doorway, whipping a dozen long-stemmed roses from behind his back. "Surprise, surprise."

She sauntered his way. "What brings you home so early?" she said, giving him a loose hug.

"I took a morning flight this time." He squeezed her tighter and kissed her on the cheek. "I missed you and the boys so much, I couldn't stand being away another hour." He lifted her slightly off the floor. "I'm so glad to be home."

He deposited her back on the floor and pushed her gently away from him, still holding her hands. He surveyed her body. "Wow, look at you. I haven't seen you with those kind of pants on since we first got married." He spun her around like a ballerina on top of a music box. "You look great. I can't believe how much weight you've lost. You"—he grinned—"look really good." He pulled her back to him and enveloped her with his arms. "I love you, Laurie. I miss you so much."

She kept quiet.

"I know we've talked about you and the boys moving to Chicago in a few months, but that's too long. I know you don't want to take them out of school in midyear, but this isn't working. I need my family with me. That's all there is to it."

That couldn't be all there was to it. She didn't know what to do or what to feel. She tightened her arms around Greg's waist. She loved Greg when he was like this. If only his heart had thawed out six months ago, before the weight loss, before the change in her heart, before John. Was it possible to need two men simultaneously? She wiped away the thought. At least for her, whatever it was with John wasn't adultery. As long as she didn't touch him, she was safe.

"Greg, we can't pull the boys out of school."

"Why not?" he said, leading her by the hand into their bedroom. "Except for Junior and Mitchell, the boys are in daycare and elementary school. They'll adjust easily."

"What about Junior? He's in middle school. He's not going to want to leave his little friends."

"I hate it, but this is the way it is," he said, closing their door.

"I don't think we should disrupt their schooling this year. Let's just wait until the summer. Moving later will be better for the boys, much better." Better for her mostly, but he didn't need to know the details.

"Laurie, look, I want my family with me whether it's in Illinois or Georgia. It's already been three months. If I have to wait another two months to get you moved, then I might as well quit my job in Chicago and come back home."

"What?" she said, staring him in the face.

"That's right. I'll come back home and find a job here or in Atlanta. That's all there is to it."

"But, you can't," she stammered.

"I can't what, quit and come back home to my family? Oh yeah, I can. Watch me."

"Greg, that doesn't make any sense. You finally have the job you want, paying what we need. You can't just give up because you miss us."

"Yes, Laurie, I can. When are you going to understand? You and the boys are the most important thing in this world to me. Without you and them, I don't have any reason to live. Don't you understand that by now? You're it for me. It kills me not being with you."

Ugh, stop. She felt ashamed before God. It wasn't as easy to cut off communication with God as she thought. He kept dipping into her thoughts, tapping at her soul. The guilt of rejecting him was eating away like cancer. Rationalizing her friendship with John wasn't winning this battle. Her commitment to Greg was about to land a TKO.

Standing in the center of their bedroom next to a basket of clothes, Greg continued talking to Laurie while unbuttoning her shirt, one button at a time. She buttoned them back as fast as he undid them.

"Come on, Laurie," he begged. "I came home early because I knew the boys would still be at school. This way we'll have a little bit of time to ourselves." He hugged her again. "I missed you so much."

"Greg," she wailed, "I have to get these clothes started before the boys get home."

He pushed the basket with his bare foot. "Don't worry

about those clothes. The boys and I will wash them tomorrow. You can take a break." He began to undo her buttons again. "Now come on over here."

This time she didn't resist. What was the point? If he'd gone to the trouble of getting an earlier flight, the least she could do was be a wife for the afternoon. Life was good for them right now, plenty of money, space, affection, and peace around the house. Best to maintain what was working.

Chapter 38

Laurie typed like the building was on fire. She had about a half hour to get out of the house and downtown for lunch. Danielle didn't mind a little tardiness, but Drake thrived on punctuality. She typed:

> I know you want to meet and I've been thinking about it, a lot. Give me another day or so and I'll have an answer.

She knew he wasn't going to take no for an answer. In the beginning, he didn't push. Now that feelings had crawled into the friendship, he was becoming more insistent about getting together. The truth of the matter, it wasn't just John who wanted to meet. She wanted to see him too. Sometimes the urge was bigger than reality. Perhaps coming face-to-face would be the water she needed to douse the flame. Meet him, get it over, and move on. That was the plan. She read his response.

> Why are you holding back? Is it because of your husband?

Of course it was because of her husband, her faith, and her confusion. Mostly her hesitation was the fear of jumping off the stable cliff, the one she had familiarized herself with for thirteen years, into the valley of the unknown. The right and wrong tug-of-war was tussling. She wanted to wipe her mind clear, remove all thoughts, good and bad. If she could just have fun, unaccountable, unmonitored, clandestine, without guilt, just one time, that would be her wish.

John continued:

> Is it your children? Because you don't have to worry, I'm not going to attack you. J All I want to do is meet this woman who makes me feel so good about everything. This woman who has me laughing out loud staring at a computer screen. I'm not trying to cause you any problems, believe me, but if there's any way to see you in person, I want to make it happen. I'm willing to meet you anywhere, anytime, any place. Whatever you want, I'm willing to do.

Did he really mean anywhere? Atlanta was big but maybe not large enough to keep her secret. Crossing the state line into South Carolina and going to Aiken might have been a viable option if it were more than twenty minutes from Augusta. Savannah, Georgia, her former home, was a possibility. It was far enough away to avoid the risk of running into neighbors. Secluded, yet vibrant. Perfect.

How about Savannah?

Her finger was bent to complete the transaction, and then it dawned on her. If she went, it would have to be on a Monday, Wednesday, or Friday when Baby Rick was at daycare, the boys were in school, and Greg was out of town. Nine in the morning to three in the afternoon was her window. So Savannah was out. The three-hour drive each way would eat up her entire block of time. Maybe that was a good thing.

Did you run away, beautiful lady?

She ran her fingers through her freshly permed hair, sailing across the salon-permed strands. Her fingers used to stop at the kinks when she did her own hair. With Greg's new job, her allowance, personal needs, and shopping power had dramatically increased.

I'm still here. ☺

Savannah wasn't going to work. She needed a closer location. She scrambled to come up with another spot.

Where could they go? She toyed with the mouse. Columbia. That's it; Columbia was an hour and a half away, straight down Interstate 20. If she barreled down, she could make the drive in close to an hour, leaving plenty of time to meet, talk, and get back home before her family had a clue.

> How about Columbia, SC?

She clicked to send without filtering her suggestion through her conscience. Her courage, which had been soaring, shrieked in the face of commitment. What had she done? What would he say? Maybe he would decline and the pressure would be over. She could only pray. Then again, that's the one act she couldn't do.

> Columbia it is. When? The sooner the better. I can't wait to see you, finally.

She slapped her palms against her cheeks, drawing them slowly together over her nose. She drew in a boatload of air and let it ooze out, guarded. The ponies were out of the corral, running wild along with her emotions, and she wasn't sure how far they'd stray before, if at all, she could get them reeled back in.

Chapter 39

The lukewarm breeze smashed between chilly February and balmy April nipped at her cheeks. Spring was stepping on stage, shoving winter to the back. She hustled into the restaurant, the pencil point of her stiletto boots clicking along the way.

"Can I help you, ma'am?" the hostess asked.

She waved the hostess off, seeing her siblings sitting directly ahead. She strutted to the table with her Chanel purse swinging. Drake's eyes locked in and ushered her to the table.

"Close your mouth," she said, joking with her brother who was clearly in awe of the changes happening to his baby sister.

"My gosh, what have you done?" he asked, dropping his napkin onto the table.

"I told you," Danielle echoed. "Your little sister is coming up," she said, snapping her fingers randomly in midair.

"You look great, Laurie," Drake complimented.

"Think so?" Laurie responded. She raised her arms, palms facing up, like an evangelist inviting sinners to the altar. She spun around casually two times. Her jubilance wouldn't stay hidden. Teeth showing, dimples dipping, she sat down in the chair feeling like a queen.

"Girlfriend, you know you have it going on," Danielle said. "How many pounds have you lost all together?"

"Almost thirty." She scooted in her chair, taking a swig of water.

"Are you still exercising?"

"Every Monday, Wednesday, and Friday."

"Whatever you're doing is definitely agreeing with you," Drake said.

"It's that husband of hers being out of town, okay? Let's just keep it real."

"You're so pitiful," Drake told Danielle.

"Well." Danielle combed the menu. "And what's up with the boots and pants?"

"Yes, what is up with the pants? Your clothes are tighter than Danielle's," Drake said.

Laurie read the menu, rolling her glance up and back down punctuated with a partial smile.

"I'm scared of you," Danielle said, going back to her menu. "What do I want to eat?" She perused the offerings. "Anything but fish. I've dreamed about fish three nights in a row, and I know I'm not pregnant. Must be you," Danielle said, smirking.

"Please, I've had my last baby. Enough is enough. I

love my boys, but I need to have a life, too." Laurie folded her hands. "Thank goodness I've had all of my children." She shivered like cold water was running down her back. "I couldn't handle another one. I'd probably have a nervous breakdown. Remember how panicked I was last August? I almost lost it." The sisters chattered.

Drake set down his menu. He generally knew what he wanted when they went out together. "Assuming nobody is pregnant at this table, in all seriousness, what are you and Greg going to do about this long-distance situation? Are you still planning to move to Chicago?"

Laurie laid her menu flat on the table and clasped her fingers on top. She took a gulp and turned her glance away from the table.

"Hello," Drake persisted.

"I'm not sure," she said with reluctance.

"You've been dragging this move out for a while now," Danielle said. "What's the deal, are you separated on the QT?"

"No, we're not separated on the quiet tip," she told her sister with a pitch.

Danielle returned to the menu. "I hope you never move to Chicago. It's too far away, and you'd be on your own, without your family or any kind of real support group."

"Remember I have a friend there, Rachel Matthews."

"Yeah, but you know what I mean. Somebody who can keep Greg in line, scare him. If he gets you to Chicago, he'll probably act a fool. That's probably why he went so far away in the first place. But it doesn't matter," she said, closing the menu once again, "because I can tell you don't want to move anyway, do you?"

Before Laurie could speak, the waitress came to their table. After the order was placed, Danielle took her interrogation off pause and got a bit loud. "Now, back to our little conversation. Why haven't you moved?"

Laurie refolded the napkin. "A new twist has developed since he's been in Chicago."

Danielle sat up in her seat. "I know Mr. Greg didn't go to Chicago and mess around on you? I know he didn't. Tell me he didn't."

"No, no, Danielle, nothing like that."

"Are you sure?" Danielle said with her eyes wide as a quarter.

"I'm sure. He's not messing around as far as I know."

"Okay, he better not be, because you've had all of his babies. Don't think I'm going to let him produce all my nephews and leave you for some young thang in Chicago."

Drake shook his head.

"What, I'm not kidding. Laurie is too easy on that man. He knows I don't have good sense. So it can be on at any time."

"So tell us what's going on. What's the new twist?" Drake asked.

"Greg wants us to move now, but I don't want to uproot the boys from school. I figure we'll move sometime during the summer," she told her siblings. "That is, if I go."

Drake and Danielle's necks stiffened, and they pushed back from the table. "What do you mean if?" Drake asked.

Laurie propped her elbows on the table, clasped her hands together, and used them as a resting post for her chin. How much did she need to share with her brother and sister?

"Come on, spill it, girl," Danielle said. "You can trust us with anything. You know that," she said, tapping her sister on the leg. "No other adults on this earth, including Greg, love you more than me and Drake. Isn't that right, big brother?" Danielle said, shifting her gaze to him.

"I can't speak for Greg, but the two of us"—Drake flicked his finger back and forth between himself and Danielle—"are definitely in the top three." He snickered.

Laurie agreed in her heart. Her siblings were safe. Their unconditional love was a fact. She wanted to leap forward and tell them about John, how special he made her feel.

"Where do I begin?"

"At the beginning," Danielle jumped in. "And don't leave anything out. I want to know all the details," she said with lips poked out.

Laurie stirred the straw in her water glass. "I'm seeing someone."

"What," Danielle said, practically leaping on top of the table. "You're joking, right?"

Laurie shook her head no. "Actually, I shouldn't really say I'm seeing somebody."

"Wait a minute, sis. That's like being a little pregnant. Either you are or you aren't. Which is it?" Danielle asked.

Drake sat back with his arms crossed.

Thank goodness the waitress was bringing the food. Her interruption was the break Laurie needed to get her story ironed out. Only problem was Danielle didn't let the interruption derail her quest for information. She continued talking while the waitress worked her way around the table.

"Well, which is it?" Danielle persisted.

"Yes and no."

"Come on, Laurie, what does that mean?" Danielle asked, letting the sound of the letter *n* stretch across the Grand Canyon.

Quick and swallow, like taking a laxative. Do it and get it over, letting the flow bring relief. "I've been in contact with a man since November."

"Since November," Danielle blurted out, "and you haven't told us anything. I don't believe you. That's four months."

"Anybody we know?" Drake asked.

"No."

"How do you know? It's a small world," Danielle jumped in.

"You don't know him, trust me."

"But how do you know. What's his name?" Danielle kept asking.

"John Gallagher."

Laurie could tell both Drake and Danielle were running the name through their databases looking for a match. Silence indicated their searches had come up empty.

"Told you. He lives in Atlanta. That's why I didn't think you'd know him."

"How did you meet someone in Atlanta?" Drake asked.

She hesitated, preferring to drink a gallon of cod-liver oil rather than be subjected to this interview. "I met him online."

"Oh, no, you didn't." Danielle rolled her glance around the ceiling with her head flung back. "Don't tell me you met some guy online you don't know anything about. He could be some pervert for all you know. Even Greg would be better than this complete stranger."

"Have you met him yet?" Drake asked.

"No," Laurie said, "but I'm planning to meet him, not next Wednesday but the one after that, two weeks from today in Columbia."

"I can't believe you, girlfriend." Danielle laughed out loud. "Greg messed up when he took the job in Chicago. His wife, my sister, the mother of my six nephews is strutting her stuff in tight pants, stiletto heels, and a man on the side. I have to give it to you, sis, you have it going on." Danielle raised her hand to give Laurie a high five. "I'm single, no kids, no husband, in shape, always been in shape, and can't get a man. You and Drake don't have any problems getting dates. It's clear to me that I need to take lessons from the two of you."

Drake grinned at his sister. "Any time you want to come out to the golf course, let me know."

"I know that's where you hang out. You're Mr. Golf and"—Danielle then directed her comment to Laurie—"you're Mrs. Online. I guess those are my two options." Danielle took another bite of her grilled chicken salad before tossing down the fork. "I still don't know what to say about you, missy."

"What can I say," Laurie responded, hunching her left shoulder.

"I think you need to be careful," Drake interjected.

"Me, too."

"I'm going to be careful," Laurie told her siblings. "We're meeting in an open place in the middle of the day."

"Great, but I'm talking about Greg. What if he finds out?" Drake questioned.

"He won't," Laurie answered, swishing her half-filled water glass so hard it spilled onto the table.

"Famous last words of a cheating spouse caught on tape," Drake said, filling the table with merriment.

"Oh boy," Danielle jeered. "Here we go. I know that laugh when I hear it."

"Is that what you call it, cheating?" Laurie asked Drake.

"What else is it, little sis? I hate to be the one to say it, but you're seeing someone outside of your marriage." His eyes widened. "That's"—he hesitated, and then spit it out—"cheating. I hate to use the word, especially when talking to my sister who I love, but I'm telling you what I honestly think."

"But we haven't touched, not at all."

He pressed his thumb repeatedly against his brow, gazing down at the table. No one spoke while he deliberated. "I don't know what else to say. If it's not technically cheating, it's a close relative."

"Well, I don't agree. This is only a friendship."

"Okay, friendship. Is that what you really want to call it?" he responded.

Danielle spoke up. "I don't care what you call it. Greg needs to know my sister still has it going on, even after six babies. He had his chance to treat her right. Now it's her turn to live." She turned to Laurie and said, "You go for it."

"Laurie, if Greg was communicating with a friend over the Internet for months without telling you, how would you feel? Would you consider it a legitimate friendship or something more?" Drake asked.

"That's different," Danielle said.

"How?"

"Because Greg better not cheat on my sister."

"So it is cheating," Drake said.

"All I know is that Greg gets whatever he gets; that's all there is to it," Danielle said, plucking her wallet from her purse.

Drake picked up the bill, which the waitress had dropped off earlier. "I'll take care of it. But the two of you owe me the next one."

"Sure thing, so long as it's not out at that country club of yours. I can't afford those lunches," Danielle said.

"Wherever you're paying, that's where I'll go," Drake told Danielle.

Chapter 40

The Sentra was retired and the old van took its spot in the garage, progress on every front. Greg wanted to ensure that Laurie had reliable transportation with him being out of town. He picked out the SUV, but she chose the color. The brand new spitfire red Suburban zipped down Interstate 20 due east with the April breeze keeping pace. The CD player hosted the recently purchased Minnie Riperton's soundtrack and blaring into the vehicle was "Lover and Friend." That was what she really wanted, tapping her thumb and making small rocking motions in the driver's seat. Greg was turning out to be the man she wanted, at least the one she'd hoped and prayed to have for years. Only challenge was, the Greg on order arrived a bit too late to get full attention. He was the entrée, the physical component to her buffet of love. Mr. Deep was the emotional factor, the spice rounding out a satisfying meal. The right amount of spice could either stir the flavor in the entrée, causing it to be better, or add too much and ruin the entire meal. She needed to figure out the right dose of John, the amount constituting friendship in the eyes of a particularly nosy community. The eyes of Greg and God were another story. If she could fool the people, deception would have a start.

COLUMBIA 8 MILES the sign read as she whisked by. Her heart fluttered, pounding so loudly she needed to turn up the music. The steering wheel soaked up the dampness spurting from her hands. She cranked the A/C down to sixty-seven, feeling her armpits perspiring more rapidly than her deodorant could absorb. Her thoughts raced around, trying to outline his image in her head. She remembered every detail in his profile photo in addition to the few other ones she'd asked him to send. She had wanted to be equally forthcoming and send him a photo but couldn't muster the courage.

Laurie fanned her face and upper body, careful to keep from sweating through her silk shirt with matching fitted bodice. She pulled off the road at the five-mile rest stop. She made the final touch-ups to her makeup, forced every strand into place, and sucked in fresh air. She had to keep breathing without a great deal of reasoning. Too much thinking this close to the rendezvous point was dangerous. Toying with whether this meeting was the right move or not continually raised its head on the ride, demanding an answer. She continued to ignore the question, shoving it into the recesses of her mind every time it popped up front declaring guilt and conviction. She wrenched her hands, stopping so abruptly that her thumb twisted. What were the odds? Practically impossible. Over an hour from home and there she was, in plain view. God didn't show up himself. He sent Mrs. Williams. Too late to dash away, Mrs. Williams had her spotted. Her mind was churning, looking for a lie that would suffice an old smart woman like Mrs. Williams. Laurie hopped out and approached her spiritual mother, unprepared.

"Hi, Mrs. Williams," Laurie said, embracing her.

"Laurie, my, my, I sure didn't expect to meet you way down here near Columbia," Mrs. Williams said, pushing back and getting a good look at Laurie. The outfit seemed perfectly fine until Mrs. Williams gave her a look from head to toe. All of a sudden she felt indecent. Not that her black silk top overhanging a pair of size ten fitted red linen pants with a zip up the side, accenting her black pumps, was wrong, but something about the way Mrs. Williams looked at her made Laurie uneasy. It wasn't quite guilt, but close. If Mrs. Williams made her feel like this, she didn't want to think about God's eyes on her.

"What are you doing down here?" Laurie asked.

"You know some of the church members come down here once a month to pick up used books that the college donates. We take the books and give them out to the children in the community. We've been doing this program for about three months now. Pastor's been raving about it practically every week. I know you've heard him talk about it?"

Laurie cringed, hoping Mrs. Williams didn't notice.

"I see that husband of yours just about every Sunday with those handsome little men of yours, but I haven't seen you in a while. I know you're a working woman now but don't forget what side your bread's buttered on. You know the Lord is a jealous God. He didn't bless you with a job, a good man, and a whole house of boys for you to turn your back on Him."

"You're right; I've just been tired."

"We're never too tired to serve the Lord, just like He's never too tired for us," she said, looking over Laurie's outfit again. "My, you look wonderful, young lady. What have you done to yourself?"

Laurie perked up. "I lost weight."

"I can see. Maybe you can help this old woman lose a few pounds, too," she said, chuckling. "Marriage must be agreeing with you. See, I told you if you just wait it out and give God time to work, you were going to be okay."

No sense responding. Mrs. Williams had one philosophy: God's way and that was it, no matter how tough the situation got, and living with Greg Wright was definitely a tough situation.

Laurie gave hugs and hellos to the other four church members as they randomly ascended from the restroom areas and boarded the van, saving a solid embrace and good-bye for Mrs. Williams.

"I'll see you at church Sunday, young lady, the Lord

willing," Mrs. Williams said as she took her seat. Laurie slid the door closed and took a step back, catching a peek at her watch. Precious minutes had escaped in a blink.

10:15. She had to get moving in order to make the 10:30 engagement. She hustled back to her vehicle and eased the Suburban onto the ramp, then the highway, giving enough gas to make up time, determined not to let Mrs. Williams derail her plans. She'd come too far to let anyone talk her out of this meeting.

The little pesky voice was back, more powerful now, unwilling to be ignored, telling her to turn around and go home. No way, she had driven nearly eighty miles in barely an hour. She was meeting John. It couldn't hurt. Two friends meeting for lunch in the middle of nowhere, that was it, no more, no less, innocent and easy to explain. She kept rehearsing the line. It wasn't strong enough to use on Mrs. Williams but maybe someone would believe it. Then a shower of comfort rushed her body when she was reminded that Greg was over 800 miles away in Chicago, probably in the middle of a meeting. She glided into the city limit looking for the Columbiana Hotel on Bush River Road. She stroked her hair once again, rapidly, and smacked her lips during a quick glance into the image maker. Every aspect of her appearance that could be done was. She was wearing a gut-sucking bodysuit under her attire as backup.

She saw the back of the navy blue Buick Century that he'd described to her. She drove past the lot, hoping to catch a glimpse. She went a half block up the road and swung back around, hesitating. This was it. No turning back. Friendship, friendship, friendship was the explanation should anyone ask. She whipped into the other side of the parking lot, two rows from John, out of his eye view. Laurie nodded, giving her heartbeats a chance to slow down before exuding more effort. She took a breath. Get it together. She fumbled with her hair one more time, giving her stomach time to settle. Still, her fingers couldn't move toward the door handle. Why? Why? Why? Why the confusion now when she was so close? Go ahead, get out, her brain said with no reaction from her body. Her armpits were no longer masking moisture, they were openly flowing.

It was already 10:35. She watched him open his car door and walk into the restaurant. He was about Greg's height, around five-foot-nine, skin the color of a chocolate-covered peanut cluster, short dark hair, and a baby gut brewing, which didn't seem unusual for a man who appeared to be in his mid to late forties. She sighed in relief. The worst was over. He looked better in person than his photos but not as good as Greg. It didn't make a difference. His physical attributes weren't her motivation for meeting him in a remote location far from her reality. John had no idea, but he'd done wonders for her, including giving her the incentive to lose the thirty-three pounds, knowing one day she would have to meet him in person. He made her feel good about herself, an element Greg hadn't learned to master.

Having John in her life had to be all right. There was no other way to explain how someone who made her so much better in a list of ways could be bad. Lock the voices in the car. She was going into the restaurant with John, and nothing and nobody would be the wiser. Of course, God knew, but she would have to deal with Him later, when she'd come up with a better story, one more believable.

She attempted movement to no avail. Her hand was on the door, wanting to burst free, but she couldn't get out. Now what? The anxiety felt like cement blocks on her shoulders, crippling her ability to move. She flopped back in the seat, with tight grips on the steering wheel, suppressing her desire to scream. Why did Mrs. Williams have to show up? Laurie knew it was God. He must have sent her. Why else would the church members pop up all of a sudden in Columbia for a bunch of charity books? Books were everywhere. They could have gotten those in Augusta; but no, Mrs. Williams had to come down to Columbia, today of all days. Why was God forcing Greg on her? Greg hadn't treated her right in all these years. Why did he get such good treatment? Even Mrs. Williams was praising him as a good husband, going to church with the boys. What about all the times she went with the boys and no one praised her, but then that was her job, undeserving of accolades. Appreciation was exactly why she needed to see John. He didn't take her for granted. He made her feel alive, fresh, smart, valued, a sensation Greg hadn't nurtured in years. Actually, maybe he hadn't ever, but he was still Greg. As ridiculous and confusing as it sounded, he was the man she married out of love.

Might as well face reality. She couldn't go through with meeting John, whether it was God, Mrs. Williams, guilt, or her few remaining drops of hope for the marriage that won out. Meeting John was wrong and she knew it.

Chapter 41

Greg handed the limousine driver a ten-dollar bill and swung his garment bag over his shoulder. Most of his work clothes were in Chicago. Traveling home every other weekend was light and without fanfare. He was unsuccessful in changing Laurie's mind about moving to Chicago before the spring. She wouldn't budge on the subject. Guess he never realized how important Augusta was to her. Waiting was difficult, but he was getting by. Biweekly visits, a challenging job, and a bucket of excitement about the impending relocation of his family was getting him through the lonely periods.

Greg unlocked the front door, a rare entry point for him. He eased to the kitchen door, opened it, and found the Suburban gone. Excellent, Laurie and the boys weren't home. He would run upstairs, take a quick shower, and be ready to surprise her when she got home.

He ran up the stairs, his ribs barely able to contain his heartbeat. He was home, only a few minutes from holding the love of his life tight within his arms. He couldn't wait. The boys would be thrilled, too, about having their father home on a Wednesday. A few personal holidays, coupled with a week of vacation, would give him almost two weeks at home, off the road, with Laurie and the boys during spring break. He turned on the water, already stripped, and jumped in singing like the blessings of heaven were showering upon him.

Laurie trudged down the road in the SUV, oblivious to her surroundings. John Gallagher, smooth, plain as a sheet of paper, unique. For weeks he'd made her laugh so hard she still felt twinges in her stomach, but not today. He never got a chance. Her two-week-old cell phone rang as she tapped the door opener above her visor, waiting to enter the garage. This was the first call in the past hour that wasn't coming from John. Finally, a call she would answer.

"Yes, Danielle," she answered.

"How did you know it was me?"

"Because your name came up on my caller ID and your number, too. You're so nosy. You couldn't wait for me to get back and fill you in on the details."

"That's right," Danielle admitted.

"Hold on," Laurie said, accelerating into the parking spot, shifting into park, and turning off the Suburban. "You are so nosy," she said, climbing down to the ground, refusing to let disappointment cloud the value and worth John had brought to her life.

"I had to check on you. Shoot, I didn't know if this guy was for real or some kind of a pervert."

"He's for real," Laurie said, cutting through the kitchen and going upstairs, wanting to put the afternoon behind her.

"I shouldn't have let you go, but since you did, tell me everything. I've been watching this clock for hours, waiting," Danielle said in a catty voice.

"I hate to break this to you Danielle, but nothing happened," she said, barely making progress ascending the stairs. "I—"

"Right, right, right, skip all that noise. What does he look like?" Danielle asked.

Laurie just wanted to let Danielle ask what she wanted, and then forget today even happened. "John is, um, about Greg's height, about your complexion, maybe a little bit darker, a little heavy in the stomach," she said with voice rising. "Danielle, I drove all the way to Columbia to meet John in person and I—" she belted, opening the bedroom door before freezing in her tracks. Greg's eyes were wide as baseballs. "I have to call you back," Laurie told Danielle.

"What? Oh no, you can't get to the juicy part and hang up. Tell me the rest. You can take the phone in the bathroom with you."

"Danielle," Laurie said, crisp and firm, "I have to go. Greg's home." She disconnected before her sister could respond.

Greg stood to his feet, slow, acting dazed.

What? Why? How? raced through her mind. She literally couldn't move. She was having an out-of-body experience. "Greg," she stuttered, clambering to find the right words if there were any.

"Don't Greg me, who did you go all the way to Columbia to see?" he said with arms folded.

"What are you talking about?" she asked, avoiding direct eye contact. Lying was hard enough but necessary for survival.

"Come on, Laurie, don't play me for a fool. Who were you telling Danielle about?"

She went into the closet, trying desperately to pull a story together that would appease a potentially betrayed and angry man. "Oh, she was telling me about one of her friends from work," she said, taking off her pumps and leaning on the inside door frame for support.

Greg stalked the closet. "Where did you go today?" he asked, scouring her body from head to toe, pausing at the fitted red pants.

"I, uhm, went to the uhm, the uhm."

Greg laughed and kept laughing, getting louder, uncontrollable. Laurie looked but didn't speak. "I can't believe you're going to stand there and try to lie to my face when you know you're busted." He let his laughter turn into scorn. "Who is he?"

"Who?" she asked, sliding out of the closet past him.

"Laurie, don't be a fool. You know who I'm talking about," he said, closing the distance between them.

"Greg, it's not what you think," she said, retreating to the corner of the room.

"Exactly what am I thinking? Huh, Laurie? I'm thinking that I can't believe my wife is actually messing around on me." He kept closing in on her.

She peered at him, stiffening in the corner.

"Here I am working my black behind off in Chicago, putting a future together for my family, and you're back here in Augusta sneaking around behind my back with some other man. Huh, Laurie?" he said, lunging within inches of her, causing her to brace the wall and turn her face sideways. "Huh, huh," he yelled. Control, control bellowed in his head, but his body was overriding the request. How could she cheat on him after all he was doing? It couldn't be happening. A bad dream. He felt the rage swelling but kept dashing waters of reason on top.

"You promised in counseling that you wouldn't hit me," she whimpered.

"Have I hit you?" he shouted into her ear. "Have I? No." He took two steps back. "You probably want me to hit you so you can be the victim and not have to deal with your cheating. Not this time. Nope, this is all on you." He moved to the bed and let his head flop into his hands. He sobbed for a few minutes; Laurie slumped to the floor and sat in the corner. His anger was like a fire burning out of control, slowing for a moment and blazing to full intensity the next. "How could you do this to us?" he howled, wanting to cut deep enough to get out the hurt. He looked at his wife, radiant, deceitful, loving, adulterous. If he could strangle her and stab himself in the process, his pain could be over. What else could bring the kind of relief he needed? He lunged at her again. "Who is he?"

"It's nobody you know," she insisted.

"You don't know who I know," he said, standing over her.

"What's his name?"

He heard her whimpering but wasn't going to let up. If she was woman enough to get into this kind of jam, then she should be bold enough to deal with the consequences.

"You don't know him."

"I'm not going to ask you again."

She rose up, almost knocking him to his feet. "Or what, what, Greg? What are you going to do if I don't tell you his name? Are you going to hit me? I wish you'd try it," she said, snatching the cordless phone from her nightstand and raising it above her head.

"So that's how it is, huh, Laurie? You cheat on me and our boys. Then you get all bad with me and what, beat me with the phone? Ha, I don't think so. I don't know who this man is or what he's filling your head with, but you better not act a fool and touch me with that phone."

"I have to pick up the kids. I don't have time for this, Greg."

"Don't pretend like you care about the kids or our family. Any time you're running around with other men, you can't play the good mother act. It doesn't fly, honey."

"You better move out of my way, because I'm going out that door and you can't stop me."

"Or what, huh, you're going to call your sister to come and stop big bad Greg from hurting her cheating sister?"

"I don't need Danielle to help me."

"So what, you're going to get your brother? Like I'm scared."

"If you were smart, you would be, but I guess that's all up for debate."

Her insults were pouring ammonia on his exposed wounded heart. Where was his Laurie? She couldn't be this lioness standing in front of him hurling innuendoes. He wanted to figure out when he'd lost the woman he'd married. He'd made sacrifices for the Chicago job, being away from his sons and her. Didn't she know how his heart ached night after night, wanting to be home with them, counting down the days to his visits and their summer relocation? Didn't she know how many times he picked up their family photo in a day? Broke and working in the dungeon at his old job with an eight-year-old van and a wife who wanted him was better than having a pocket of money, a career, and a woman who was finding fulfillment elsewhere. No matter how bad life got, he always had Laurie and the boys. What was he supposed to do if they were gone?

Laurie pushed past him.

"I don't know who you are anymore. You've changed, and I'm not just talking about your weight, or this new career thing you have going on, or even those clothes you're wearing now. I mean really changed. It's like you're not my wife anymore."

"Whose fault is that?"

"You really don't care, do you? I can't believe you're doing this to us." He dropped to the bed and clutched his hand around his face. "I gave up my life here in Augusta for a job in Chicago. I found a job that's making our life better, for us and for the boys, and this is the thanks I get."

Laurie extracted her pumps from the closet. "Actually, truth be told, I got you the job in Chicago, or did you forget that, too?" she said, rushing out of the bedroom, down the hall and stairs while the words of rebuttal were still on his lips.

Greg heard the garage door open and the SUV back out. He burst into a gut-wrenching cry that could only be done by a man when the coast was clear. No one could hear his agony. The thought of Laurie being with someone else felt like one of his limbs had been severed without anesthesia. The threat of losing his family was unthinkable. He needed relief at all costs. There was nowhere to go and no one to turn to, except the one friend he met a few months ago and with whom he was doing a fair job of keeping in touch, not daily by any means but frequent enough to maintain an acquaintance-level relationship. He slid to the floor by the bed, clasped his hands together, and pressing beyond his sobs, he cried out, "Lord, it's me and I really need help this time and I don't have anywhere else to go. Please,

please, help me," he said, tailing off at the end and letting his upper body rest on the bed, praying for relief, believing that something would come; it had to if there was any hope of him enduring the night.

Chapter 42

Four hours darted by every night at work, except tonight. Her emotions and thoughts were warring. John wasn't real, not yet. He made her giggle and see life clearly, uncluttered by marital woes, responsibilities, and hang-ups. He made her feel pure, attractive, and worthy of attention for no other reason than she was a woman whose conversation he enjoyed. She'd missed that kind of connection with a man for years, relying on the daily interaction of a toddler to feed her yearning for validation. Now she was getting it from an adult, a decent man, freely. But why did the price seem so high?

Laurie searched the rack for her time card and punched out.

She'd suffered in a wishy-washy relationship for so many years, never realizing until recently the depths of her despair. She had been walking around with love for the marriage seeping out of her pores, without detection, now rendering her maritally anemic. The amount of transfusion required to get the love level back to where it needed to be for marital recovery was questionable. She still loved Greg, a part of her always would, but the taste of freedom and stability were quenching. The desire to stay was flowing like still waters, ever present, carving deeper into her existence, but tugging at the surface was the daunting yearn to go, so powerful that to resist might cause a catastrophic calamity in an already shaky reality. She longed to make the right choice, but how could she deny herself a sample of happiness, or whatever the feeling for a John-like person was, without betraying her vows, not so much to Greg, but to God. She wasn't listening, but it hadn't stopped the Lord from talking. She was angry with Him and angry with Greg, and for good reason. Like an employee in an unfulfilling job with great pay and benefits, Laurie had no grounds to leave but no desire to stay for so long. Greg put her there, and why had God let her stay so long?

Steps translated into miles as she trudged to the car, not so successfully balancing anger, fear, and guilt. She put the car in gear and took the long ride home, dreading round two with her husband. Another option was to avoid going home altogether, but common sense kicked in. Regardless of what happened with her and Greg, she was a mother to six boys who needed her whether they knew it or not. She sauntered into traffic and stayed in the right lane, letting whisking cars pass on the left. She would get home tonight, just not in a hurry. Her torment would be there, whenever she arrived.

Laurie stopped at the local diner and tinkered with a slice of warm apple pie with her cell phone to her ear.

"Can I get you anything else?" the waitress asked, as she'd done three other times over the past hour.

"No, I'm fine, thanks."

"I'm just checking because the kitchen closes in fifteen minutes."

Laurie glanced at her watch. 11:15. "Do you close at eleven-thirty?"

"The kitchen does, but the diner doesn't close until midnight."

"Oh, okay," Laurie said, taking a swig of water and pulling out her wallet. "I might as well leave now."

"You don't have to rush off. Nobody's going to need this booth." She poured more water into Laurie's glass once it was back on the table. "Stay as long as you like," she said, finishing with a no-teeth grin and walking away.

She'd finally listened to one message from John and two from Drake. It was a wonder John was still interested after being stood up. Although he accepted her apology and repeatedly told Laurie he understood, she wasn't completely convinced that some of his zeal hadn't been lost. Why not, some of hers was.

The remaining five calls were from Danielle, each becoming more frantic with the last one threatening to bring over the entire Augusta Police Department if Laurie didn't call her by midnight. She would call Danielle in the car again. Apparently calling Danielle on the way to work earlier and giving reassurance that Greg hadn't hit her sister wasn't settling. Calls to Drake and John would have to wait.

Laurie placed a five-dollar bill next to the check, took one more drink of water, and left. Outside, the air was warm enough for her to recognize spring but too cool to be jacketless. No surprise. In the middle was exactly where the rest of her life was, a dreadful place to be, in the middle of nowhere and no direction on how to get moving to one side or the other. She tried everything, being submissive, getting bolder. She probably could have shown more commitment to counseling, whether Greg went or not, but she wasn't taking blame for that either. Greg's shoulders were broader and so were God's. Yes, now that she'd let the whole picture materialize, she was definitely put off by God for not fixing her marriage sooner. She'd asked so many times when it would have made a difference, or at least she thought so according to her timing.

Chapter 43

Solitude and time was normally the recipe for the making of sound judgment. Tonight's ride home went a long way toward exacerbating the problem, Greg. She left the car in the driveway, not wanting to potentially wake anyone in the house since the lights appeared to be off from the street. There was no reason for her to take all of the blame this time around. Yeah, so what, she'd been building a friendship with John. No big deal. How many times had Greg broken her trust? Maybe not with another woman, but through all of the times he scared her into submission and made her feel inadequate as a wife. Only in the past six months had he started to make her feel like a partner. He had fifteen years in total to get his act together. It wasn't her fault if he hadn't. He was as much to blame for the circumstance as she was. If she could lock in on her outrage and not move from her spot of bitterness, then decisions would be easier. But she couldn't. Hurt, anger, and rejection jumbled together still wasn't enough to totally squash her trickle of love for Greg and the desire to keep her family together. Glimmers of hope didn't mean she could bear laying eyes on Greg at the moment. She needed time to sort things through.

Laurie climbed the stairs, carefully, silently. On the landing, she paused. She saw the couch in the family room; she could sleep there and avoid the impending round two with Greg. She debated for a minute, standing in the dark, perplexed. Deep breath, get it together. She resumed motion, reaching the bedroom door, holding the knob and twisting with the deliberate speed of a tortoise, no rush. Success. She had the door cracked without a sound. Her size ten body, which would soon be an eight if she had anything to do with it, squeezed into the narrow opening, undetected. She waited to hear movement from the bed area. Nothing. She went inside the closet, closed the door, and turned on the light.

Being in the bedroom, back in his presence, stirred a reaction she couldn't contain. The cordless phone plagued her mind and the emotions she felt when wielding it over her head this afternoon emerged. She vowed, right there, Greg would never intimidate her again, under any circumstances. Times had changed and he better get into acceptance mode. A warm, burning sensation lined her core. The sprig of hope that had crawled into her soul minutes before darted out like the house was on fire. The first four years of marriage were wonderful. Memories of the last nine years dashed at her. They felt like daggers as she remembered every mean word, every argument, every time Greg had her so terrified she winced in the corner, every moment of despair suffered at the hands of that man. Their old love was gone. She stuck her head in the crack of the closet door, allowing adequate light to see the bed and him. She remembered every time he'd broken her spirit. The sensation was breaking down the gates, overtaking her feelings, and jetting toward her judgment. How could someone she loved so much cause her to feel so badly?

She tried to get comfortable. Disgust was rising, no, not disgust, more like anger. He slept without a care in the world, leaving the anguish for his victims to harbor for days, years. Maybe getting to know John was wrong, but what she was feeling was bigger than a friendly relationship, as clandestine as it might be. For the first time, it dawned on her. She'd gotten over all those painful times in the past with Greg. She'd sat through counseling, nodded her head in unison with the counselor, and told herself how to feel. Those actions were all lies.

Greg was still sleeping; she needed to stay in control. Her eyes were fixed on him. Anger was fully formed and looking for room to expand. She was the good wife, at least she had been, the one who put up with his poor treatment and swept it under the covers. Well, the covers were off and the ugliness of their relationship was exposed, and he deserved to pay. Right and wrong were of no consequence. They looked so much alike. *Get it over, the pent-up hurt, unresolved emotions. Pick up the phone and crack him over the head. Fast, poof.* Maybe that would stop the pounding in her head. Rage was rolling, careening out of control. She tussled with her reason but couldn't get it harnessed. *Do it; forget the phone, he might wake up in the middle of the act. Be precise,* the voice in her head said, describing a gun, maybe a knife, even a hammer. How absurd, she didn't have a gun. That wouldn't work. She was pressing so hard against the crack in the door that when she stepped back, the pressure released sent a tinge of pain through her face, snapping her back to a rational state. What was she thinking? Greg wasn't the one involved in an extramarital relationship, she was; but it was a relationship, not an affair. That would sound too wrong and she wasn't in the wrong, Greg was. He had to be. Otherwise, she'd be forced to deal with the demons of her own decisions. It was easier to blame Greg. He'd planted enough seeds over the years to take claim for this crop of marital destruction. She turned out the light and went to bed, staying close to the edge, where the rest of her was.

Chapter 44

Stress graciously took the blame for the last two times her monthly visitor showed up late, twice since August. She flopped down on the bed, still clutching the plastic-covered strip. It couldn't be correct, but six babies to her credit, the test didn't tell her any more than she already knew. Before this long two-week stretch, Greg was coming home less frequently, no more than every other weekend since the company stopped paying for his trips at the end of February. She was his wife and didn't mind occasional intimacy, at least until clarity came about what to do—stay or go. Allowing herself to get caught up in their moments of affection on his quick visits had her in this undesirable spot, capitulating toward child number seven, the very act she had dreaded and tried to avoid. She wanted to cry, or wail, or pull her hair, or something drastic that could dissolve the anguish. She stared at the ceiling, hoping for an answer. Making the decision wasn't easy. It was like choosing between chemo and surgery, baby or not, further tied down or free. Both had their records of successes and failures. John was a dream, for now, but so was Greg in the beginning. Regardless, the future was on the back burner; more important matters were at hand.

Laurie rolled around on the bed, pondering her brain about whom to call. She wanted to talk to somebody, anybody but Greg. She had to think. Less than two hours to figure out a solution before Greg and the boys came home filled with plans for the weekend. There were only two options: tell Greg and have the baby, or get rid of the baby without telling Greg.

What was she thinking? How could she even think it? She was in a pit of desperation. Honestly, she didn't feel good about the second option, but the low voice in her spirit was getting fainter and fainter in recent months. She spent less time at church and even less time in prayer. She was grateful to Drake for turning her on to religion and to the Lord during the rough periods in her marriage, but life had been looking up, except for the slipup when Greg found out about John. She was on the right track, and for a change, she was setting her own course. Another baby was throwing a wrench into the plan.

She tucked her knees into the fetal position and restrained from agonizing. The timing couldn't be worse. There was so much to be considered. It was Greg's fault she was in this tight spot, but he didn't have to suffer the consequences, only her as usual. She hadn't decided whether to stay with him or to strike out on her own with someone like John. Why now, this new child, why ever? She had enough of Greg's children. It was time for her to take care of Laurie's needs. No one else was.

There wasn't anyone to call. If she told Rachel, there was a strong chance she'd encourage her first to tell Greg, and then move to Chicago next week. Rachel was not a good candidate to confide in on the pregnancy issue, since she'd had her own unplanned pregnancy when her twins were born. Danielle wasn't a consideration. She'd drain too much energy harping on why birth control pills weren't used all along. Laurie wasn't up for battling Danielle. Drake was her only other option. She thought about calling him and decided against it. Without having to ask his opinion, he would definitely be against getting rid of the baby, knowing his position against divorce and living together before being married. No sense wasting precious brain cells about a concept he'd surely reject.

His words echoed in her head as she held the plastic-covered strip to the light, hoping for a color change. "Life comes from God. If he gives it, go with it." She'd heard Drake say those words on several occasions. Her brother couldn't help, no one could, except God, but she didn't want to use Him this early on, not after turning her back on Him for so many months. He'd be a last resort if and only if she couldn't work this out on her own.

Chapter 45

Two more nights and thank goodness, it would be glorious Monday, the day when Greg would get out of town, finally, after nearly two weeks at home. She would have packed his bag for him, but he'd stopped bringing clothes back and forth several months ago. Besides, adding pepper to an already spicy set of circumstanses wouldn't be wise. She paced in a daze, struggling to block out the test results. What was there to do? She drew a glass of water from the new water cooler as half the boys played upstairs. The rest staked out their territory in the family room, prepared to watch cartoons.

"Don't forget to wash your faces and eat your breakfast before you watch TV." Not a voice was heard. "Did you hear me?" she asked, escalating her voice.

"Yes, Mom," responded Jason and Keith.

"Where is Rick?"

"He's upstairs with Daddy," one of the boys said.

"No, he's not," Greg said, clearing the stairs. "He's playing in his room."

"Can you bring him down so he can eat before I go?" she said, pulling the snug-fitting workout pants over her tiny pouch and wiggling the matching midriff tank top down. She made a mental note to go shopping before the week was out for more appropriate workout gear, given her permanent or not-so-permanent predicament.

"He'll be fine. He's with Junior. I'll get him later," Greg said, turning to her and firing off a look that made her gasp. "And where are you going dressed like that on a Saturday morning?" he said, walking past her to open the refrigerator. "Or do I even need to ask." He sailed her way, slamming the door shut once the juice was retrieved.

"I'm going to the gym like I do every Saturday morning and every other day, for that matter, except for Sunday. You know my routine," she said, taking the last drop of water and putting the glass into the sink.

"No, I don't. To be honest, I don't know much about anything these days."

"Greg, don't start again. We've been arguing this whole week."

"I know. What a way to spend a week of vacation with my family. But then, whose fault is that?"

Don't get sucked in. Let him think whatever he wants. She hadn't and wasn't planning to see John. As long as she and God knew, who cared about Greg. She couldn't deny how Deep made her feel fulfilled and complete as a woman. But he wasn't the answer. That much she knew. Mrs. Williams's advice about marriage was ringing in her ears. No, John wasn't it, but living in misery indefinitely with Greg wasn't an option either. Keep rolling toward the door. Hang in there. Another day and he would be out of town, ushering in the space she needed to make real decisions. For now, she needed to tread water as the shark hovered.

He kept at it. "Are you on your way to see him?"

She was bubbling inside again. Don't do it. Don't let him incite a riot. She was already worried, tired, mad, and pregnant. If he only knew just how volatile his pushing was. Times like this she questioned why she had decided to stay in the failing marriage for so long. But she maintained her dab of composure.

"I guess no means yes."

"Greg," she drilled with jaws locked in place, lips perched like she'd eaten four limes, not moving, as the words charged out, "don't talk about this around my children."

"News flash, lady, these are my sons, too. What's the big deal anyway; if he's only a friend, why are you so afraid to talk about him?"

"I'm not, I just don't want to be ignorant about the whole conversation," she said, snatching her keys from the counter and going for the door leading to the garage.

"Oh, so I'm ignorant. Maybe"—he laughed openly,

and then cut it off in an instant—"but I'm not an adulterer. Which is worse?"

She slammed the door, causing the walls to rumble. She walked to the SUV, wearing a smear of dejection. Without much effort, he'd managed to take her lower into the realm of despair. A so-called cheating pregnant woman who confessed to the general public that she was religious, what a joke. She let the vehicle drift out of the driveway with no momentum to get far. She pulled to the side and got on the cell phone, dialing Drake's number first. Two rings and he was on.

"What's up, little sis?" he asked in a chipper voice. She pushed and pulled, but the words were lodged too deep to surface. "Hey, Laurie, what's going on?" he asked in a baritone, serious-sounding voice.

"I don't know what to do," she said, holding back the floodgates.

"Where are you? What's going on? Talk to me."

"I'm at home, or actually in front of my house."

"Are you okay, did something happen?"

"Yes, I mean no, Greg didn't hit me or anything like that. It's more than that."

"You're not making any sense. Hold on, I'm coming over there."

"No, no, you don't need to. I'll come to your place," she said, sliding the gear into drive and creeping from the curb.

"Laurie, are you sure, because I can come to you."

"I'm already in the truck and on my way. I'll be there

in twenty minutes." That gave her sufficient time to collect her thoughts and arrange them in a way that would make sense to both her and Drake.

No traffic, a string of lights, and a few winding curves deposited her at Drake's subdivision. The Toyota Camry? What was Danielle doing at Drake's this early on a Saturday? She slumped in the seat, wanting comfort and unconditional support. What she hadn't planned on was for Danielle to be there, possibly forcing Laurie to defend her raggedy marriage and a list of other choices not to her sister's pleasing. She needed to pull it together and get inside, fast and over.

Laurie traipsed up the walkway, finding the screened door closed with the main one behind it open. She stuck her face near the screen, visible from inside. "Knock, knock," she said, opening the door and entering.

Danielle swooped in. "Girl, what's wrong with you? Drake called me and said something had happened to you." She grabbed Laurie's shoulders. "What happened, because if that fool hit you, play time is over; he will be dealt with whether you like it or not. I am not playing," she said, flailing her arms.

Drake grabbed Danielle's shoulders. "Hold on, little sis. First of all," he said, turning to Laurie, "are you okay?"

"Yes, I'm fine, sort of."

"See," Danielle lashed out, dipping her shoulder from Drake's grip, "I knew it. I should have jacked his behind up a long time ago; then we wouldn't be having these issues today."

"Danielle, please, will you calm down? I can't find out what's really happening if you're going to keep flying off the handle," Drake said.

"Humph," she said, pouting her lips and locking her arms but silencing.

"Start talking, young lady," Drake said to Laurie. "I want a yes or a no, not maybe, kind of, sort of. Are you okay?"

Laurie took a sigh of breath, spewing it out forcefully. "Yes, I'm fine. Greg didn't touch me. This is about way more than Greg hitting me."

"What else is there?"

"I'm pregnant," she said, before verbiage and good sense could gel.

"What?" Danielle shouted, bending her body in half.

Laurie dropped onto the sofa. "Yes, I'm pregnant."

"Oh my gosh, you can't be pregnant. I mean, how? Who? Oh my gosh."

She could have closed her eyes and described Danielle's reaction ahead of time. It was Drake she didn't know how to read.

"Danielle, you know this is Greg's baby."

"How do you know for sure? Oh no, you didn't. And, Drake, you thought I was the wild one," Danielle said in a giggly tone.

"This is Greg's baby because you know I've never met John in person."

"Yeah, right. Come on, girlfriend, we're not Greg; this is me and Drake. Now you know you have to tell us the real deal."

"I'm serious, I've never met him."

"You're lying," Danielle said, plopping down on the seat next to her sister and leaning close into her. "You're trying to tell us you drove an hour and a half?"

"Barely an hour," Laurie corrected.

"An hour, fine, whatever. But you drove all the way to Columbia to meet this man and you didn't do anything, especially if you were dressed like I think you were, all slim and trim looking."

Lauric pulled at the base of her top. "I'm serious," she said in a lighthearted tone. "I'm not lying. I didn't meet him. I've already told you this three times. I got there and saw him from across the parking lot. He didn't see me. I never got out of my truck, just turned around and left."

"Just like that?" Danielle prodded.

"Just like that." No need to tell them about running into Mrs. Williams. They didn't know her anyway. Why add drama to an already complicated fiasco. "It was innocent."

"Innocent my big toe," Danielle said, laughing hysterically while leaning back on the sofa and covering her mouth, which couldn't contain the volume. A circus tent couldn't have.

"What did Greg say?" Drake asked, taking a seat on one of the winged-back chairs facing the sofa.

"About John or the baby?"

"Both," Danielle interjected.

"Well, he is very angry about John and doesn't know about the pregnancy."

"So you told him about John?" Drake asked.

Danielle let her glance drag the floor.

"Not exactly, he overheard me talking to Danielle last week after I'd gotten back from Columbia."

Drake nodded his head in acknowledgment of the information, propping his elbow on the arm of the chair and letting his knuckles brace his forehead. Silence. *Speak up*, she thought, wanting her brother to give some reassurance. "What have you done about John?"

"Nothing. We've talked a little, but that's all. I have enough problems without adding another man to the mix." Dealing with the pregnancy was a full-time issue plopped on top of everything else going on. Laurie ran her hand down the side of her head and slowly let it massage the side of her neck. Just her luck. When life was starting to go her way, treating her as a valued being, Greg indirectly found a way to mess it up. "I haven't talked to John since last week. I didn't know what to do before, and now that I'm pregnant, I really don't know what to do."

"That's exactly why I can't believe you're giving John up so easily. And you had it going on, too. This John is all in love with you even with six children; maybe he'll take seven, never know," Danielle suggested, unsuccessfully containing her humor.

"Come on, Danielle, this is serious. I don't know what to do. I can't tell Greg about this baby."

"But you have to," Drake said. "It's his child, too. You don't have a choice."

"Why can't you tell him? It's not like the two of you haven't been here before. You should have stock in those home pregnancy kits. You'd be millionaires by now," Danielle said, barely able to push the words past her laughter.

Laurie leaned against her sister. "Stop, I'm serious. I need advice."

"What's there to say? Congratulations Mommy on your new baby boy, because you know it's going to be another boy. Greg obviously can't make a girl. And she'd be so cute too with your little ears, his smooth skin, and big round eyes. It would have been nice to have a niece." Danielle reared back on the sofa. "I'll have to wait on Drake to bring a girl into this family," she said, shifting her glance in her brother's direction. "Please, Mr. Holy Man, spend less time on the golf course and more time tracking down Ms. Right while I'm still young enough to take my niece shopping."

Drake and Laurie both shook their heads. Drake massaged his face with his hand. "You need to tell Greg you're pregnant and work through this together."

"I'm not even sure"—she paused, not certain what was to follow needed to be birthed in this forum—"if I'm going to keep the baby."

"What, you mean adoption?" Danielle said, tickled. "I'll take him, might as well."

"No," Laurie responded in a whisper, "I'm considering other options."

Danielle's glee dried up. "There aren't any other

options, not for my sister. I don't care how pitiful that husband of yours is, you can't be getting rid of none of my kinfolks. Mama and Daddy would be turning over in their graves if they knew you were considering that option. Ooh," Danielle moaned. "Don't even think it."

"You need to tell your husband about the baby," Drake reiterated. "The sooner the better."

"That's true. You'll be showing soon enough," Danielle added.

"I'm scared."

"Of what?" Danielle asked with an attitude.

"Of how he might react. You should have seen the look on his face when he found out about John. Remember how I told you he acted and for no reason, really," Laurie reminded her sister. "He was so mad and has been mad ever since."

"Can you blame him?" Drake asked. "Most men would be upset."

"But it's not like I'm into some kind of affair."

"What would you call it?" he asked.

"Please tell me we're not back to the whole affair issue," Danielle pleaded.

"I don't know, but it's not an affair. I never touched John. We've never been together. I don't care what you say, it's not an affair. Right?"

"Sounds good enough for me," Danielle chimed in.

"I don't agree," Drake added. "Don't you see the issue here, sis? It doesn't matter whether you were intimate with John. Actually, I take it back; it's better that you weren't physical with him. We would be talking straight-out adultery. But don't be fooled; the moment you developed a relationship with another man that your husband couldn't be a part of, you were in violation of your commitment to Greg and to the marriage."

"Basically you're saying that I've been cheating."

"You must be kidding," Danielle said, rolling her neck with her head following. "He's only getting back a taste of what he's dealt her over the years. What goes around comes around. Good for you, girl," she said, preparing to high-five. "Better you than me, because I would have done Mr. Greg in a long time ago and hid the body. Humph, if nothing else, he's lucky she didn't pour some grits over him a few times. I sure would have. That's probably why God hasn't given me a husband. The first time he looked at me crossways, he'd be hearing a kettle hissing in the middle of the night getting ready to fix his behind. He'd better learn my rule: Hit me and you better sleep with one eye open, because it's on."

"In Matthew it says what God has put together, let no man put asunder."

"Oh boy." Danielle winced. "Here we go. I tried to help you, sis, but now he's throwing the Bible on you." Danielle sat back, tilted her head up, and closed her eyes. "You're on your own."

"You said with your own lips just a month or so ago that Greg had changed and he was a better husband than he'd ever been. It sounds like your prayer is finally getting answered and now the enemy is throwing a temptation at you to derail the answer."

Laurie was expecting more compassion from Drake. She needed to hear that what had happened wasn't her fault, not really, not the getting-to-know John part. Instead, he was echoing the same stuff that faint voice deep in the cavern of her mind was saying, forgive Greg, forgive herself, forget the pains of the past, let go, and walk in faith for the marriage. If she could figure out how to block out Drake and the other voice, then she'd be okay, able to make her own decisions, however disastrous they turned out.

Chapter 46

Laurie sat in the parking lot of the Y listening to music from the radio, songs she didn't recognize, but that didn't matter. The music fit. She was in unfamiliar territory. The cell phone was slightly damp as she clutched it in her hand. If she could just do it, call John and tell him that her situation had changed, that she couldn't keep in touch anymore. The confusion was agonizing. Ending the whatever-it-was with John was better; that's what she had to believe. Letting go wasn't for Greg, it was for her own conscience. He'd understand. He had to because there was a real chance no one else would truly appreciate the tragedy of her circumstances. Twelve years ago, she had everything going for her. She was smart, married, and never in her wildest dreams back then had she thought about ending up like this—desperate for respect, for love, and for validation to the extent that she had been willing to see another man for it. Shame tried to squeeze in, but there wasn't any more room; guilt, hurt, sadness, and loneliness hogged all the space. She dialed the number and waited. Time elapsed and she hit CLEAR. Two more songs, a bit more fortitude, and another dialing frenzy. A total of five rounds of dial and ditch. Finally on the sixth attempt, she wiped the phone on the seat, dialed, and pressed SEND. Her heart leaped forward. It wasn't too late. She could hang up, but what would be the point. Most people in the free world had caller ID. He would see the number and call her right back. Maybe not today, or tomorrow, but one day she'd have to tell him; it might as well be now. His familiar voice answered on the other end.

"Hello."

"John"—she hesitated—"it's me."

"I was hoping it was you. I almost answered and said, 'Hello, gorgeous, my beautiful, super-fine Foxy mama.'"

Anxiety began to melt. He always knew what to say. The words she longed to hear, was desperate to hear, he dropped freely and without prompting. He was what she needed, at least for the moment.

He continued, "I didn't answer the way I really wanted to because you never know who might decide to use your phone and give me a call."

Ugh, him again. Couldn't she get away from Greg for one conversation? Was she forever going to be plagued with his infiltration of her thoughts, deeds, and actions? Wasn't there a part of her that still belonged to Laurie and not to Greg Wright? If there was, she had to be found and quick before hope took the paddleboat over the waterfall.

"I'm sure nobody will be using my phone anytime soon," she offered, not sure if it was true.

"You never know. Anyway, I've missed talking to you, but I know how busy you are. It's been tough suffering through entire days without hearing your voice or reading your e-mail. Talk about torture. So, how is my sweetheart on this bright Saturday morning?"

She didn't know where to begin. Tell him the truth and get it over, or sugarcoat and buy some time? Clarity didn't spring forward, so she held off.

"I know I've said this plenty of times, but I can't say it enough, I will be so happy when you finally agree to meet me in person. I'm hooked and I don't mind telling you."

"Stop, you're embarrassing me." She giggled, forgetting about the mound of anxiety that rested on her shoulders a brief ten minutes ago. The warm compliments heated her lukewarm soul. Determined not to get lost again in the pleasantries that she craved, Laurie pushed past the fairy tale and grasped reality.

"I'm not trying to embarrass you. I'm just being honest. There's no sense in playing games. I want you and that's all there is to it."

"But you know I'm married."

"Unh-hmm."

"And have six children."

"Unh-hmm."

"And none of that bothers you?"

"Nope."

She didn't know what to say.

"I don't have any problems with you having six children. Hey, they come with the package, and with a package like you, how can I resist? Look, I'm not saying your being married is the ideal situation for us, but like you've told me on several occasions, you're separated for all practical purposes. Your husband is in Chicago, and you're in Augusta. Divorce is next."

Hearing him say the "d" word sounded heavy piled on top of her other decisions, ones that wouldn't wait much longer for answers without making themselves known. She rubbed her abdomen.

"John."

"Yes, sweetheart."

"I have something to tell you," she said, gritting her teeth and letting her neck tilt up. Her fingers tapped the steering wheel while she glared out the side window.

"Anything, lay it on me."

Remove the stopper. Squirt hard. No hesitation. "I can't talk to you anymore."

"What?"

"I have to end our relationship. It's wrong and I can't do it anymore." If Mrs. Williams could run into her out in the middle of nowhere, then surely God saw her, too. Maybe she could fool Greg for a while longer, maybe even herself, but God wasn't someone to play with.

"That's it? We're done? You're calling it quits just like that?" he said, letting frantic reign. "What did I do?"

"You didn't do anything. It's me and Greg and the marriage, the kids, you name it." She hesitated, taking time to construct the proper lead-in for what was coming next. "On top of everything else, I'm pregnant." Quiet muffled the line. Not even a sigh escaped. "Did you hear me?" Still nothing. "John, are you there?"

Finally he responded. "I'm here."

"Did you hear me?" she asked, feeling anxiety returning.

"I did."

"Talk to me. Say something."

"What do you want me to say?"

"Anything, something," she said, burying her fingers in her hair, scratching her forehead in the process. They weren't going to keep in touch anymore, but at this moment, how he felt about her was important.

"Okay, I'm shocked." He paused.

"Trust me, I'm shocked, too. I don't know what to say. You have no idea how I feel." Maybe, somehow, some way, he could forgive her. Then her world could stop spinning out of control and rest back on its normal axis, rendering her peace of mind. "I'm sorry, John."

"I don't care about you having six children. That doesn't bother me at all, not at all. The fact that you and your husband are still sleeping together, I wasn't expecting this."

But he knew she was married. She'd always been

upfront about Greg. Certain actions came with the role. She and Greg slept in the same bed; it was bound to happen.

"Obviously you're not quite as separated as I thought, as you led me to believe."

"But I never lied to you about me and Greg."

"No, perhaps you didn't. Maybe I just didn't put the puzzle together soon enough."

"What does that mean?" she asked.

He sighed. "Laurie, you are a phenomenal woman, and I would have loved spending the rest of my days making you happy, but I see that's not possible."

She wanted to respond but couldn't.

"Laurie, I realize you have a lot to work out with your husband. If I'd met you fifteen years ago, Greg would have had a run for his money; but as much as I hate to do this, I will back off. I agree, you don't need any more variables added to your equation. I'm an extra wheel, just complicating things."

"No, don't say that," she said. "You made me happy. You made me laugh all the time." He didn't have to know, but he did more for her self-esteem in a few months than Greg had done in twelve years.

"I don't know what else to say, except you're a beautiful woman and you're going to be okay. I hope your husband figures out what he has. Take care of yourself, and remember, Deep thinks you're special."

After his good-bye was extended, she held the phone, wiping the river streaming down her face. She was so, so close to fresh happiness, and it slipped out of her fingers, like a man hanging over the ledge before crashing to his doom. Congratulations went to Greg. He'd managed to rip away another ounce of her joy.

Chapter 47

Once around the universal-weight circuit, pulling, pushing, and puffing, plus thirty minutes on the elliptical machine, Laurie's legs and arms felt like logs. Four pregnancies ago, she would have eased up on strenuous activity during the first trimester, but this time around she didn't need or want to be careful, or did she? Back at home, anxiety kicked in. "Where's your father?" she hollered into the family room, guzzling a cold bottle of water extracted from the refrigerator.

"He went to get some food."

She sucked down the last few ounces of water. It was 5:30 already; the day had flown by. She trudged up the stairs discounting the sounds of sons calling out for this and that. Baby Rick attempted to catch her on the way up the stairs, but his little legs gave out after the fourth step, unable to keep up with her pace. He slid back down to the foot of the stairs, whining for a bit until he was drawn into the family room where thunderous laughter bellowed as his brothers played one of their electronic games.

Good, Greg was gone. She could soak in the tub, hopefully for thirty minutes without interruption from the kids, from Greg, from life. She drew the warm water, sitting on the side of the Jacuzzi, swishing the water with her fingers, watching the mini-ripples, intense at first, then fading. She rubbed her abdomen gently in a circular motion. As much as she agreed in her heart with Drake about this baby being a blessing, it sure wasn't feeling like one, more like an inconvenience, a burden. She turned up the hot water. Why bother to be cautious? She didn't have the heart to terminate this pregnancy, but if an incident happened naturally, she might be able to live with the loss.

The water was ready. She set her watch on the tile platform surrounding the tub. A dash of lilac bath beads and the aroma ushered her into a place far away, beyond the veil of her troubles. She slid into the tub, dipping her toe in first, nice and super warm, bordering on hot. Minutes and she could be refreshed, the sins of the past washed away. She let her body submerge. If only it were that easy. She'd made the right decision. John was gone but he wouldn't go away.

The bumping sound coming from the bedroom startled her. She fumbled around the outside of the tub for her watch while sitting in a tub of lukewarm water.

6:30. Sleep had eased in like a thief and stolen her moments of solitude, the time she needed to get her situation together. She could warm the water or get out of the tub. Her fingers looked like dried prunes, wrinkly and pale. Back to reality. She lingered in the sanctity of the bathroom, surfacing thirty minutes later. Greg was lying across the bed reading a newspaper.

"I didn't know you were home," she said, wanting to make the best out of a bad and getting worse set of events.

Greg continued reading the paper.

"Did the boys eat?" she asked, sitting on the bed and rubbing lotion on her leg, keeping the robe tight across her top.

The page turning was the only other sound in the room besides Laurie.

"So you're not talking, is that it? Fine with me. The less talk, the less arguing for a change."

Greg raised his glance, let it marinate, and moved back to the paper. Usually Greg would be hounding her for affection. He finished the paper and left the room, closing the door behind him. Laurie climbed into a pair of casual pants and a T-shirt. She followed Greg downstairs. The boys plastered her with conversation, where as Greg would not.

By 10:00 every body under the age of eighteen had to be in bed, some earlier, depending on where they fell in the Wright age lineup. Weekends were no exception. It was 10:05 and not a floorboard was creaking. Laurie turned on the light next to her side of the bed and opened the novel she was reading to the spot identified by the wrinkled bookmark.

Greg pulled the cover up to his armpit. "I'll be leaving in another day," he blurted, "and we haven't solved anything."

She continued reading. He could wait. It wasn't that important, couldn't be, because she'd attempted to open dialogue with him earlier. Now it was her turn to be invisible, at least for another few weeks.

"Are you going to stop seeing this clown and give this marriage another chance?" he asked. She wanted to concede somehow since his voice sounded sincere, until he ran his mouth a few words too far. "Or are you going to keep running around acting like a teenager instead of a grown wife with six kids."

Perfect, just like him to make a small effort toward generating goodwill and then working three times harder to tear down the progress. Forget him, when she determined the verdict about a few key issues, he'd be informed, and not necessarily first. There was a long line of people ahead of him.

He rolled over close to her, just what she was wishing he wouldn't do. She leaned toward the lamp and turned off the light. She preferred to let his aggravation stir in the dark, like their glued relationship had done year after year, finally giving way to age and pressure, cracking into a ton of pieces, requiring repair yet again, maybe, maybe not. "I don't know what I'm doing yet." He didn't deserve the luxury of knowing she'd painfully ended her relationship with John. If she was willing to sacrifice her needs to do what was right, why couldn't he? She was always the one giving up a piece of herself for his selfish behind.

"Oh, so you're serious about this dude? You're really taking this adultery all the way? I can't believe you," he said, flipping on the light switch with enough force to send their four-by-six framed family photo crashing onto the nightstand, facedown. The sound sent shivers up her spine. Hurricane Greg was rolling into town. "You're actually serious about some other man when we've spent thirteen years together, no, actually sixteen if you count all the years we've been together, from the beginning. And you're telling me you're willing to throw our family away for some dude you've known for a few days."

"Four months."

"What did you say?" Greg asked her back, because she had no plans of turning around and giving him more fuel.

"Nothing," she said, realizing the mistake she'd made.

"Did you say four months?" he asked.

Big mistake. She could sense the momentum building. Best to let the sand blow around and settle down as quickly as possible. She could hear him counting and tapping his fingers.

"Four months means you met him in December," he said, tapping her back. "Are you saying you've been seeing this guy ever since I took the job in Chicago? You have got to be kidding me." He rolled his legs to the side of the bed, letting his feet find the floor. "While I'm busting my behind in Chicago for you, you're back here playing house with some other man, probably in my house with my children." Greg sandwiched his head with his hands. "I, I just can't believe this. This is a trip." He swung around, tossing his leg sideways on the bed. "What am I supposed to do about this, Laurie?"

She didn't have anything to say. He was doing all of the rambling.

"You better say something," he drilled her way in a piercing tone. "Don't I at least deserve an answer?"

He wasn't going to let up. Barring the windows and doors of her emotions wasn't strong enough to resist the impending damage coming from Hurricane Greg. The best she could hope for was that he would lose steam and tire into submission. Until that magical hour, she had to keep him calm. "What are you asking me?"

"I'm asking you what were you thinking," he said, snatching the covers off of her.

"Greg," she said, jumping from the bed, "don't pull the covers again."

He rushed across the bed on his knees. "Or what, huh, Laurie?" he said, making it to the other side and getting in her face. "What, is your boyfriend going to jump on me?"

"I don't need anybody to protect me."

"Get him."

"I'm not getting anybody," she screamed, almost hysterically. To think she'd let John go for this. Good thing her decision had nothing to do with pleasing Greg; otherwise, she'd be choking on a mound of regrets.

"I want you to get him, Laurie. I'm begging you to get this man who has been messing around with my wife behind my back."

The creaking sound outside the door caused both to break in the action for a second before resuming.

"I'm not getting anybody. You're so much of a man, you want him, you go get him. And by the way, I'm pregnant. Now chew on that for a while."

Without warning, he was in her space, close enough to hear her heart pounding, fast, faster. His eyes got darker, meaner, deeper.

Junior burst into the room. "Don't touch my mother," he said, wielding his math book.

"Junior, get out of here," Greg demanded as Laurie clung for safety.

She engulfed her arms around Junior like a tigress protecting her cub. If there was physical punishment to be dished, she would rather take the brunt of it instead of her babies, the oldest and the youngest one.

"Mom, are you okay?" Junior said, crying.

She rubbed his cheeks and kissed his forehead. "Mommy is fine, baby."

"Junior, get out of here. Nothing is wrong with your mother."

"Mom, do you want me to call the police again?"

"No," Greg interjected.

"No, baby, I'm okay. I'm going to be fine," she said, still trying to catch her breath. "You'll see. Go back to bed. Trust me, I'm going to be all right. Okay?" she said, sending him off with another kiss to the forehead.

After Junior left, Greg seemed to sputter out of steam. He turned out the light and lay back on the bed, mumbling something about being pregnant. Tides were shifting and back-to-back hurricanes were coming inland, with Hurricane Laurie up next. She'd warned him ample times. Talk time was over. She sat in the doorway, rehearsing the marriage, sifting through her emotions, and trying to suppress the rage that wanted to jump up and knock him in the head, a nice and solid one for the record. Every fight, another log on the fire of rage, every argument, burning higher, for every time he had her scared in the bedroom, was blazing now. Finally she'd figured out the puzzle.

Greg was the culprit. He had thirteen years to get his act together, and now he had finally come close thirty-five pounds and an admirer later. This was her time to step into the world, fearless, tasting the goodies of life; then she remembered the baby, a seventh one. Nope, no matter what Drake said, she wasn't going to allow herself to sink back into the marriage when the rescue boat was sitting at the dock, waiting. All she had to do was stomp out caution wrapped around guilt and seize the lifeline. Just because the floodwaters of her relationship with Greg had receded and flowers were growing, it didn't mean the stench was gone. The years of up and down, waves beating the shoreline, wore her away bit by bit until there wasn't significant substance left in the marriage.

Blackness claimed the hours as she sat in the doorway. The nightlight from the boys' bathroom illuminated the hallway, giving her a silhouette view of Greg. It wasn't the fact that he'd terrified her yet again only hours before, or that he'd caused her a bucket of pain during the marriage. What drove her mad was watching him sleep so peacefully, like he'd done so many times before, leaving her to find solitude in the darkness. He deserved a sample of her pain. He'd earned it, with every word, every harsh word, and every ounce of fear that he had fostered. She'd finally gotten to a place where she felt good about Laurie, a foreign phenomena in the Wright house. She was in a good place, and John was a contributor. But Greg had fixed that. He had won. He was entitled to his reward, and she was determined to make sure he got it. She descended the stairs to the kitchen without the assistance of light. Some tasks were more suited for the dark. That pesky voice was hollering something about stop, but she was on a mission. Greg was first, and then the voice would get dealt with next if it didn't shut up. She removed the poker from the fireplace and glided up the stairs, floating like in a dream. She sliced into the room. The floorboards knew she was serious and didn't make a single sound. If only Greg had taken her seriously sooner, they could have been spared this necessary deed. Pain was powerful and needed to be shared.

She stood over him with the poker clutched between her palms raised in the air.

"Stop," Laurie thought she heard but knew no one was in the room. She looked at Greg's lifeless body, still asleep. She raised the poker to an action position again. "Stop," she heard again, this time getting aggravated and jittery simultaneously. Shake it off, do it. There would never be a better time. Deal with the consequences later. Block other stuff out. He deserved to suffer. She raised the poker one more time, this time determined to follow through. "Stop, you are not alone. I've seen your pain and I have heard your cry. Fear not, for I am with you." It was a voice she recognized. She winced in shame and threw herself into the doorway, sobbing into her arms, muffled so as not to wake the boys or Greg. The familiar voice was too strong, no longer able to be suppressed. She had tried running away from the voice, never able to get too far. Deep down she knew her decisions weren't right, but independence and feeling in control were addicting, hard to deny. She was ashamed for the past months when she'd turned from God and attempted to solve her own problems. Instead of helping, she had made matters worse. All along she wanted to blame Greg for their problems, taking none of the responsibilities for fixing the marriage. It was easier to let Greg be the villain so she could play the victim.

He wouldn't be silenced. "I have never left you, even when you turned away from me, my daughter. My hand of grace was upon you. I have seen your struggle and know that in the midst of your pain, I allowed you to endure, for how else would you know my miraculous power, my unwavering love for you."

She felt comfortable talking like a daughter to her father, honest but respectful. "Why didn't you answer my prayers? I needed you to help me a long time ago."

"You didn't ask for my help. You told me what you wanted me to do, but my child, my thoughts are not your thoughts, neither are your ways my ways. You looked at the situation on the surface while I looked at Greg's heart. You're concerned about where you are today, whereas I'm concerned about where you'll be in eternity." She cried out to God for forgiveness. "I will never leave you or forsake you, for I know the plans I have for you, plans to prosper you and not to harm you, plans to give you hope and a future. Then you will call upon me and come and pray to me, and I will listen to you. You will seek me and find me when you seek me with all your heart. I will be found by you and bring you back from captivity. I did not give you a spirit of fear, but of power, love, and a sound mind."

For the first time, she was by herself, but she didn't feel alone. A warm sensation, comforting, loving, careened through her body, rising in her spirit and cresting in her soul. The words of her church mother sailed in, reminding Laurie that she was a blessed woman with a houseful of God's gift, including the one on the way. She wasn't a victim. No way could she be, knowing the Lord was with her, her mighty and victorious Father. The sweet aroma of repentance rocked her to sleep with the poker still planted in her hand.

Chapter 48

A hawk, that's what he was. Out of sight, waiting for the right time to fly in. He could protect the birds, the little animals without anyone knowing. He crawled out of the dark corner on his knees. He'd watched her cry and fall asleep a while ago. It was hard to tell how long, because there weren't any clocks in the hallway. Late is all he knew. It was all right, though. He'd learned how to make himself stay awake until after they went to sleep. That way, he knew everything was okay. She was okay. He was so glad he'd been able to stay awake tonight. This was harder; it felt much later than usual. He parked as close to her as he could get without touching, wondering what to do next. He knew why she had the fireplace stick. He'd watched her all three times. He hated when his father was like that, mean like. He was nice to him and his brothers. Why couldn't he be nice to Mom all the time, too? Still, he knew

Mom would get in trouble if she did this bad thing. She couldn't do it. She needed his help. He moved his hand a millisecond at a time toward the handle. He would get the stick and finish up. He prayed hard, just like he learned in Sunday School, silent, believing that no one would hurt his mother again. He was sure of it. Finally, after careful movement, he secured the stick. Done. Now he could take care of the rest before his father woke up. There was still a chance.

Chapter 49

Blood flowed like a spring brook through a desolate forest, nothing in its way. Bright fiery red. Too fast. Stop. How could this happen. He needed help and wanted to scream, but the words wouldn't come forth. Trapped in the pit of his consciousness, just like so many other words that should have been released to clear the air, to change the tide with Laurie, even with Sterling Sr. Looking back, maybe he had gone too far. Maybe certain actions weren't well thought out; but why was his penalty always the steepest, more than anyone else had to pay for the same indiscretion. He lived a lifetime of tragic moments intermixed with a heap of more tragedy and a few dashes of good, like his children and Laurie. The doses of joy in his life had sustained him. It's what kept him trudging through the mire. Life was turning around. He was getting it together, a few bumps but nothing he wasn't going to work out, especially with Laurie. Too late. The blood continued flowing, unhindered, like his tirades had been for years.

Everything was blurry.

Odd, there wasn't any pain. He wanted to cry out, but who would hear? Worse yet, who would care? Maybe Virginia Wright, but her reaction would depend on timing, whether or not the judge had upset her bowl of contentment. He need to sit up and take it like a man. He was the one who dug this hole and now the liquid of his existence oozed. Maybe it wasn't too late to repent and get serious about God, for real this time, not just when it felt easy. There wasn't anyone else to save him. God was his only hope at this point. "Lord Jesus, forgive me for my sins. I've done a lot of bad things. I can't change what's already been done, but I really do believe in my heart that you died for me and that you rose from the dead. If it's not too late, I want to accept you as my personal Savior. Please help me to be a better man, a better husband, and a better father. Lord, I'm so tired of running," he bellowed into the depths of the night, not knowing if today was his last tomorrow.

Junior stood over him.

"Daddy, wake up," Greg heard far in the distance. It repeated, "Daddy, wake up."

Greg popped up. Laurie woke up about the same time and stared at Junior with a worried look. "What?" he said in a groggy voice, while still in dream mode but able to recall every detail. He patted his arms fiercely onto his chest and head. Everything was in place. He wiped the sweat from his brow with the back of his hand. He took a breath, blew it out, and turned on the light.

"Junior," he said, "what's wrong?"

"Nothing now. I fixed everything."

Laurie broke out in tears.

"What are you talking about?" Greg asked, tossing back the covers and scouring the mattress for blood, coming up instead with a drenched sheet. What a dream, no, more like a nightmare. He patted his chest again.

"I asked God to make us a family again," Junior said.

Laurie rose to her feet and took two steps, sobbing and burying her face into her hands.

"We're already a family, Junior."

"No, I mean a real one, where we all get along."

Greg was ashamed in front of his son. His efforts to make Junior's boyhood better than his own had failed.

"I fixed it, Daddy."

"How, son?"

"I prayed and I asked God to help us fix our family. I also promised him that I'd treat my brothers better and give up the computer and every video game I have if he'll answer my prayer. I know he'll do it."

Laurie stood but didn't approach. She covered her nose with her hands as tears and sobs flowed.

"How do you know?" Greg asked, standing up and pulling his son into his arms, holding the water on his eyelids in place.

"We learned in Bible school on Sunday that we can ask

God to fix stuff that we can't fix, and he can do it if we have faith, and I do."

"What is faith, son?"

"Believing that God can do everything because we can't. I believe God is going to help you and Mommy." The words couldn't make it out. He was choked up hearing his son speak more passionately about the Lord than he had. "It's going to happen, Daddy," Junior said, hugging his father tight. "I know it will."

"Son, if you believe it will, then I'll believe it, too." God was using an innocent child to bring adult-sized hope and faith to what seemed like a dire situation. Only God could create a miracle in the midst of mayhem, creating something good from what appeared to be all bad.

Greg held on. His lifeline had arrived, smaller than he expected but no less powerful. During the fiascoes at work, the ups and downs with Laurie, he thought both of his fathers, God and the judge, had forgotten about him, left him to fend for himself. Most of the time the weight he bore in trying to keep his family together had him teetering the fine line between life and death, but change had arrived on the wings of his soon-to-be thirteen-year-old son. He wanted to, but he couldn't hug Junior any tighter for fear of crushing him. Nothing would ruin this moment, not even Dad, for this hug was for him, too.

Epilogue

Eight Months Later

The holiday season was hectic with six boys each wanting time, attention, gifts, and their way. No matter how chaotic the house was or how worn-out her body felt after last week, Laurie hadn't missed sending out Christmas cards from the time she turned eighteen almost fifteen years ago. This year wouldn't be the exception. She plopped the cards, family photo, and stamps in the center of the bed and followed suit with her body. She sniffled, staring at the photo. Big eyes, milk chocolate–colored skin, and a smile that lit up the family. How could she dare dream of not having her, their first and probably only daughter? Laurie was amused reflecting on the cliché that a son is a son until he takes a wife, but a daughter is a daughter for life. She took a breath and cast out the spirit of guilt. No such animal resided in or around her anymore; it hadn't for months, eight to be exact. Thank God he intervened when he did, instead of letting her continue down the path of doom she'd created. It took sinking into the pit of despair to realize that happiness was a state of mind, a choice, not an uncontrollable feeling. She looked up at the crib to see Erica sleeping peacefully as a newborn should. Chicago was bitterly cold, but it couldn't hold a stick to the warmth and love burning inside the Wright household. Marriage wasn't perfect, but with the change in her attitude and God's abounding grace, which she had no intention of letting go of this time, happiness was here to stay.